Megan

JACK WEYLAND

BOOKCRAFT

SALT LAKE CITY, UTAH

To Sherry

*My companion for eternity and
the best part of every day*

The talk given by Elder Richard G. Scott, quoted on pages 259–60 in this book, was given in the October 2000 semiannual general conference. See "The Path to Peace and Joy," *Ensign,* Nov. 2000, 25–27.

Library of Congress Cataloging-in-Publication Data

Weyland, Jack, 1940–
    Megan / Jack Weyland.
        p. cm.
    Summary: Infatuated with an older boy who is not a member of her church, seventeen-year-old Megan, a Mormon, goes against the values she was raised with and becomes pregnant.
    ISBN 1-57008-732-6 (Hardbound : alk. paper)
    1. Mormons–Fiction. 2. Pregnancy–Fiction. 3. Conduct of life–Fiction.
I. Title

PZ7.W538 Me 2001
(Fic)–dc21

Printed in the United States of America   70582-6862
Phoenix Color Corporation, Hagerstown, MD

10   9   8   7   6   5   4   3   2   1

1

Megan, seventeen, a senior in high school, stared in the restroom mirror at Leo's Pizza and, with her black, almond eyes, scowled at her reflection. Her thick, dark brown hair was out of control. In the fluorescent lighting, the tan she had worked on so hard gave her skin a near-death, grayish tint. She was wearing the purple eyeliner that her older brother, Bryce, said made her look like she'd been in a fight. Now, in that light, she could see why he'd said it.

She stepped back and turned to catch her profile in the mirror. Her hip-hugging khaki pants fit really well, even though her mom thought they were too tight. Megan had bought them a week earlier with her paycheck from Burger King, where she worked part-time.

Underneath the oversized T-shirt she'd permanently borrowed from Bryce, she was wearing a black tank top. She'd bought it at the same time she got the pants but, up to then, hadn't had the courage to wear it in public. She was wearing it tonight just in case Kurt showed up.

What if he doesn't come? But he will. Thomas said he was coming, so he'll be here. And even if he doesn't come, I'll have fun. I always have fun with Thomas.

She took a deep breath, opened the swinging door, and entered the Friday night after-hours world at Leo's Pizza. Although the restaurant was closed, Thomas Marconi, her best friend from school, was one of the managers, and he often let his friends come in while he was cleaning up. They'd make their own pizzas, push the tables and chairs into a corner, and dance. On the weekends they'd be together until one or two in the morning and then Thomas would get them to help clean up and then he'd boot them out.

"Is this okay with Leo?" Megan had once asked.

Thomas laughed. "There is no Leo. The owner's name is Phil Silverstein, and he hates pizza."

Thomas was six-foot-two. His wire-rimmed glasses with small frames made him look intelligent, yet somehow detached, as if he were a dispassionate observer of the follies of mankind. His nearly black hair was so thick and coarse, it hardly ever got out of place.

"Well, then, is it okay with Mr. Silverstein?"

"I asked him once. He said it was okay as long as I take full responsibility for what happens and pay him back for what we use for our pizzas. One thing it does is reduce the chance of anyone breaking in."

Megan had known Thomas since seventh grade. Through the years they had remained devoted friends. In fact, because he knew Megan liked Kurt, it was Thomas who had invited him to drop by.

"Are you sure he's coming?" she asked.

"He said he'd come."

"I wish he'd hurry up."

"Me, too, so you'd quit bugging me about it. To get your mind off him, how about making me a pizza? Write a special message on it, just for me."

2

She suspected that rather than trying to help her, he just wanted a pizza, but, even so, she couldn't turn him down. He was her best friend. "I guess I will," she said.

"That's my girl," Thomas said, patting her on the arm as he sat down to enjoy watching his friends have a good time.

Of the ten people who came regularly to Leo's after hours, Thomas only let three or four actually make pizzas, people he could trust not to make a big mess. Megan was one of those few.

She remembered when Thomas had tried to teach her how to toss the pizza dough in the air to shape it. By the time they were through, she had an extra large, doughy crust draped over her head, and they were laughing so hard they had to lean on each other for support.

She loved working in the kitchen at Leo's because it was well-equipped, and people were always drifting in, asking when the next pizza would be done.

After getting Thomas's pizza ready to go in the oven, she decided to write him a message using chopped green peppers to make the letters. She thought of several possibilities, some of which would be funny, but then she thought about how much happiness he was giving to his friends and so, in the end, she decided to go with THANK YOU!

By the time she'd done THA, she realized she wasn't going to be able to finish the whole phrase, so she changed it to THANK U!

In her excitement to prepare this tribute to Thomas, she almost forgot about Kurt, but ten minutes before the pizza was done, she peeked out to where Thomas was sitting and saw Kurt at the same booth with him.

"Oh, my gosh! I can't believe he's here!" she said to herself.

Thomas and Megan had first gotten to know Kurt a year earlier in choir in high school. From the first time she saw him, she'd been attracted to him. He had great looking, dark brown hair and brooding eyes and a terrific smile, when he chose to show it. But the thing that attracted Megan the most was his self-confidence. It was almost a cockiness that made it seem as though he didn't need anyone's approval.

Kurt was also into adventure. He loved to surf and camp and hike and scuba dive and sail.

Since their paths seldom crossed now that he'd graduated from high school, she'd cooked up this way to stay in touch. This might be her only chance with him. He was a moving target and might never return to Leo's.

She went to the restroom and took off her T-shirt to see how she looked in the tank top. She turned sideways and admired herself in the mirror. The tank top was tight, and it left her midriff and belly button exposed. She liked the way she looked, but because she'd never worn something that daring in public, she began to have second thoughts. *Well, it's not what I usually wear, but it's no worse than what they show on TV. Besides, this may be my only chance to get Kurt's attention.*

She stepped back to take in the overall effect. *Good thing none of my Church friends are here,* she thought with a cynical smile. *No worry about that. Their mommies wouldn't let 'em out this late. They're probably all home praying.*

Heather would have a fit if she saw me in this, she thought. Heather was her twenty-two-year-old sister, who was serving a mission in Montana. Heather wasn't like anyone else in the family. She was quiet and reserved and had an inner compass that caused her to always make good choices.

The tank top's not really that bad. It just seems weird to me because of what I usually wear. But it's no worse than what everyone else is wearing these days.

Megan remembered Heather going through her clothes just before she went to the temple, getting rid of anything that would be inappropriate for someone who'd been to the temple.

4

She'd have gotten rid of this, if she'd had it, Megan thought. *But so what? I'm not going on a mission, and I'm not going to the temple. At least not for a while, so why not wear whatever I want until then? It's like they say, you're only young once.*

She pursed her lips, trying to decide if she had the courage to leave the T-shirt off and just go with the tank top. *I bought it, so I might as well wear it. I'll probably get used to it after I've worn it a few times. Besides, it's not that bad.*

She took the pizza out of the oven, cut it into slices, and carried it out to where Kurt and Thomas were talking.

"Here's that pizza you ordered, sir," she said to Thomas.

Thomas's eyebrows rose at seeing her for the first time in a tank top.

Please don't ask why I changed, she thought. *At least not in front of Kurt.*

"Is this pizza any good?" Thomas asked.

She loved bantering with Thomas. "My friend, this is the best pizza that's ever been made!"

"I'll be the judge of that. And let me warn you, I have extremely high standards. Sit down and let's see how you did. Oh, you remember Kurt, right?"

She sat down next to Thomas, facing Kurt. "Oh, sure. Hi, Kurt. You want some of the best pizza in the universe?"

"How could a person turn that down? I'd better wash my hands though. I just got back from horseback riding."

"So you're the one who smells like a horse. I was wondering."

He seemed surprised by her boldness, but then flashed his trademark, understated grin, and left for the men's room.

"So, what's with the . . . uh . . . new look?" Thomas asked.

"Is it okay?"

Thomas was doing his best to avoid looking at anything except her face. "Yeah, sure, why not? It's just that, uh, it's not what you usually wear. So why did you change? For Kurt?"

She was blushing. "I just wanted to see how I'd look, that's all. Do you think he noticed?"

"Oh, yeah," Thomas said with a silly grin. "You can trust me on that."

"It was a dumb thing to do, wasn't it?" She folded her arms over her midriff because she felt self-conscious.

"You don't need to do anything, you know. You're great just the way you are."

"Yeah, right," she said with a scowl.

"I'm serious."

"Whatever."

"Why do you like Kurt, anyway?" he asked.

"Look at him. And because he's so sure of himself."

"He's like you then, right?"

"Do I seem that way?"

"With people you're good friends with, you are."

"That's what I want to be."

"That's what you are."

"Thanks." She kissed him on the cheek.

"What's that for?"

"For being my friend."

He raised his hand to fend her off. "Don't go thinking that kissing me is going to make me give you a better evaluation of your pizza. I can't be bought, you know."

She laughed. "Well, it was worth a shot."

"All right, it's payback time. I made you feel good about yourself. Now you do the same for me."

"You want me to lie?"

He grinned. "Yeah, pretty much."

"Well, you're my very best friend, and I love spending time with you."

"That's not a lie, though, is it?"

"No, it's the truth."

He put his hands behind his head and leaned back. "Tell some outrageous but flattering lies about me, okay?"

6

She ran her fingers through his hair and spoke in a husky, seductive voice. "You are, without a doubt, the sexiest guy in the world."

He chuckled. "That was okay, but this time try to exaggerate."

She mussed his hair with one swipe of her hand.

"Hey, don't mess with perfection, girl."

She folded her arms across her chest. "You think I'm dumb for wanting to spend time with Kurt, don't you?"

"Well, yeah, I do actually."

"Why?"

"Because Kurt doesn't need anyone. Not you, not me, not anyone. That's the way he's always been."

"I like that in a guy."

He shook his head. "Great then, if that's what you want."

"Are you jealous?" she asked, putting her hand on his arm.

"Maybe a little, but I'm not that worried. You and I will always be close. And Kurt will be out of your life before long."

"You're probably right."

Kurt came back and sat down. He looked at Megan as if expecting her to say something. "Well?"

Megan didn't know what he meant. "Well, what?"

"How do I smell?"

She leaned over the table and sniffed. "A lot better."

"Good. You ever try to wash up in a restroom? It's not that great. Especially trying to dry yourself with paper towels. The wet towels kept sticking to me. At one point I looked like a mummy."

She laughed. "I would've loved to see that."

"I should've invited you in."

"Actually, I usually stay out of men's restrooms."

"Except for when you clean for me after everyone else is gone," Thomas said.

"Oh, well, sure, but that doesn't count."

7

Thomas put his arm around Megan and patted her shoulder. "After our little party is over here, most everyone chips in and does a little work, but Megan stays around and works until everything's done. She saves me a ton of work."

Kurt gave a halfhearted smile. "What a trooper." He looked bored.

He's going to leave now and never come back. What am I doing wrong?

Kurt started to talk about his dad's sailboat. Megan leaned forward and tried to look very interested in everything he was saying, even offering animated comments like, "That sounds so fun!"

It must have worked. "You want to go sailing?" Kurt asked.

"Sure, when?"

"Now."

"Now?"

"There's a full moon, so we'll be able to see where we're going."

She didn't know what to say. She turned to Thomas. "I'd better stick around and help Thomas clean up after everyone else goes."

"No, that's okay," Thomas said. "You go ahead. I can get by without you."

To Kurt the decision had been made. He stood up, grabbed what was left of the pizza and a handful of napkins, and said to Thomas, "Sorry to take your best worker and the best pizza in the universe."

"No problem, man."

Megan felt like she was betraying Thomas. "Are you sure you don't need me?"

"No, you go ahead," he said with what looked to her like a slightly forced smile.

Kurt drove a late model, bright yellow Jeep Wrangler, complete with roll bars and with the top removed. He turned to his favorite radio station, started the engine, and turned to her and smiled. "You buckled up?"

"I am."

"Good," he said.

She worried, because of his reputation as an outdoors adventurer, that he'd drive like a maniac, but he didn't. In fact, she felt very safe with him. He didn't talk much while he drove, but that was okay. It gave her a chance to enjoy the ride.

An hour later he pulled up to a parking area next to the private dock where his father's boat was moored.

She looked at the clock on the dashboard. It was two o'clock. Her mother would expect her to be home by now. Her dad was a Scoutmaster and was on a camp out with the boys.

She knew she should call home and tell her mother what was going on but didn't because her mother would want her home right away. Megan didn't want to cut short her time with Kurt. She figured they'd be out on the water for maybe an hour, and then it would take another hour for Kurt to drive her home. But at least she'd have a good explanation of why she was late.

She decided not to tell Kurt she needed to be home.

It was a beautiful thirty-foot sailboat, sleek and long and slender.

"This is amazing!" she said as he extended his hand and helped her step onto the polished, wood deck.

"It's even better on the open water. Let's get to work. I'll need some help from you."

"Sure, what?"

"I'll tell you, but first we need to have a few lessons. Listen carefully because there will be a quiz afterwards."

"Sounds serious," she teased.

"It can be. If you mess up at Leo's, you end up throwing away a pizza. You mess up here, and you could die."

"Okay, teach me what I need to know."

"The right-hand side of the boat is called the starboard side. The left-hand side is called . . ."

"Wait a minute. Why not just call it the right side of the boat?"

"Tradition."

She smiled. "And calling it by the right name is going to save my life? I don't think so. I think you just want to impress me with how much you know."

He started laughing. "Well, I can see you've got me figured out."

"Not quite, but almost. I just need a little time."

"I think that can be arranged."

An old man with a flashlight walked down the dock toward them.

"Who's that?" she asked privately.

"Night watchman."

The man got close enough and then shined the flashlight in their eyes. "Kurt, I see you're at it again, hey?"

"It's a beautiful night for sailing."

"Yes, it is. And how is Samantha doing tonight?"

Kurt rolled his eyes. "Actually, this isn't Samantha."

"Oh, sorry. Who's this one?"

"Tell him your name," Kurt said.

"You don't know my name?"

"Sorry. I forgot."

"I'm Megan," she said to the night watchman.

"Oh, Megan. Well, good to meet you. I can't keep track of 'em all."

"Apparently, Kurt can't either," Megan teased.

"He brings a lot of girls out here, that's for sure."

"I'm sure you have other things to do," Kurt said, sounding annoyed.

"This is our first Megan, isn't it?"

"Yes, it is. It's been great talking to you."

"You're right. I need to go. Well, be careful out there. The sea is a vengeful mistress."

"We'll be careful."

"The sea is a vengeful mistress," Kurt mimicked as the night watchman continued on his way.

"So, how many girls have you brought out here?" she asked.

"What difference does it make?"

"Maybe you should have a guest book so you can keep track of 'em all."

"I haven't found what I'm looking for yet," he said.

"What are you looking for?"

"Someone I can talk to about things that really matter."

She could find nothing about his answer to make fun of. That was what she wanted, too.

The things Kurt needed her to do as they left the dock were easy enough—shining a flashlight ahead of them to make sure there were no hidden obstacles and steering the small outboard motor while Kurt rigged the sails as they left the inlet.

And then they were under way. It was a magical experience to be silently sailing under a moonlit sky with the lights of the city across the bay, shining like sparkling diamonds.

It was cooler on the water. She had goose bumps and wished she had something to put on over her tank top; but she didn't say anything about it. "It's so beautiful out here," she said.

He nodded. "This is where I come alive."

"I can see why."

"I'm happy to share it with you. Oh, there's some wine in a cupboard in the galley. Why don't you go see if you can find it and then pour us both a glass?"

Ordinarily she didn't drink. Just once in a while when it would be awkward to say no. But never to excess. For instance, she'd never been drunk. And she was always very

11

careful so her parents wouldn't find out. Even if she'd been drinking on a Saturday night, she always made sure she made it to church the next day because she didn't want her parents to get suspicious.

She knew what the Church taught about not drinking, but she couldn't see how a beer or two with friends once in a while was that big of a deal. It was like the boy who talked her into taking her first drink at a party two years earlier had said, "It's just one beer, okay? It's not going to kill you. C'mon, loosen up. You're ruining the night for everyone else."

She found the wine, located two glasses, and poured a little in each glass. Drinking wine on an expensive sailboat in the middle of the night seemed like a very grown-up thing to do.

On her way out of the galley, she saw a sweatshirt on a hook. It would keep her warm and make her feel less self-conscious, but she decided not to ask if she could wear it. Kurt was paying attention to her. She wasn't sure how much of that was due to the tank top, but she definitely didn't want to ruin everything.

She made her way back to Kurt and gave him one of the glasses. He took a small sip and set the glass in a nearby cup holder.

They sipped their wine and looked at the stars and at the lights of the city, enjoying the sound of the wake as the sleek hull knifed through the dark waves. In the distance she could see the Golden Gate Bridge in one direction and the Bay Bridge in the other. Megan could hardly believe it. Being here, alone with Kurt, was about the most exciting thing she had ever done.

"You love this, don't you?" she asked.

"I do. More than I can say." He seemed to be struggling to open up to her. "Out here is the one place where I feel . . . like I've found my place in life." He paused. "And . . . that I'm not a complete failure."

12

"It's hard for me to believe you'd ever feel that way about yourself."

He nodded. "I don't admit it to most people." He paused, then sighed. "Actually, I've never admitted that to anyone else." He smiled. "You know what? You're very easy to talk with. Not like the other girls I've brought out here."

"Why am I different?"

"With everyone else, it's like I'm putting on an act. My dad once told me, 'Never let 'em see you sweat.' I guess that's what I do with everyone else. But sometimes I get tired of it all and wish I could just find someone that I'd feel free to talk to about my hopes . . ." She was seated next to him as he operated the wheel, and he reached over and rested his hand on her leg just above her knee. " . . . and my dreams for the future. Maybe you're what I've been looking for . . . all this time."

She wasn't that comfortable having his hand on her leg, but she was reluctant to ask him to remove it when he was revealing his innermost thoughts and dreams for the future.

A moment later he removed his hand and asked, "Are you cold?"

"Well, maybe a little."

"You should have told me. Let me go get you something."

He brought out the sweatshirt she'd seen. "Here, put this on."

She put it over her head. It had that new sweatshirt smell she loved. Being warm again, along with the wine, made her feel relaxed and comfortable.

"The truth is, I don't have anyone . . . I can really open up to," he said. "About the things that really matter, I mean, like what I'm going to do with my life."

"What do you want to do?"

He sighed. "That's just it. I don't know. Oh, of course, my folks have plenty of suggestions. But it's all what they'd do if

13

they were my age. Well, they had their chance. Now it's my turn."

"Have your folks ever said you had to be exactly like them?"

"No, not in so many words, but the message is always there."

"You don't have to follow in their footsteps."

He nodded. "You're right. You're absolutely right. You know what I'd like to do? Have a marine store and sell boats like this."

"Do it then."

"It wouldn't bring in much money."

"You don't have to be rich to be happy."

He smiled. "Now that's a new thought."

"It's true."

"Are you happy?" he asked.

"Most of the time."

He sighed and took another sip of wine. "You're doing better than me then, that's for sure. I'll go get us some more wine."

She didn't want any more wine but didn't tell him that because she didn't want to ruin the evening. When he returned, he brought the bottle. "Do you want me to fill up your glass?"

"Just a little."

She noticed a pattern in his drinking. He would fill the glass maybe a fourth of the way full as if he just wanted a sip, and then he'd take small sips occasionally, giving the impression he was just a social drinker. But then, a few minutes later, he'd repeat the whole process over again.

The more he drank, the more he confided in her. "I just want to be left alone to let me find out who I really am. Is that asking too much?"

"No, not at all."

"This is so great having someone I can talk to like this.

14

And this night, well, it's perfect. It's a gift, really, a gift made for us to share together."

She looked at her watch. "Well, that gift is going to have to end pretty soon because I've got to get home and get some sleep."

He put his hand on her arm. "Why go home?"

"Because my mom will be starting to wonder where I am."

"Any other reason?"

"I need to get some sleep, so I can go to work tomorrow."

"This is such a beautiful night. What if we stayed out here all night? You could sleep in the cabin. I'd sleep out here under the stars. It'd give us more time to be together."

"I can't stay here tonight with you."

"Why not?"

"Well, for one reason, my mom would freak out. And my dad, too, when he gets home tomorrow."

"Where is he?"

"He's a Scoutmaster. He's on a camp out tonight."

"Your dad is a Scoutmaster? You're not serious."

"He's been Scoutmaster for the past five years. He bought a Scout uniform when he first began. It fit then, but now his stomach spills out so you can hardly tell if he's wearing a belt or not."

Kurt laughed. "I guess I shouldn't complain. My life could be a lot worse. Like, my dad could be a Scoutmaster."

"He loves it."

"Good for him."

Kurt sat down next to her and reached for her hand. "I told you there would be a quiz about sailing tonight. So here it is. What if the wind were to suddenly die down and we were left stranded out here until morning? We'd have no way of getting back to shore."

"Except for the outboard motor," she said.

"Let's say we don't have an outboard motor."

"But we do."

"Pretend we don't. It's my quiz, okay?"

"Well, even if we didn't have an outboard motor, the fact is the wind isn't dying down."

"True, but your mom doesn't know that, right?" he said with a grin. Even in the darkness, his straight teeth glowed white.

"Well, actually, Kurt, I'm not comfortable spending the night out here with you."

"Hey, I know what you mean, but we need to get to know each other better. Nothing will happen, okay? Except we'll have a few more hours on the water on the most beautiful night for sailing I've ever experienced. Let's call your mom and tell her about the wind dying down and us out here with no motor. What is she going to do? Swim out here and rescue us? I don't think so."

Even though she still had reservations, Megan took his cell phone and punched in the numbers.

It rang several times before her mom answered it.

"Mom, hi, it's me. Don't get worried, okay? Everything's fine. I'm with Kurt. We were in choir my junior year."

She listened for a moment.

"Well, I met him at Leo's, he's a friend of Thomas, and he took me out on his dad's sailboat, but now the wind has died down, so we can't get back."

She glanced at Kurt, and he gave her a thumbs-up.

"So I won't be home until morning. I didn't want you to worry." She listened again.

"Yes, I know it's late. Sorry. There's nothing I can do about it now, though. We're stranded out here. I feel as bad about it as you do."

"Let me talk to her," Kurt said.

She handed him the phone, and he put his hand over the mouthpiece.

"What's your last name?" he asked.

"Cannon."

He put the phone to his ear. "Hello, Mrs. Cannon? I'm sorry about this, really I am. Don't worry about a thing. Megan will be perfectly safe here. We should be back around ten in the morning. . . . Yes, that's right. If you want, I can give you my cell phone number in case you want to get hold of us. . . . Okay, here it is." He gave her his cell phone number, assured her once again of Megan's well-being, then said good-bye.

"There's a bed in the cabin. When it's time, I'll make it up for you." He paused. "You'll be safe in there."

"Thank you."

They spent another hour sailing. At first she just stood next to him as he steered, but after a time he had her sit in front of him and he let her steer as he pointed out the lighted landmarks on the shore—Fisherman's Wharf, Ghiardelli Square, Coit Tower, and the big hotels on Nob Hill. Megan had never done anything so romantic and couldn't believe she was actually there with Kurt, cradled in his arms, listening to the wash of the boat's wake, the lights of the city reflecting off the water.

Finally, they went toward the shore and anchored the boat for the night, and then he showed her where there was an extra blanket, said goodnight, and closed the door to the cabin on his way out.

She was self-conscious about the arrangements and didn't think she'd sleep at all, but just after nine-thirty in the morning she awoke, sat up, looked out a porthole, and saw that they were under way.

She glanced into a mirror on the galley wall, tousled her hair with her fingers, and wished she had a toothbrush or some gum. Then she left the galley and climbed the stairs to the deck. Kurt was standing at the wheel. He smiled when he saw her.

"Good morning," he said.

"Good morning."

17

"Did you sleep okay?" he asked.

"Yeah, really good. What about you?"

"No problem at all, except I was a little lonely not having you to talk to. I can't remember when I've opened up so much to anyone. You probably know me better already than anyone. Thanks for being such a good listener."

"I enjoyed talking to you, too."

"You want to call your mom and tell her you're okay?"

"She's at work by now."

"She has a phone at her work, doesn't she?"

"Yes."

"Let's call her then. I don't want her worrying."

"What about your folks?" Megan asked. "Why haven't you called them?"

"They know where I am."

"How do they know that?"

"GPS tracking. They always know where I am when I'm out on the boat . . . or at least they could know if they wanted to. My parents and I have an arrangement. I stay within their limits of acceptable behavior, and they don't ask too many questions. It's a good arrangement. They're very busy people, you know, and very influential. They don't want any negative publicity about me, but other than that, I'm on my own."

"That seems strange to me."

"It's like being in a very big and very expensive prison. As long as I don't try to escape, things go well for me."

Five minutes later Kurt was talking to Megan's mother at work. "Hi, Mrs. Cannon. This is the guy who got your daughter stuck in the middle of the bay last night," he laughed. "I just wanted you to know that everything's fine. I didn't want you to be worrying about her. Also, we drifted a little during the night, so we're just a few miles from Sausalito. I was wondering if I could have your permission to take her to breakfast there before we head back."

This was all new information to Megan.

18

"Yes, thank you. Would you like to talk to her?"

He handed Megan the phone. "Hi, Mom. Everything's okay here. I'll be home soon. Okay. . . . Yeah, me, too. Bye."

She handed the cell phone back to him. "I need to be at work at one o'clock," she said.

"Where do you work?"

"Burger King."

"Can you get the day off?"

"No."

"Have you ever missed work?"

"Yeah, sure, when I'm sick."

"How long has it been since you called in sick?" he asked.

"About six months."

"Well, I think you're about to get sick again. C'mon, one day isn't going to make any difference. If you call now, your boss will be able to get someone to fill in for you."

"That's not how it works. If I'm not going to be there, I have to get my own substitute."

"Even better." He handed her the phone.

"Why should I sluff work?"

"Because this is going to be a spectacular day. And that should never be taken for granted. We'll go to Sausalito and have an early lunch, looking out at the bay while we eat, and then we'll walk through Vina del Mar Park and see the elephants and the fountain, and then we'll go back, have a snack, and come home. We'll be home about the same time you'd be getting off work. This will be our day in the sun. Everyone deserves a day in the sun, a time-out, and this will be yours. It's my gift to you." He was grinning at her. An inviting kind of grin.

"What about you? Don't you have a job?"

"I work for my dad, but my hours are my own."

"What do you do?"

"I write code for computer games. I do most of my work

19

at home, usually between the hours of eleven at night and two in the morning. I'm all caught up this week."

"Let me think about it while I get cleaned up, okay?"

"Sure, take all the time you need. We'll be at Sausalito in half an hour, but we can always turn around and head back."

She went into the boat's cabin, closed the door, and began to wash her face. As she did so, she thought about her job. She worked harder than any of the other student workers, and she was often called upon to fill in for them when they got sick.

It was hard work, and her boss hardly ever said a nice thing to anyone. The best part of the work day was when he left and put her in charge. They worked harder but had more fun when he was gone.

Her boss had grudgingly made her assistant manager but at no increase in pay. Three nights a week she closed and took care of the night depository.

She was tired of the people she worked with. Most of them told dirty jokes and made cutting remarks about the people who came in to eat.

Kurt is right. I deserve a day off.

A few minutes later she came back on deck. "I need to use your phone to try and get someone to go in for me."

He smiled. "I promise you won't regret it."

"I may not be able to get a substitute."

"I'm sure you'll get the job done."

It took six phone calls to get someone to go in for her. By that time they were pulling into Sausalito. After docking the boat, they walked along the waterfront and bought food for a picnic lunch, which they ate at a park.

"This is where I want to live someday," Kurt said. "I'll work from an office in my home. I'll work three hours a day and then spend the rest of my time sailing."

"How would it be?"

"It would be even better if you and I were enjoying it together."

"It sounds like it could be fun."

When they were done eating, they tossed their trash in a dumpster. "But right now it's time to go shopping. All the big stars from Hollywood come here. Let's go back to the boat. You can ditch the sweatshirt, and we'll put on sunglasses like we're rich and famous and don't want anyone to know who we are, and we'll walk through this town like we owned it."

As she followed his advice and took off the sweatshirt, she was still a little self-conscious about the tank top but felt more confident than she had when she first put it on the night before.

They spent an hour pretending to be rich and famous, wandering in and out of the quaint shops and art galleries, acting sufficiently bored, pretending to nearly buy artwork valued at over twenty thousand dollars and then, when they couldn't keep a straight face anymore, running outside and laughing about it all the way to the next shop.

Kurt had brought a digital camera from the boat. "Let's pretend you're a famous fashion model and we're here today on a shoot."

She smiled and shook her head. "Just take the stupid picture, okay?"

He took the picture. "Work with me, baby! Show me some good stuff!"

At first she was too self-conscious to do much more than just smile at the camera, but after a while, with Kurt's encouragement, she got into it. She told herself that she didn't know any of the tourists milling around and would never see any of them again. After that she tried to pose as if she really were a fashion model.

Kurt loved it. "Oh, yeah! You're hot now! That's it! Give me more of that."

When a group of Japanese tourists stopped to watch and

take their own pictures of her, Megan decided it was time to quit. "Kurt, I can't do this anymore. It's too embarrassing."

"Sure, I understand. Let's go someplace else."

They walked along the harbor front for a while, enjoying the view of the city across the bay, then sat down on the lawn in the warmth of the sun. While he lay on the lawn, half sleeping, she sang to him. After a couple of songs, he opened his eyes and smiled. "Let's do this every day for the rest of our lives."

"I think after a while my boss would catch on that I wasn't coming in to work."

"So what? It's a dumb job anyway, right?"

"But it's the only one I've got. We can't all have *rich* parents."

"Look, my parents aren't rich, okay?" He spoke with bitter resentment.

"How can you say that? That boat alone is worth more than the house I live in. Looks to me like you've got it made. You work, what did you say, three hours a day? I know this will be a surprise to you, but some people work eight to ten hours a day. Like my mom and dad. They both work hard every day."

He cupped her chin with his hand and turned her head so they had eye contact. "There's something you need to know about me."

"What?"

"When it comes to writing computer code for video games, I'm . . . well, . . . I'm one of the best. I'll just leave it at that. I know I go around looking like all I do is have fun, but that's just because when I do work, it takes so much concentration that I can only do it for a few hours at a time."

She didn't appreciate him lecturing her. "Okay . . . sorry if I made you mad. I didn't mean anything by it."

"It's kind of a sore point with me. All the guys I graduated from high school with think I'm totally irresponsible for not

22

going to college like them. But I'm already making more than they ever will, so why should I follow in their footsteps?"

"No reason to."

He sighed. "I'm glad you understand. Sorry if I came on too strong. Sometimes I just get tired of trying to explain to the world why I'm not like everyone else."

She was quiet for a moment. "That's why I like you."

He put his arm around her shoulder as they continued their walk. He whispered in her ear. "Do you have any idea how beautiful you are?"

She blushed. "No, not really."

"Well, you are."

"Thanks."

"Especially your eyes. Did you know they sparkle when you smile? And your mouth. I bet when you were a kid, you could give your folks a pouty face better than anyone in your family."

She stopped walking. "Excuse me? Are you saying I was a difficult child?"

"No, not at all. It was a compliment."

"Yeah, right," she laughed.

They stopped to admire the sailboats dancing on the water. "It's such an amazing day, isn't it?" he asked.

"It is."

"The sun, the water, the clouds, it's all just perfect. But even with all that, the most beautiful thing on this island is right here beside me."

"You're making me blush."

"What do you say we stay here tonight?" he asked. "We'll find ourselves a fancy hotel, and we'll call up room service and order every chocolate dessert they've got. How does that sound? You like chocolate, don't you?"

She was alarmed by how innocent he made it seem. "Kurt, I can't drop everything just to be your playmate for a day."

He kissed her cheek. "I think what we've got going here is

way more serious than just two people coming together for a day or two."

"You do?" she asked hopefully.

"Oh, yeah. Something like this doesn't come along every day. I mean, at least not for me. What about you?"

She cleared her throat. "I've never had more fun with anyone."

He gave her his confident grin. "I'm so glad to hear you say that. I was worried I was the only one who felt this way."

Megan was worried. This was moving way too fast. *I need to let him know what I believe. But where do I start?*

She cleared her throat. "There's something you need to know though."

"What?"

She paused. "Did you know that I'm a Mormon?"

"Let's see, did I know that? I think somebody told me that once."

"We're taught that life is more than just having fun," she said.

"Since when?"

She rested her hand on his shoulder. "Kurt, you have so much to give to the world. The reason you were sent to earth is to help others less fortunate than yourself."

"Helping others? You know what? I've never thought of that as a reason for living. Well, okay, Megan, if you really want to help someone, help me become a better person."

She smiled. It was the one offer she couldn't refuse.

2

On Sunday Megan went to church but found it hard to think about anything except Kurt. It was Scout Sunday, which meant the deacons and her father wore their Scout uniforms to church. It was an old ritual, and Megan had long ago gotten over being embarrassed about it. She just tried to pretend that the totally enthusiastic, nearly bald, middle-aged man with stomach protruding under his faded Scout shirt was not her father.

Sometimes she wondered if her dad actually thought they were close. *He might*, she thought. *That's because we never really talk. Or if we do, I try to say what he wants to hear. It's not that hard to do. Anyone can learn to do it.*

Megan's family always sat in the same place in sacrament meeting, usually the third row on the right side of the chapel. That allowed her mother, who was ward chorister, to sit with them after the sacrament until the closing song.

Megan always sat on the end of the row nearest the wall, with her fifteen-year-old sister, Brianna. Their father, Walter, sat next to Brianna, and Carolyn, their mother, sat on the end of the row, next to the aisle. Megan liked having Brianna serve as the buffer between her and her parents.

Her twenty-one-year-old brother, Bryce, didn't go to church anymore. At first it was because he worked Sundays at The Home Depot, but then, after a while, he quit coming, even when he wasn't working.

Because it was Scout Sunday, the deacons gave talks about the values of Scouting in their lives.

I've heard these same talks every year since I can remember, Megan thought.

She took the program for the meeting and drew four lines to set up a game of tic-tac-toe with Brianna. It was something they'd been doing for years. She showed Brianna the paper.

"Only if I can be first," Brianna whispered.

"You're always first," Megan answered.

"That's because I win. The one who wins gets to be first the next game."

"The reason you win is because you go first all the time."

Brianna smiled sweetly. "Who else have you got to play this game with?"

Megan shrugged, and they started to play, passing the paper back and forth as they made their marks.

A few minutes later, Brianna stopped their game long enough to listen to the special music. A girl Brianna's age sang a hymn.

"You're way better than her," Megan whispered.

Brianna smiled. "I know."

Megan studied her sister's face. They didn't look much like sisters. Megan was darker in complexion and had more of a dramatic look to her. Brianna was like the cheerleader for the whole human race. She talked with more energy and volume and enthusiasm than any of her friends. And she had a gift for comedy. Just watching her was enough to make anyone smile, even more so now that she had developed her own rap vocabulary.

Privately at least, Megan had begun to think of her parents as Walter and Carolyn. They were less threatening that way. *Walter and Carolyn,* she thought. *If you're named Walter, what else can you end up being but a joke to the rest of the world? How did those two ever get together? Mom says they became friends first and then they fell in love.*

Sometimes when they talked about their courtship, her father would say with a big smile, "You never know what a little friendliness can get you."

She'd grown up listening to her dad, a sales representative, talking on the phone, saying, "Good morning, this is Walt from Consolidated Industries. How's it going? Say, I was wondering . . ."

As critical as she was of her father, she found it difficult to be too hard on her mother. *She's still pretty, even though she's been doing her hair the same way for as long as I can remember. I remember when she seemed so tall, and now she's the shortest one in the family.*

The girl finished her song and the game of tic-tac-toe continued.

Brianna, when she won, which she always did when she was first, leaned over and whispered, "I took care of it, right?"

"You hottie," Megan whispered back, a phrase she'd learned from Brianna.

Megan skipped Sunday School because it was boring. She went to Young Women, though, because the news would get back to her parents if she weren't there.

Before Young Women began, Alexis, the Laurel class president, approached her. "We're having a presidency meeting right after church. Can you come?"

Megan was the secretary of the Laurel class. "I'm not sure. Probably not. Sorry."

Alexis paused. "I called yesterday morning but you were gone. I left a message."

"Sorry, I didn't get it."

27

"We could meet at my house later today, if that would work out better for you."

"No, you go ahead."

Alexis looked troubled. "Is anything wrong?"

"No, why do you ask?"

"No reason." Alexis looked directly into Megan's eyes.

"What?" Megan snapped.

Alexis pursed her lips. "Nothing. You just seem different today, that's all."

"I'm the same as I've always been."

In her Laurel class the lesson was about the importance of staying true to the standards of the Church. To keep her mind occupied, Megan took a piece of paper and wrote Kurt's name over and over.

As they drove home from church, her mother asked how their classes had been.

"Real good," Megan said.

"What was your lesson about?" her mother asked.

"Keeping the standards," Megan said.

All afternoon she stayed by the phone, hoping Kurt would either call or come over to see her, but he didn't, so she took a nap and then watched some reruns of *Friends*. She'd taped all the episodes so she could watch her favorite programs anytime she wanted. Someday, she wanted to have a life like the cast on the show.

◆　　◆　　◆

The family waited until Bryce got home from work before they had their big meal on Sunday.

He always entered a room like he was a cop making a drug bust.

"Hey, bro, what's happenin'?" Brianna asked.

"Don't talk to me about work! I hate working Sundays."

Bryce was the tallest one in the family. He had a high-domed

28

forehead and a strong jaw. He prided himself on his barrel chest and what he called his "washboard abs," something he had developed by buying every ab machine offered on infomercials in the past year. Most of them were now stored in the storage shed next to the house.

Bryce went to wash up before supper.

Brianna had gone to a dance the night before and wanted to talk about it as only she could do. "Well, this hottie Derin was talking to me, and I was like, 'Wow, he way is diggin' me,' so I was all, 'Hey, pap, what up, stud?' So he was all, 'Not much, mama, how you doing?' So we talked, right? And then when I was making my cool exit, I tripped. So I turn to him and I'm all, 'Good thing I didn't just trip and look stupid, huh?'"

"Please pass the mashed potatoes," Walter said.

Bryce returned to the dining room and sat down. "Why do you talk like that?" he asked Brianna.

"Like what?" Brianna asked.

"You know what I'm talking about. You think it's cool, but it isn't. It's stupid."

"How do you want me to talk?" Brianna asked.

"Like a normal person."

"Yeah, right," Brianna said. "Like you're the expert on normal."

"What went wrong at work?" Carolyn asked.

Bryce shrugged. "Sundays are when all the desperate women come out."

"Desperate women? I don't understand," Walter said.

"You show me a woman wearing tight jeans and a too-small tank top who says she needs a five-eighths socket wrench, and I'll show you a desperate woman."

"Are you saying a woman can't buy a wrench?" Megan asked.

"No, I'm not saying that. I can tell the ones who are trolling for men though. They've spent at least four hours getting ready. They wander around the store looking like they're lost, hoping to find a man to help 'em. But they never buy anything. And some of them have left kids at home with a sitter."

"Are they looking for a husband?"

"They're looking for anything they can find. My favorite time to work is Mondays, where all you see are contractors buying supplies for the week. But not Sundays."

"If you didn't work Sundays, you could come to church," Carolyn said gently.

Bryce smiled. "I don't hate Sundays that much, but keep trying, Mom."

After they finished eating, they read one chapter from the Book of Mormon. It was a Sunday tradition.

"I'd like to interview each of my children today," Walter said.

"Count me out," Bryce said, getting up. "I'm going to help a friend sheetrock."

"Megan, how about if we start with you, and then I'll do Brianna."

Megan had grown up having monthly interviews with her father. The last time she'd been totally honest in talking to him had been when she was in the ninth grade. He'd asked if she had any questions about sex, and she'd asked him a question about something she'd heard in school that someone had done. It flustered him so much that he had to leave the room for a glass of water. When he came back, he said, "I really don't think you should be thinking about things like that."

"It's just something I heard at school, that's all. I just wanted to know what it is and what the Church teaches about it."

"The Church is against anything like that. That's all you need to know."

From that moment on, she began holding back from him.

And now she said very little that would let him know what her life was really like.

But, still, they dutifully went through the ritual once a month.

This interview always took place at the dining room table. Everyone in the family knew to stay away during these times.

"How are things going for you?" he asked. He would be going to a court of honor later that day and was still wearing his too-tight Scout shirt.

"Just fine, Daddy. Just fine." She looked at all the badges he had on his shirt and wondered why he insisted on disgracing himself so publicly.

"Your mother says that on Friday night you went sailing with a boy and when the wind went down you couldn't get back, so you and the boy stayed the night in his boat."

"Yes, Daddy, that's true. We both felt bad about it. Oh, in case you're wondering, nothing happened. We didn't even kiss."

"Well, that's good to hear. Some boys might have tried to take advantage of a situation like that."

"I know, but I'd never spend time with a boy like that."

"You can't always tell these days."

"I'm real careful, Daddy."

"Good, I'm glad to hear that." He cleared his throat. "There's one more thing. Your mother says she's not happy with some of the clothes you've been buying lately."

"Like what, Daddy?"

"She says you bought a tank top with your last paycheck."

"I did, and I know that doesn't sound very modest, but, the thing is, I'm going to always wear a T-shirt over it, so it's not that bad."

"Oh, I see. I didn't know that." He seemed puzzled. "If you always wear a T-shirt over it, then why'd you buy it?"

"It's what people are wearing these days. Except they wear it without the T-shirt. But not me."

31

Walter cleared his throat nervously a couple of times. "Sometimes a boy will get a certain . . . message when a girl wears immodest clothes. It might not be the kind of a message a girl like you wants to give."

"I know all about that, Daddy. We talk about it all the time in Young Women."

He gave a sigh of relief. "Well, good, I'm glad you know." He got up and got himself a glass of water. "You want any?"

"No thanks."

He took a big gulp and sat down. "One more question. How are you doing in regard to chastity?"

"Fine, Daddy. Everything's fine."

He seemed relieved. "Good. Do you have any questions for me?"

"No. Like I said, we cover all that in Young Women."

"What about the Word of Wisdom? Any problems there?"

"Not really." She chuckled. "Except . . . I shouldn't have had so much dessert today."

He laughed, patting his stomach. "Well, I don't think we want to get into that. If we do, I'll end up having to go on a diet."

"You're just fine the way you are, Daddy."

"Well, I should watch what I eat more than I do." He finished off the rest of his water. "I think we're done, unless you have anything you want to talk to me about."

"No, Daddy. Everything's going real good for me now."

"I suppose you'll be applying for college any day now, won't you? You think you might go to BYU?"

"I'm not sure my grades are good enough."

"How about BYU-Idaho?"

"I don't know. I guess I could try."

"Or if not that, you could go to a California school where they have a strong institute program."

"That's a good idea, Daddy. I'll look into that, too."

32

He stood up and hugged her. "You're growing up so fast. A year from now you'll be away to college. We'll miss you."

"Thank you, Daddy. I'll miss you, too."

"Go tell Brianna I'm ready for her."

"Yes, Daddy. Thank you for taking the time to talk to me."

"My pleasure. I know I'm not home much during the week, and then with Scouts I'm gone some Friday nights and Saturdays, but I want you to know you're my number one priority."

"I know that, Daddy."

She was relieved that was over for another month.

◆　　◆　　◆

Monday nights were usually slow after hours at Leo's Pizza, and the next day was no exception. The weekend had taken its toll on Thomas's friends, but Megan showed up. She wanted to spend some time with Thomas.

They worked in the kitchen cleaning up. She was on her hands and knees washing the worst spots while Thomas was scrubbing down the counters with soap and water. He always told her she didn't need to do the floors on her hands and knees, but she liked to do it the way her mother had taught her on their kitchen floor at home.

"So, how was it with Kurt?" he asked.

She tried being low-key. "It was okay."

"Just okay?"

She smiled. "Better than okay, actually."

"Tell me all about it."

Megan told him everything.

"So, you stayed the night with him on his boat?"

"Yeah, but nothing happened. I slept in the cabin, and he slept under the stars."

He grinned. "Yeah, right."

"It's the truth."

He quit smiling. "I believe you. I was just teasing. So, do you like him?"

"Yeah, actually, I do."

"What do you like most about him?" Thomas asked.

She thought about it before answering. "He really opened up to me. I mean once you get to know him, he's not anything like the way he comes across. At least not with me."

Thomas chose his words carefully. "Did he tell you that he was opening up more to you than anyone else he's ever known?"

"What if he did?"

"Well, that's great . . . if it's true. I mean it might just be what he says to girls to get them to trust him."

"He's not like that."

Thomas held back saying more. "Great then. I'm happy for both of you."

"You don't trust him, do you?"

"I don't know. I'm not sure what to think."

"I'll be careful."

"Good. I think you should."

She was standing next to Thomas at the sink while he worked. He was wearing a ragged, gray T-shirt. She slowly ran her hand down his arm. It was part of a running joke between them. The hair on his arms was like the hair on his head—dense and coarse. She'd once told him that if an ant ever fell on his arm the other ants would have to send out a search team to find him.

"Well, did you find that silly ant yet?" he asked her.

"No, it's still lost. What are you going to do after you graduate?"

"I guess I'll take some classes and work here at night. What about you?"

"I don't know."

"Harvard hasn't called yet?" he asked.

"No, they must have lost my number."

"Mine, too. You and me, we're pretty much average, right? No better, no worse."

"I want to be more than average," she said.

"Look on the bright side. We're way ahead of those who are below average."

She smiled. "You sure know how to cheer a girl up."

"Glad to help out."

They stepped back and admired the clean kitchen. "We're almost done here," he said. "We just need to wipe off the tables and take out the garbage."

"I can start on the tables."

A few minutes later, Thomas joined her in the eating area as they wiped the tables clean.

"Thomas, can I ask you a question? How come you don't drink?"

He shrugged his shoulders. "Drinking messed up my cousin pretty bad. He got drunk and ran his car into a bridge. So now he's in a wheelchair. I was nine years old when it happened. After that, I decided I wasn't ever going to even start."

"That's good. One other question."

"Okay."

"You don't go after girls like some guys do, you know, to see how much you can get."

"No, that's not my style."

"How come?"

"The girl I marry deserves better than that."

"You'd make a great Mormon. Better than me, that's for sure."

"Being religious isn't my style, either."

They finished up opposite each other, wiping up the same table. "Can I ask you a really personal question?" Thomas said.

"Sure, I guess so."

"You don't have to answer it if you don't want to. What are you going to do when Kurt suggests you sleep with him?"

35

"Thomas! We haven't even kissed yet. Besides, I'm not that kind of girl."

"It might be just a matter of time, though. So answer my question."

She shook her head. "I don't know."

"You'd better start thinking about it."

"I guess it would depend."

"What would it depend on?"

"If I really cared for him."

"So what you decide will be based on how you feel about him?"

"Yes, I guess it will."

"Sure, why not?" he said, walking away from her.

"You think I shouldn't?" she called out after him.

"I didn't say that, did I?"

"I know, but the way you're acting I can tell."

"Once you start that way with him, you'll never have time for me."

"That's not true, Thomas, I'll always have time for you."

He shook his head. "I know how these things work." He started for the kitchen again and then turned to her. "It's okay, though, as long as you're happy. That's the main thing, right? To be happy."

She wanted to assure him she'd always be there for him, but she wasn't sure she could guarantee it.

I wonder how this will turn out, she thought.

◆　　◆　　◆

From then on, because Thomas had raised the question, Megan tried to decide what she'd say if Kurt wanted her to sleep with him. Even after two weeks of dating him and thinking about it, she still couldn't make up her mind.

To help her decide, she picked up a copy of teen a magazine at a convenience store. An article entitled "Your First

36

Time" advised a girl not to rush into something like that but ended with "You'll know when it's right."

Whenever she watched *Friends*, the answer seemed to be, *If you like the guy and he seems really nice, and if your friends like him, too, and if you want to, then it's okay.*

She knew what the Church taught, but all the people who talked about chastity in the Church were old people with families—like her bishop, or her Laurel adviser. She couldn't imagine any of them being tempted. And it was gross to think about any of them making love. *Things are different now than when they grew up.*

Kurt isn't even a member of the Church. If I start trying to change him, he's not going to want to spend any time with me. Is that what I want?

After a lot of thought, she finally decided that if she felt that Kurt really loved her, she might agree to sleep with him.

When she told Thomas her decision, he got mad at her. "Are you saying that all any guy has to say to you is, 'I really like you,' and you'll sleep with him?"

"I didn't say *any* guy. We're talking about Kurt."

"How can you base a decision like that on what a guy says to you? Don't you know that some guys will say anything to get what they want?"

"Kurt's not that way."

"No, that's just it. He is. Why don't you base your decision on some kind of overriding principle, not just on your feelings?"

"You're just jealous."

"That's not true. I just don't want you to get hurt, that's all."

"I won't get hurt. I know what I'm doing."

"Why don't you talk to some of the girls Kurt's been with? Why don't you ask them what he's like?"

"I have," she lied.

"What did they say?"

37

"Nothing bad. Look, I can take care of myself, okay?"

"No, that's just it, you can't. You'll get hurt and then you'll come crawling back to me."

"That's not going to happen. I can take care of myself."

"Good-bye, Megan. I can't stand to sit by and let this happen to you. I can finish up here by myself tonight . . . and from now on."

Megan left Leo's Pizza that night for good.

◆　　◆　　◆

Megan continued to see Kurt. Sometimes when they were together, he opened up to her like he'd done the first night on his dad's boat, but at other times he seemed preoccupied.

"Is anything wrong?" she asked one night.

"No, not really. It's just that I've been working really hard writing code for a new computer game. After doing that for ten hours straight, it's hard to let it go. My dad's really excited about what I've done so far. He's thinking of us starting up our own company. So that'd be great."

There was one thing she could do to get him to focus totally on her, and that was kissing. At those times she had his undivided attention. She loved the feeling of having power over him. "You thinking about computers now, Kurt?" she once teased him.

"No, not at all."

"Really? What a surprise? So what are you thinking about?" she asked.

"You. Just you."

She grinned. "I know."

Sometimes things got a little crazy, but she was always able to stop what they were doing before it got out of control. And he never pushed beyond what she felt comfortable with. The only trouble was that the more time they spent together, the harder it became to hold the line.

She didn't worry about it too much when she was with him. But there were times when she worried where this was going. Like one morning when she woke up and saw her sister Brianna kneeling by her bed saying her prayers.

Brianna thought Megan was sleeping, and so she was saying her prayer out loud in a soft voice. Megan pretended to still be asleep and listened to the prayer.

"Please help me live the commandments," Brianna said softly.

I never pray anymore, Megan thought. *I should. It might help me. What would I pray for? To be happy. That's all I want out of life. Just to be happy.*

She didn't feel comfortable attending Young Women anymore because every lesson seemed to be on morality. *Why do they have to keep harping on that all the time? If I hear one more lesson about wilted flowers and the symbolism of white dresses, I'm going to puke.* She kept going, though, because if she didn't go word would get back to her parents, and she didn't want them to get on her case or be suspicious.

When she and Kurt first started seeing one another, Kurt preferred to pick her up at school or at her work, because then he didn't have to deal with her parents. But when her father found out she was continuing to see him, he said he wanted to meet Kurt.

"My dad wants to meet you," she told Kurt one night.

"Why?"

"He just does."

Kurt shrugged his shoulders. "All right, I'll do it. Tell me about your dad."

She told him more about his involvement in Scouting and about his job as a salesman.

That Friday night Kurt dropped by Megan's house to pick her up. Her dad answered the door, but her mother rushed in to have a chance to get better acquainted.

Megan wasn't quite ready when Kurt arrived. By the time

she entered the living room, he was telling Walter about how much he had enjoyed Scouting when he was a boy. Her parents were hanging on his every word.

"So, you're an Eagle Scout?" her father asked.

"Oh, yes, that's where I got my love for the outdoors."

"I can't tell you how many college-age, young men have come back to tell me their Scouting days gave them not only a love for hiking and backpacking but a solid foundation for life."

"That's certainly the case with me," Kurt said. "And not only that. What I know about patriotism, obedience to laws, respect for authority, and an appreciation for the spiritual side of life all came from Scouting."

Walter was fairly beaming.

Megan was standing in the doorway to the living room watching Kurt win her dad over. "Well, I'm ready."

Kurt stood up and shook hands with Walter. "I've really enjoyed getting to know you both."

"Since you have an appreciation for spiritual things, what would you think about hearing something about what we believe?" Walter asked.

"Well, that'd be great. Megan has already told me a few things about your church. It sounds very interesting."

"We'll see if we can arrange to have our missionaries come around sometime and teach you," her father said.

"Great. I'm looking forward to it."

A few minutes later, they were on the road. They drove to his dad's sailboat, then sailed out into the bay and followed the coast to a secluded cove where Kurt threw out the anchors and cooked them steak over a charcoal grill.

Megan sat in the boat, sipping wine and watching him. She loved the confidence and skill Kurt demonstrated as he prepared their food. And when she asked if she could help, he wouldn't let her.

After eating they drank some more wine and listened to music and watched a glorious sunset.

At nine-thirty they went swimming off the boat for half an hour.

While they held onto a float in the water, he kissed her and then whispered, "You know how I feel about you, don't you? I think about you all the time." He was nuzzling her neck with his lips.

The closeness made her shiver. "I'm the same way."

"Since we both feel the same way, and this is such a special night, why don't we do each other a really big favor?" He was smiling as he said it.

This is it, she thought. *I knew it was coming. I just didn't know when.*

There was just one thing left to find out. "Do you love me, Kurt?"

He laughed. "I think you know the answer to that, don't you?"

"Yes, I do."

"Let's go back to the boat then."

They swam to the boat, dried off, then went in the cabin, and she gave in to him.

When it was over, she wanted to stay in his arms all night and never leave him, but at ten-thirty he got up, dressed, and slipped out of the cabin and pulled up the anchor and prepared to leave.

"Are we leaving?" she asked a minute later.

"Yes. I think it's better if we don't stay out too late tonight."

"Why's that?"

"We don't want your parents to be suspicious, do we?"

On the way home, she wanted to talk, but he didn't say anything. She couldn't figure it out. She thought that what they'd done would bring them closer together.

She didn't know how to even begin a conversation. Finally she asked, "Are you really an Eagle Scout?"

He looked at her and scowled. "Why are you asking me that?"

"I just wanted to know."

"Well, it's a stupid question."

"Well, just tell me and then we'll talk about something else."

"What do you think?"

"I don't know what to think. That's why I asked."

"No, I'm not an Eagle Scout. I just said that to impress your father."

She wasn't sure why, but she felt very depressed. "That's what I thought."

"Then why did you ask the question?"

"I was just curious, that's all. It's not important."

She did have another question, though, but she didn't have the courage to ask it. The question was, *What lies have you told me just to set me up for tonight?*

"You do love me, don't you?" she asked.

She'd seen the look before. When he was upset or angry, he clamped his jaw tight. It wasn't easy to detect, but there was a set of muscles along his jawline, which became visible. Other than that, he left no clue how the question affected him.

He drove silently for a time and then turned to her, reached for her hand and kissed it. His jaw muscles were relaxed once more. "You know how I feel about you. It's even more now than ever before, because of tonight. This was your first time, wasn't it?"

"Yes," she said timidly.

"That makes it even more special to know that I was the first."

She nodded.

A minute later he looked at his watch, let go of her hand, and began driving faster.

They pulled into her driveway just after midnight. In spite of his assurances, she felt confused.

"Call me in the morning," she said as he walked her to the door.

"I've got a few things I have to do tomorrow, but I'll call you as soon as I can," he said.

He held her in his arms and whispered in her ear, "Thank you for a wonderful night. You're the best."

As soon as she got in the house, she hurried upstairs, took a shower, and then crawled into bed without turning on the light. Brianna was already asleep.

Megan couldn't sleep. She kept going over in her mind what had happened that night. At first she tried to focus on the closeness she'd felt with Kurt. But something else kept nagging at her. *I've done the one thing I've been warned all my life not to do. Now what happens? Do I go to church on Sunday and pretend nothing has happened? How can I sit through church anymore knowing what I've done? I knew this is against the teachings of the Church, but I did it anyway.*

The reason I did it is because I love Kurt. And when you love someone, you want him to be happy. I knew that doing it would make him happy. And it did for a few minutes. And then he turned weird. Like he couldn't get rid of me fast enough. I don't understand that.

At ten the next morning, a Saturday, thinking that Kurt might drive over and surprise her, she carried her phone into the bathroom. While she did her hair, she kept listening for his call.

At eleven-thirty she finished putting on her makeup and got dressed. She was scheduled to work at Burger King, at one-thirty.

At twelve o'clock she went in the kitchen and made herself a sandwich and ate it in her room. *He probably slept in this morning. That's why he hasn't called yet. But I'm sure*

43

he's up by now. He's probably taking a shower and getting ready. And then he'll call.

She half expected Kurt to drop by and see her at work, not to stay, just to say hello and maybe tell her he'd been thinking about her all day, and with a private wink telling her how much the night before had meant to him, and then asking when she got off work so they could spend some more time together.

But he never showed up.

She worked until eight and then went home. She asked if Kurt had phoned but was told nobody had called for her.

At nine-thirty that night, feeling abandoned because she hadn't heard from Kurt, she called his home.

"Is Kurt there?"

"No, he went kayaking with his friends," his mother said.

"Well, do you know when he'll be home?"

"He took his sleeping bag and camping gear, so I'd guess he won't be home tonight," his mother said.

"Oh."

"Would you like me to give him a message when he comes home?" his mother asked.

"Yes, please. Tell him Megan called."

"Megan, all right, I'll tell him. Are you the girl from the kayaking club?"

"No, I'm another Megan."

"Oh, of course. Look, maybe you'd better give me your number."

By the time she hung up, she was near tears. *How many Megans does he know? Did last night mean anything at all to him? Why doesn't he call? Will he ever call? Will I ever see him again?*

On Sunday she went to church with her family as usual. She skipped Sunday School but forced herself to go to Young Women, although it nearly made her physically ill to have to stand and recite the Young Women's theme. She wanted to

44

run out of the room and never come back, but she couldn't because Brianna would see it, or her Laurel adviser, a friend of her mother, would notice it, and questions would be asked.

Alexis sat next to her in Laurel class. "Can you meet after church for just a few minutes? We need to plan an activity with the priests quorum. It's coming up in two weeks."

"I can't meet. I have to go home."

"How about later this afternoon then?"

"No, we're having a family activity this afternoon."

"We can work around it. Just call me when it's over. We'll even come to your place if you want."

"Why do you need me?" Megan asked. "I'm just a secretary. Anyone can do that."

"You're not just a secretary. You're part of the presidency. And you always have such good ideas. I need your help."

"Sorry, but I can't help you," she said, feeling a sense of loss and estrangement.

The first thing she did when she got home after church was to check to see if there were any phone messages.

There were no messages.

At three-thirty, while she was taking a nap, there was a knock on her bedroom door.

It's Kurt! she thought excitedly.

"Yes?" she asked.

It was her mother. "Alexis is here to see you."

I told her I couldn't meet with her. Why can't she get the hint? I don't want to have anything to do with her anymore. She sat up. *If I don't at least talk to her, Mom might start getting suspicious.*

"Okay."

Her mother opened the door for Alexis to enter. "I'm sorry if I came at a bad time."

"It's all right. I needed to get up anyway. When are the others coming?"

"They're not coming. I came to visit you."

45

"Why?"

Alexis closed the door and came over and pulled up a chair next to where Megan was sitting on the bed. "I'm worried about you."

"There's no reason to be."

"You sure?"

"Of course."

"We are friends, aren't we? I mean, if you had a problem, you'd tell me, wouldn't you?"

"If I had a problem, I'd tell you. Right now my only problem is you grilling me about whether or not I have a problem. Well, I don't. I'm still the crazy, girls camp tentmate I was when we were Beehives."

Alexis gave a sigh of relief. "Good. I'm glad to hear it." She stood up. "Well, I'd better be going."

"Thanks for coming."

They walked outside together. While standing in the driveway, Alexis announced her plans for the summer. She would be leaving right after graduation to attend summer school at BYU. "What are you going to do after you graduate?"

"I'm not sure yet," Megan said.

"You should come with me to Utah. We'd have a great time together."

"We would. That's for sure. I'll think about it, okay?"

Privately, Megan was glad she'd soon be graduated and that Alexis was moving away and that she'd have the freedom to live her life the way she wanted to without any interference from anyone.

◆　　◆　　◆

On Monday, in school, she saw Thomas in the hall, but she turned her head and pretended not to see him because she didn't want to talk to him. Because if she did, he would find out what had happened. She could never hide anything from Thomas.

Kurt called on Monday night, at seven-thirty, just after family home evening. She had come very near to deciding not to see him again. She was not only mad at Kurt, but the guilt was eating her up. She'd have to go to her bishop and tell him what had happened and try to get her life back on course again.

Brianna answered the phone, then handed it to her. "It's for you."

"Who is it?" Megan mouthed.

"How should I know? It's a boy."

"Hello?" she said.

It was Kurt. "Hey, I just got back from my trip! I thought I'd call and see how you're doing."

"Okay, I guess," she said sullenly, taking the phone to her room so she could have some privacy.

"You don't sound all that great."

"Why didn't you call earlier?"

"Like I said, I went kayaking with some friends, and we were having so much fun we decided to stay an extra day."

"Oh."

"You should've been there."

"I wasn't invited."

"It's just an expression."

"I know."

"But if it's any consolation, there weren't any other girls there. Just guys."

"Oh."

"The reason I called was to see if you'd like to go sailing tonight. It'll be a perfect night for it. I can have you back by ten o'clock."

"I'm not really in the mood for sailing."

"What would you like to do then? Your choice."

She still felt betrayed. "I'm not sure."

"I just wanted to tell you that Friday night was really good for me."

She didn't say anything.

"How was it for you?" he asked.

The feeling of being abandoned afterward overshadowed any physical pleasure she might have experienced. But she knew he wouldn't understand that, and she didn't want to hurt his feelings. "It was really good," she lied, trying to sound as though she meant it, but, at the same time, feeling like she was not being honest with herself.

"For me, too," he said, then paused before adding, "So I was wondering if we could get together and do something tonight."

She wasn't sure what to do. The reason she had done what she'd done with Kurt was because she wanted to show him how much she cared for him. It wasn't just because she wanted to experience the physical act of love. She wondered if he would have been equally happy with any girl.

She had thought that giving in to him would make their love grow deeper, but now she wondered if all it had accomplished was that from now on, every time they got together, he would expect them to be intimate.

Even so, she was reluctant to stop seeing him because, if she did, it would mean that her decision to give herself to him the first time had been a mistake.

I have too much invested in this to just quit now, she thought. *Maybe in time he'll come to love me the way I want him to.*

"You still there?" he asked.

I know what I'll do. I'll show him so much love he'll never want to leave me.

With that decided, she said, "You know what, Kurt? I've changed my mind. I'd love to go sailing with you tonight."

"Good girl. You won't regret it."

Even then, she wasn't sure that was true.

48

3

I'm expecting a baby! Can you believe it?" Melissa Partridge, barely twenty years old, who had been married in the San Diego Temple only two months before, announced to the other Young Women leaders in her ward just before a presidency meeting.

"That's wonderful! Congratulations!" Colleen Butler, the Young Women president, herself the mother of five children, exclaimed as she hugged Melissa.

"It must have happened on our honeymoon!" Melissa, red-faced, said with a huge grin. "Can you believe that? It might have even happened on our wedding night! We were totally blown away when we found out. We thought it'd take a whole lot longer."

Ann Marie Slater, thirty years old, the tall, blonde, and usually very in-control first counselor in the presidency, fought to keep her composure.

Melissa continued. "When we were talking about getting married, we talked about maybe having six children. But we didn't think we'd start so soon."

The Young Women president and Melissa were still hugging.

What if everyone else hugs her? Ann Marie thought. *What will I do? I'll have to hug her, too. I can do it if I have to. I can do anything if I have to. I can go to baby showers. I can look at new babies when a new mother shows one to me. I can send little notes to new mothers. I can listen to a child cry and not rush over to pick her up. I can do anything. Anything except get pregnant, that is.*

To her great relief, the other counselor as well as the age group advisers did not hug Melissa, and so all Ann Marie had to do was force a smile and return her eyes to the agenda they would soon be covering in their planning meeting.

The meeting began with a prayer and minutes and then they proceeded through the agenda. When asked, Ann Marie gave her report on the upcoming service activity.

An hour and a half later, the meeting was over. There were refreshments, but Ann Marie made some excuse why she needed to get home.

She pulled into the driveway of her home ten minutes later, activated the remote, and closed the door of the garage.

She could hear Weston, her husband, cheering as he watched an NBA game with his thirteen-year-old nephew and ten-year-old niece from Utah, who were visiting with their parents from Pleasant Grove. They'd arrived in time for supper and would be staying three more days.

I can't go in like this, she thought. *I need a few minutes to try to get better control of my feelings. If I go in the way I am, I'll burst into tears.*

She cupped her hands to her face and permitted herself to have a few minutes of sorrow.

All I've ever wanted from the time I was a little girl was to be a wife and mother someday. I never wanted a career like some of my friends.

Father in Heaven, what do you want from me? I never did

50

anything growing up that violated the law of chastity. I kept myself morally clean. I didn't even kiss a boy until I first kissed Weston shortly before we became engaged. We wanted a baby and, from our first night together on our honeymoon, didn't do anything to stop one from coming. So why won't you let me get pregnant when that's all I want?

She ended her prayer. She'd said it all before, hundreds of times, and it never did any good.

I'm not asking for anything. I've given up asking. God never hears my prayers. It doesn't matter how many times I ask. It never does any good.

When we were first married, being intimate with Weston was a celebration of our love for each other, but now it's something else. She struggled with her thoughts. *Now it's a test, a test that I always fail at because I never get pregnant.*

They had gone to several doctors who specialize in helping couples get pregnant. They had kept a daily record of her temperature until she began to think of herself as a science project.

For the first couple of years of marriage, Ann Marie had stayed at home, fully expecting she would be getting pregnant soon. She wanted to be a stay-at-home mom, but after they'd purchased a home, Weston made an offhand comment that it would be nice to have a little additional income. And so, Ann Marie got a job as a secretary for an insurance agent. She worked full-time and soon became invaluable to her boss—efficient, careful, and friendly to everyone she dealt with.

"The best thing that ever happened to me is when I hired you," Burton McLaughlin, a portly man with an infectious smile, said to her nearly every week.

"I enjoy working for you, too," she said with a forced smile. *But it's not what I want. It's not what I expected my life to be.*

She searched in the glove compartment for a tissue but couldn't find one. She searched again through her purse to no

51

avail, so she did something she hadn't done for twenty years. She used her sleeve to wipe her face and nose.

I am so pathetic, crying in the dark in a garage. I should go inside and sit down and watch the game with Weston's niece and nephew—both above average in intelligence, both extremely talented, both advanced for their age. And neither of them belonging to me or Weston.

It's not just me who's suffering from this. It's Weston, too. He's so good with kids. When he enters a room, they just gravitate to him. It's such a waste he's not a daddy.

I am of all women most grieved, she said, quoting a scripture from the Old Testament, which now reflected her true feelings about her situation.

She used her other sleeve to wipe her face, then turned on the dome light and looked at her reflection in the mirror. Her eyes were puffy. *If I go in all cheerful and happy, then go to the kitchen and make some refreshments, nobody will notice.*

I can't let them see me down, she said. *In a couple of days, Weston's family will leave, and then I'll have a little time alone to feel sorry for myself.*

But not now.

Melissa got pregnant on her honeymoon. It's not fair. Why couldn't God give that baby to Weston and me? Has he even heard our prayers? And if she was going to get pregnant so soon, why put her in our ward, and call her to work in Young Women, so I'd know about it? Why do I have to be around women who have babies?

She sighed and opened the car door.

I will put some of the cookies I made last Saturday on a plate. And make some lemonade. If I wait long enough, maybe by the time I go in the game will be over, and I can say I have a headache and go to bed.

And be asleep before Weston comes in.

Because I can't fake my feelings to him.

He always knows when I've had a hard day.

52

She forced herself into motion, moved in the dark to the door leading into their house, and put on her best smile.

"I'm home!" she called out brightly.

4

MAY

J ust after her eighteenth birthday, Megan had her annual
interview with her bishop. Bishop Oldham was a giant of
a man. Easily six-foot-four, he weighed well over two hundred pounds, and in his college days he had played basketball
for BYU. But that was twenty years before. His only souvenir
of his glory days was a pair of bad knees.

While some bishops might go on and on with small talk,
Bishop Oldham, an engineer, although friendly, liked to get
down to business right away when he interviewed.

"Any problems with the Word of Wisdom?" he asked.

"No, not at all."

"You understand what we mean by being morally clean,
don't you?" he asked.

"Yes, of course," she said, her smile frozen on her face,
hoping she was not blushing.

"What does it mean?"

"Bishop, I'm about to graduate from high school. I mean,
it's not like I'm twelve years old. I do know what it means."

"Then tell me."

"Well, it means you don't watch bad movies, and you're careful who you date, you know, that they have good standards. And it means you don't let yourself get carried away with a guy, you know, physically. That's about it."

"You're dating someone now, aren't you?"

"Yes, I am. How did you know?"

"Brianna told me."

What did Brianna say? Does she suspect anything?

"I've been seeing a guy named Kurt off and on."

"Is he a member of the Church?"

"No, but he's really interested. He's talked about taking the missionary lessons."

"Tell me a little about him."

"Well, he's an Eagle Scout. He's a year older than me. He works for his dad. He writes code for computer games. He and his father have started their own company."

"Have you two had any problems with regard to chastity?"

"No, of course not. I'm usually home by eleven when I go out with him."

"So there's no problem with chastity?"

"No, not at all. Why do you keep asking?"

"I'm not sure. It's just, well . . . you seem a little nervous."

"Is my face red?"

"A little."

Confess something, she thought. *Something that doesn't matter.*

"Well, Bishop, to be perfectly honest, I did have a little bit of a problem with Kurt."

"What's that?"

"Well, about a month ago he talked me into having some coffee, just to see how it tasted. I knew that wasn't right, but I did it anyway. I feel really guilty about it now. But I just took a taste, that's all, and I'll never do it again."

The bishop seemed relieved it wasn't more serious.

A few minutes later, the interview was over.

When Megan left, she appeared cheerful and upbeat to him. But she only made it two blocks in the family car before she had to pull over. She felt sick to her stomach. *I can't do this anymore. I can't live a double life. It's tearing me up too much.*

And so, to get away from her family, a few weeks later, just after graduating from high school, she moved away from home into an apartment on the other side of town. She told her parents she was going to room with another girl. But there never was another girl. It was just a way to get them to agree to let her move out.

◆　　◆　　◆

July

Megan sat hunched over a TV tray and ate her supper, a warmed up can of beef stew. While she ate, she watched one of her tapes of *Friends*. Her hair smelled of fried foods, and her skin felt greasy. All she wanted was to eat, take a shower, and go to bed.

She worked the morning shift at Burger King, and then, as her second job, assembled computers in a high-tech production line. It was mind-numbing work, tedious and boring.

She no longer went to church. It was easy to justify because she always scheduled herself to work Sundays.

I wonder if Kurt will show up tonight. He'd better not. He knows how I feel about him showing up in the middle of the night and expecting me to welcome him with open arms.

After watching *Friends*, she decided to clean up a little before taking a shower. She liked to keep her place neat and tidy. Kurt liked things that way. And she never knew when he'd show up.

The furnished apartment wasn't much, but it was all she could afford. On the outside the apartment building looked like it should be condemned, but inside it wasn't so bad. At first she had prided herself on making it look good. She bought posters to hang on the walls and hooked up her stereo. She had high hopes. She had even invited her mother and Brianna to come and see it. They came and were politely complimentary.

"Of course, it's not exactly what I had in mind, but I won't be here long. As soon as I get a better job, I'll move to some place better, some place overlooking the beach."

"Wouldn't that be nice," her mother said diplomatically.

The better job never came. With only a high school education and very few job skills, she was never considered for the jobs she really wanted.

Megan was always surprised how little was left over after a paycheck. Not enough to fix up her apartment. Not enough to take college night classes. Not enough to afford a better place to live. The old, beat-up car her parents had let her take always needed gas and repairs, and she couldn't believe how much the insurance cost.

She and Kurt had talked about getting their own apartment, but so far nothing had come of it. They'd looked at a couple of places but none of them seemed good enough for him. "It's probably better for me to stay at home," he said. "That way I can save up money so we can move into a really nice apartment someday."

Sometimes when Kurt dropped by, he stayed only part of the night because his friends and what they wanted to do always took precedence over her. At other times she didn't expect him, but he'd knock on her door, sometimes late at night, after she'd gone to bed.

The last time he showed up past midnight she told him it was too late for him to come in. He said he just wanted to talk to her for a few minutes. She gave in and let him in, and he ended up staying. But when she woke up the next morning, he was gone without even a note.

The closeness she had hoped for in their relationship wasn't there. They were, of course, close physically, but when that was over, it was to him almost like it had never happened. She was beginning to feel she was being used. *He takes me too much for granted*, she thought.

The company Kurt and his father had started was beginning to be very profitable. In many ways Kurt lived a charmed life. He could always get time off work, and he always had plenty of money. All his parents asked was that he stay out of trouble.

What attracted me to him at first was that everything came easy to him. That was true of me, too, she thought with a growing sense of bitterness. *I came easy, too.*

She turned off the TV and sat in her apartment in the dark and listened to the sounds coming from other apartments. Mr. Podolsky, in the apartment next door, was going through another of his coughing fits. He'd been wounded in the Vietnam War and hadn't worked since then. He'd been living in the same apartment since being released from the veteran's hospital in the mid-seventies. Mr. Podolsky still walked with a limp due to his war injury. He had no friends or family. He spent hours each day tending a small garden along the side of the building, not because it required that much care, but because he had nothing else to do. While he worked, he waited for someone to come by so he could lecture them about world events. He liked to talk about the corruptness of city, county, state, and federal officials. Megan had learned to avoid talking to him.

He got lost in the system and nobody cares about him anymore, so now he's a prisoner here and will be until he dies, just like everyone who lives here. The same thing might be happening to me. What if I'm still here in ten years?

In the other apartment next to her was Mrs. Capriatti, a dried-up, fragile woman in her eighties who never left her apartment. Megan had seen her once at her door, taking food from a boy who was delivering a week's worth of groceries to her in one small bag. Because Megan seldom heard anything from Mrs. Capriatti's apartment, she sometimes imagined the woman was dead but had not been discovered yet.

Once in a while she heard a man and woman on the floor above her arguing late at night, but she didn't know who they were.

I hate living here, she thought.

She felt betrayed. The only problem was she couldn't decide who to blame.

What she wanted from Kurt was not what she was getting. If anything, he was more detached now than before they'd become intimate.

He's the master of putting his life in nice neat compartments, she thought. *He's able to keep his life with his friends separate from his attachment to me. I'll never be a big part of his life as long as they're around. He's having too much fun to give them up. He likes having his physical needs met by me and spending the rest of his free time with his friends.*

So what do I do? If I don't let him come and stay the night, then he'll quit coming around entirely. And if he does that, then what do I do? Move back home and admit to my family what's been going on in my life? I can't do that.

If we had our own apartment, if he'd give up going out night after night with his friends and spend more time with me. If it was more like we were . . . She sighed *. . . If it was more like we were, well, married,* she thought. It was a bitter pill because it was what her mother had warned her about long ago.

I'll make this work out. I won't let things stay the same. I'll get Kurt to go with me to find a place for the two of us to live, and then I'll be happy. Anything to get out of here. And then in a couple of years, we'll get married and everything will be fine.

But even as she thought about it, she doubted if it would

ever happen. *Kurt wants the best of what life has to offer, but only if it requires no effort on his part.*

She brought strands of her hair to her nose and sniffed. She hated it when she smelled of greasy foods. *I'll clean up and then I'll take a shower and then I'll go to bed.*

In the tiny kitchen, she filled the sink with water to wash two days' worth of dishes. Because it was a warm night, she opened the window. It had begun raining. There was a screen on the window to keep the bugs out. Over the years its wooden frame had been painted permanently closed.

As she set the last dish to drain on the counter, she glanced out the window. In the light from the street lamp, millions of raindrops glistened, shooting out beams of colored light in all directions. It was the most beautiful sight she had ever seen.

Looking at the scene, she felt a longing for something she couldn't even define—something to fill the emptiness in her life. Tears welled in her eyes and, when she blinked, began running down her cheeks.

She dried the dishes and silverware while continuing to look out at the light show being put on by nature.

She wanted to pray. She closed her eyes and folded her arms the way she'd been taught in Primary. "Dear God . . ." she said quietly, then stopped because it sounded so out of place. "I can't even remember how to do this anymore. I used to pray all the time, but then I stopped because I was doing things that I knew were wrong. Thank you for the rain and the way the lights are shooting out. It's very beautiful. That's all I wanted to say. Amen."

Tears continued rolling down her cheeks. She realized she had more to say, much more.

She went to the bedroom and closed the door and fell to her knees.

"Oh, God, please help me. I'm trapped in this apartment and I'm trapped in my jobs and it seems like I'll never get out of this. I'm afraid I'll go the rest of my life trapped. Please, get me out of this. Please, dear God, please. Amen."

She ended the prayer, still embarrassed she'd done it. And then she sat down on her bed and tried to figure out where things had gone wrong.

◆　　◆　　◆

AUGUST, FIRST MONTH

Megan stood in front of a display of home pregnancy tests in a mall drugstore. She'd come in just before closing, hoping there wouldn't be many customers. She didn't want to run into anyone she knew.

It's probably nothing, Megan thought, trying to subdue the panic that had been building in her over the past few days. *It happens all the time. Like that girl who sat next to me in English last year. She told me once that she missed all the time. All the time she was running cross-country, she missed every month. So missing once doesn't mean anything. It could be I'm just working too hard and not getting enough sleep.*

There were other signs, too, but most of them could be attributed to other causes. She was going to the bathroom more often than usual, and she felt sick in the morning when she woke up. Also, she seemed to be tired all the time.

She looked around to make sure nobody was watching her and then grabbed one of the packages and then almost as quickly returned it to the shelf. *I can't take this to the counter and have the clerk see it. I can't do it. There's no reason to even worry about it anyway. Women miss all the time. It doesn't necessarily mean . . .* she couldn't even think the words *. . . that there's a problem.*

Out of the corner of her eye, she saw someone with a shopping cart coming toward her. She panicked, moved ten feet down the aisle, reached for a package of foot powder, and then quickly walked in the same direction down the aisle so she wouldn't have to face the customer.

She waited at the far end of the store until the customer left the store. And then she walked quickly down the aisle and picked up a home pregnancy test kit and headed for the checkout counter.

I can't have this be the only thing I buy because if it is, then the clerk might say something to me, and I couldn't stand that.

She picked up some eyeliner and a copy of *Cosmopolitan* magazine.

Later that night, in her bathroom, she stared in disbelief at the results of the home pregnancy test, her heart pounding and her thoughts racing. *Oh, no! This can't be right! I can't be pregnant! There must be something wrong with the test.*

She felt like she was going to faint. She sat on the floor and fought the overwhelming panic.

This can't be right! There must be a mistake! I must not have done the test right. That's it. That's what happened. It's because I've never done the test before. There must be some step I left out. I just have to find out what I did wrong and then get another test and do it again.

She pulled out the directions and tried to read them, but she couldn't make her eyes focus. And then she broke down. She rested her arms on the side of the tub and sobbed. *What is Mom going to say? It will break her heart.*

Mr. Podolsky next door turned down his radio. "What's going on over there?" he yelled through the paper-thin walls.

"Nothing. Everything's fine."

"You sure?"

"Everything's fine. I just stubbed my toe, that's all."

The radio went back to loud again.

She washed her face and went into her room and crawled into bed and pulled the covers up. Lying there in the dark, she couldn't stop thinking. *I can't be pregnant. If I am, everyone will know. They'll think I'm a fool. I can't be pregnant. I'm not ready for this. And neither is Kurt. Someday we'll be ready to settle down and have kids, but not now.*

I'm not worried about Kurt, though. If I am pregnant, we'll get married. He told me he'd take care of me if anything happened. It's just that we're not ready for this.

I don't trust these tests. I've got to find out for sure tomorrow. I've got to go to a doctor. I'll call in sick at Burger King, get the test, and then go to my second job. I'll feel a lot better once I know I'm not pregnant.

♦   ♦   ♦

Megan's family had gone to the same doctor all her life, but she couldn't go to him because she was afraid it would get back to her mother, and she didn't want her mother to know about this. And so she picked a public health clinic out of the Yellow Pages.

She was hoping she would get there early enough that she wouldn't have to wait, but by the time she got there the waiting room was full. The woman next to her was there with four kids, all under six years old. The mother was impatient and spoke Spanish to them.

I bet these people are all on food stamps. You can always tell.

And then she began to wonder if anyone was looking at her, wondering why she was there. She looked around, but nobody seemed to be paying any attention to her.

She saw a girl her age, or maybe even younger, with a baby in her arms. Because Megan felt so isolated, she went over to sit by the girl, who wore no makeup and hadn't done anything that morning with her hair.

"Hello," Megan said.

"Hello," the girl said quietly, and then turned her gaze away from Megan.

63

"Busy place," Megan said.

"It always is."

"Really? This is my first time."

Megan tried not to be critical, but the baby obviously had a messy diaper. The smell was making her sick.

"Are you out of diapers?" Megan asked the girl.

"I brought two diapers, but he's gone through them already."

"Do you want me to go see if I can get you one at the desk?"

The girl avoided any eye contact but nodded.

Megan went to the desk to talk to the receptionist, a distracted woman who was shuffling papers.

"My friend has run out of diapers. Do you have one she can use?"

"We don't supply diapers."

"I know, but you must have one or two lying around. The thing is, it's stinking up the whole place."

The woman pointed to the end of the room. "You'll have to go see a nurse . . ." She pointed. "Over there."

"Thank you."

Megan walked to the back of the clinic. Finally, she found a nurse. "I need a diaper. It's for a girl in the waiting room. Her baby has a messy diaper, and it's smelling up the whole place. The secretary told me I could get one back here."

The nurse went into a storeroom and brought back a diaper and handed it to Megan.

Megan returned to the girl and gave her the diaper. "There you go."

The girl took it. "I have plenty of diapers at home. I just forgot to bring enough here, that's all."

"I understand."

"I am a good mother."

"I'm sure you are."

The girl went into the restroom to change her baby's diaper.

That could be me in a year, Megan thought but then quickly disregarded the thought. *No, not me. The worst that could happen would be that, if I am pregnant, Kurt and I will get married a little sooner than we'd planned. That's all. I will never be like that girl, alone, afraid, and dependent on government support.*

Forty minutes later a nurse with a loud voice that filled the clinic called her name. Hearing her name announced in a place filled with people she'd spent her life looking down on made Megan want to run away.

An hour later Megan was told by the doctor she'd been assigned, "Well, you are pregnant."

"Are you sure?"

"Positive. I assume you'll want an abortion. That's not something we do here, but I can give you some names of clinics where you can get it done."

"An abortion?"

"Yes. You're not married, are you?"

"No, but I'm sure that once . . . my . . ." She couldn't think of the right word. *Husband* wouldn't work. *Lover* seemed too intimate a word to use in front of a doctor.

"Your partner?" the doctor asked.

"Yes, once my partner finds out, he'll want to marry me."

The doctor raised his eyebrows. "Well, I'm not in a position to comment on that. But if it doesn't turn out for you, I'll give you a list of clinics where you can get an abortion."

Megan took the list and a short time later left the clinic and went out to her car and sat there in a stunned stupor.

I've got to tell Kurt right away, she thought. *He'll want to know. We have to talk about when we're going to tell our folks, where we're going to live, and when we're going to get married.*

She thought about waiting for Kurt to come around and

65

see her, but she didn't think she could wait that long because sometimes he didn't come by for days at a time. It was Friday, and on the weekends he was usually gone with his friends camping or sailing or hiking or whatever else they decided to do.

She didn't want to just leave a message because he never called back. He said it was because he never got the messages she left, but she was beginning to think that wasn't always the case.

She thought about going to where he worked and asking to talk to him, but she knew that would make him mad because he liked to keep each part of his life separate.

As she was trying to decide what to do, she realized her right hand was resting on her stomach. She looked down at her hand and tried to imagine what was taking place inside her, how many cells that would become her baby were being produced every hour, all of this going on without any conscious effort.

Hundreds, maybe thousands, all coming together in some orderly way that nobody can understand. How can this be happening without me even knowing that it's going on?

That helped her decide what to do. *I can't wait. I've got to see Kurt now. We need to talk. There's so much we need to do to get ready for our baby.*

She knew he wouldn't appreciate her interfering with him at work. She decided to call him first, so it wouldn't come as a complete surprise to him that she was coming.

She used her cell phone to call him.

He didn't say hello, just gave his last name.

"This is Megan. I need to talk to you . . . right away."

"Can't it wait until after work?"

"No, it can't."

"I'm in the middle of a big project."

"I know, but this is important. And it won't take long."

"What's it about?"

"We'll talk about it when I get there."

"What's so important you have to interrupt me at work?" He stopped, and then swore. He lowered his voice. "You haven't gone and gotten yourself pregnant, have you? I mean, is that what this is about?"

She was startled by the accusing tone in his voice. "I'll talk to you when I get there," she said.

"Because if you have—"

"I'll be there in ten minutes."

"I'll meet you at the front entrance."

"Bye then."

Even though she said she'd only be ten minutes, she couldn't drive right away because she was furious with him for the way he'd treated her over the phone. Her hands were shaking, and her face was flushed. She kept going over in her mind what he'd said. *You haven't gone and gotten yourself pregnant, have you? Like he didn't have anything to do with it. Like it's some germ you get if you don't wash your hands. Like everything is my fault.*

She showed up at the place he worked twenty minutes later than she said. She could see him through the front window, in the lobby, pacing the floor. *Good,* she thought, *let him sweat this out like I had to.*

"You're late," Kurt said the instant she walked in the door.

"Sorry."

"Let's get this over. I need to get back to work."

"Where can we talk?"

Kurt looked around. They were in the front office, but the secretary was away from her desk.

"Here's good. Say what you came here to say."

"Well, I went to the doctor today."

He rolled his eyes.

"And you were right. I am pregnant."

Kurt swore.

67

"I thought you'd better know right away so we can make preparations."

"Look, I'll pay for the abortion."

She was stunned. Her black eyes flashed, and she recoiled in horror. "Are you serious?" she asked, barely above a whisper.

"Of course, what else is there to do?"

"Well, we could get married."

"Forget it. I'm not marrying you."

"You said you loved me."

"I say a lot of things, but one thing I never said was that I'd marry you if you got yourself pregnant."

"Got *myself* pregnant? As I recall, you were there, too!"

He waved his hand in a gesture of disgust.

"You said you'd take care of me."

"And I will. I'll pay for the abortion."

"That's taking care of me?"

"Be reasonable, will you? The sooner you get this taken care of, the better off we'll both be. You don't want people knowing about this, do you? Your family? Your friends? It's best just to get it taken care of, and then we can both get on with our lives. That's the best way."

"The best for you, or the best for the baby?"

"It's not a baby. Besides, we never said anything about a baby."

"That doesn't matter now, does it?"

He threw up his hands. "Look, what do you want from me? Money? Is that it? How much? Just tell me and I'll get it for you . . . somehow."

"It's our baby, Kurt. Doesn't that mean anything to you?"

"It's not a baby, okay? It's just a growth that needs to be cut out, that's all, just a growth. People do this all the time, you know. It's not that bad. You go in, they take care of it, and you're back home the same day. And then there's nothing left to worry about. It's all taken care of. For good."

"How can you be so heartless and cruel?"

"I'm just looking out for myself. That's what both of us need to do now. For all I know, you got yourself pregnant to try to force me to marry you."

The secretary came into the office. Kurt took that as an excuse to leave. "I really have to get back to work now."

"Call me, okay?"

He waved her off and disappeared through the door to the carrels where everyone worked.

Megan left the office and went to her car, drove three blocks, pulled into a grocery store parking lot, and sat there stunned. She felt betrayed. And alone, with nowhere to go.

She sat in her car for two hours, and then, ten minutes before she was scheduled to show up at her second job, she called in sick.

Two hours later she was still there in her car outside the store. She might have stayed longer, but she needed to use the restroom. She looked at her reflection in the rearview mirror and tried to make herself look presentable, then opened the door and walked slowly toward the entrance of the store. She took her cell phone with her just in case Kurt came to his senses and called to apologize for the way he'd acted earlier.

As she slowly walked toward the entrance, it was like she'd been transported to a different planet. Everything seemed different to her, even things she'd taken for granted before. Like a mother with two kids coming out of the store with her cart filled with groceries, and one of the kids begging his mother to find the cookies they'd bought, and the mother saying she didn't know which sack they were in, and the boy, about five years old, asking her just to look because he wanted a cookie. And his two-year-old brother, perhaps only knowing a handful of words, but knowing the word *cookie*, who kept saying over and over, "Cookie? Cookie?"

The mother stopped and went through her groceries until she found the package of cookies. She opened it, gave a cookie to each of her boys, and, as a happy afterthought, took

69

one for herself. Then, munching together, they made their way slowly to their car, happy with life.

Megan turned to watch them, paying particular attention to the two boys, both of them with light blond hair and a fair complexion. *A boy,* she thought, *I could have a boy. A boy like one of those two.*

She used the restroom and then drove back to her apartment. She fell asleep with the cell phone in her hand, watching *Friends.*

Kurt did not call all that week.

She continued to oppose abortion in principle, but there were times, when she felt sick to her stomach, or late at night when she couldn't sleep because of worrying about her situation, when she just wanted all her problems to go away, that she considered it as a possibility for her.

On Friday she was fired from her job assembling computers because she'd missed two days in a row.

With only her part-time job at Burger King in the mornings, she wouldn't have enough to pay her rent and buy groceries.

On Saturday morning she got sick at her job at Burger King and had to leave a customer in the middle of filling her order so that she could throw up. When she came back, her boss told her to go home until she was feeling better.

"I'm okay now."

"You don't look very good. I can't have you handling food if you're sick. Just go home. Come back when you're feeling better. I'll take you off the schedule for a couple of days."

"You don't understand. I need the money."

"I'm sorry, but I have to look out for my customers. I don't want you spreading germs."

Megan returned to her apartment.

What am I going to do? The rent's due next week, and I don't have enough money. Where can I get it? I can't face this all by myself. It's too much. I can't tell my folks. It would kill

70

them to know. What other choice do I have but to go along with what Kurt wants me to do?

She called Kurt's parents' home at around two that afternoon. Kurt's mother told her he'd gone camping.

"This is Megan. He wanted me to bring him out some climbing rope, but he didn't tell me where he'd be camping. Can you help me?"

Kurt's mother said she wasn't sure where he was going that weekend but did give her directions to where he and his friends usually went.

Megan didn't feel well enough to travel right then, so she took a nap.

When she woke up, it was late afternoon. She could hear Mr. Podolsky coughing next door. He had his radio on. Someone was talking about UFOs. " . . . and it was then the spacecraft, or whatever it was, began hovering."

"What were you thinking when that happened?" the moderator asked the caller.

"Well, I'll tell you, I was pretty scared."

Megan banged on the wall. "Mr. Podolsky, turn it down!"

He yelled back at her through the wall. "You should listen to this. It's important to our survival."

"Turn it down!"

Mr. Podolsky turned the radio down.

She started to watch TV, surfing through the channels until she had a familiar wave of nausea.

By the time she came out of the bathroom, she'd made her decision. She'd go along with what Kurt suggested and get an abortion.

An hour and a half later, she drove through the entrance of the state park where Kurt's mother had said Kurt and his friends might be spending the weekend. She drove slowly from one campsite to another until she spotted his Jeep.

A group of maybe ten guys was sitting around the campfire, drinking beer and talking.

71

She knew Kurt wouldn't be happy to see her. He liked spending time with his friends, and she'd never been invited to go with him and his buddies. It was like a club, and no girls were allowed. She got out of the car and walked slowly toward the campfire. At first she didn't even know if Kurt was there.

They looked at her as if she were an intruder.

"I'm looking for Kurt," she said.

For a few moments no one said anything. Finally, one of the guys pointed. "He's down at the dock."

She turned away from the fire and walked slowly down a steep path, wishing she had a flashlight. As she approached the dock, she could hear Kurt talking to someone. It sounded very familiar to her. "Sometimes I just wish I could find someone I could really talk to about my feelings and dreams for the future."

"Really, Kurt? I feel the same way," a young girl replied.

Megan slipped on the graveled path and fell down on her seat, jarring herself.

"Someone's coming," the girl said.

Feeling stupid for falling, and angry, Megan stood up and forced herself to walk onto the dock. "If you want to talk about your hopes and dreams for the future, Kurt, I'd suggest you talk to me," she said, her voice sounding hollow and mechanical, like it was coming from a computer.

"I'd better go now, before my dad starts to wonder where I am," the girl said. She pushed past Megan and hurried up the path.

"Up to your old tricks again, right, Kurt?"

He ignored her question. "What are you doing here?"

"You said you'd pay for my abortion, right?" Megan asked.

"Yes, that's what I said."

"Good, because I've decided to do that. Can you write me out a check for it now?"

"I can't just give you a check now."

"Why not? You said you'd pay for it."

72

"Do you have insurance with your job?" he asked.

"No, I got fired."

"The insurance should still be in effect. I think you get thirty days, but I'm not sure. It's something you'd have to check out."

"Why bother? You said you'd pay for it."

"I will."

"Then give me the money. I want to get it taken care of tomorrow."

"I know, but if you have insurance and if they cover abortions, then I'd only have to pay the deductible. I mean there's no need to waste money over this, is there?"

"I don't want to wait. I want to get it done right away. Monday by the latest."

"I'm not sure we can get all this straightened out by Monday."

"Hey, I've got an idea," she said sarcastically. "Why don't you give up trying to come on to ninth-grade girls and playing 'Survivor' with your stupid friends for one weekend and help me get through this?"

"I don't see that there's any reason to rush this. I mean you can get an abortion anytime in the first three months, right?"

"It's making me sick. I can't work. I can't eat. And I'm about to lose my apartment. I want it taken care of right now. Even tonight, if I can find somebody who will do it. Just give me some money now, and we can sort out the insurance later."

"I'm afraid that with insurance it doesn't work that way."

"Are you going to pay for the stupid abortion or not?" she shouted.

"Not so loud. People can hear you."

"You think I care what your stupid friends think? Well, I don't. I want out of this. I want someone to make this all go away."

"Did you really think you could show up here and I'd just write you out a check?"

"So what are you saying, that you're not going to help me?"

"I'll help you, but only what your insurance won't pay. Do you know if your insurance will pay for it?"

"No, Kurt, I don't. Sorry. I hate to take up your valuable time like this."

"Sometimes you can get a doctor to bill you for something else that your insurance will pay for, like for appendectomy, and then he just goes ahead and does the abortion." He paused. "If you can find the right doctor, that is."

"How many girls have you had to do this for?"

He ignored the question. "I'm just saying you have to find out, first of all, if your insurance will pay for it, and then, if it won't, see if you can find a doctor that will charge you for something that the insurance will pay for."

"Why does all this fall on me?"

"Because it's your insurance policy, not mine. They won't give me information about your insurance. Look into it and then get back to me."

"Will you be with me when I . . . when I have my . . . my abortion?"

He pursed his lips. "Actually, that might be a problem. We're in the middle of a big project. One deadline after another."

She shook her head in disbelief. "Of course. I wouldn't want you to miss one of your deadlines."

"Get back to me when you find out about your insurance. I might be able to take half a day off when the doctor operates on you."

She started back up the path and then turned to glare back at him. "Can I ask you a question? Did you ever love me?"

He pursed his lips. "In my own way."

74

She nodded. "That's what I thought."

She drove much too fast down the winding mountain road leading to the highway, partly out of anger at Kurt and partly because she didn't care anymore if she lived or died.

◆　　◆　　◆

The next night, not wanting to end up in bed listening to Mr. Podolsky's radio, she decided to go to a movie. It was Sunday, but she decided to go anyway. Anything to get her mind off her own problems.

She ended up at a multiplex movie theater. There was a long line for the seven o'clock show. When she finally got to the front of the line, the gum-chewing ticket girl at the counter asked, "What movie?"

Megan had been so wrapped up in her own problems, she hadn't even thought about what movie she was going to see.

"Do I have to make a choice now?"

The girl rolled her eyes and gently slapped the counter with her hand. "Yes, I have to know. Otherwise we don't know when we've sold too many tickets."

"Well, what's showing?"

"It's up there, on the wall."

The first movie was an R-rated movie that, on the poster, promised to be a "raucous sex romp."

That's part of the reason I'm in the fix I'm in now, because of movies like this one.

The second movie was R-rated. "Is there much sex in that movie?" she asked, pointing at the poster.

The girl groaned and looked up at the ceiling as if seeking divine intervention. "Look, all I do is sell tickets. I'm not a movie reviewer."

"How long is this going to take?" the girl behind Megan asked.

75

One of the other movies was a Disney film. It seemed like the best choice. At least it wouldn't have any sex in it.

When she entered the theater, though, it was filled with kids and their parents. She found one seat at the far end of one of the side rows near the back of the theater. She excused herself and made her way past a family. The movie hadn't started yet, and after taking her seat Megan looked out of the corner of her eye at the family next to her. The father was a good-looking man with a well-kept beard. His wife was beautiful in an unassuming way, and they had three children—a girl, maybe three years old, her brother, a six-year-old boy, full of questions, and his sister, twelve years old, not quite sure if she was too old for Disney, alternating moment to moment between being a young woman and being a child.

Megan was sitting next to the twelve-year-old girl.

The three-year-old was taking all the attention of the parents.

"Must be a good movie, right?" Megan said.

The girl turned to Megan. "Excuse me?"

"I said this must be a good movie."

"Why?"

"Because of all the people."

"Whatever." The girl turned away from Megan, obviously not wanting to talk.

Megan looked at her watch, impatient for the movie to begin. She didn't like being around so many children.

A two-year-old boy in the row in front of her turned to face her. He was being fed popcorn one kernel at a time. He held out his hand to Megan and said, "More?" Except it sounded like "Moa."

"You want me to have this piece?" Megan asked.

"Moa?" he asked again.

Megan took the kernel of popcorn. The mother turned around. She was a young mother, not too much older than Megan.

76

"I'm so sorry."

"No, it's fine, really."

"Moa?" the boy asked, looking to see if Megan would eat the popcorn he'd given her.

"Thank you!" Megan said enthusiastically. She popped it in her mouth.

"Oh, gross," the girl next to Megan said.

The boy turned to his mother for another piece of popcorn, received it, and then turned to Megan. "Moa?"

Megan took the piece of popcorn and then ducked down behind the backrest of his seat, then popped up suddenly.

He started to laugh.

She ducked down again.

Same result.

The little boy laughed each time Megan appeared from behind the backrest of his seat.

The girl next to her wasn't amused. "Tommy, can I change places with you?" she asked her brother.

They changed places. Tommy joined Megan in the ducking game, ducking down the same time Megan did. The little boy in front of them was even more delighted and laughed even harder.

A few more minutes of that, and his mother turned around. "You can ignore him if you want," his mother said to Megan.

"No, it's okay. He's so cute! How old is he?"

"He'll be two next month."

"He's adorable."

The mother smiled and nodded. "I guess we'll keep him."

Megan felt a wave of embarrassment and shame. *That's more than I'm going to do. I'm having mine cut out of me on Monday or Tuesday. That's because it's only a growth, not a baby.*

"Moa?" the boy asked.

Megan shook her head. She'd had enough. This was too painful.

The theater darkened, and the coming attractions began showing on the screen.

"Moa?" the little boy asked.

Megan felt sick to her stomach. She stood up and made her way out of the row, past the family, to the aisle, and then up the aisle to the common hall linking all the movies being shown at the multiplex that night.

She went into the least offensive R-rated movie, wanting to escape from little kids who laughed at the silliest little thing.

The movie had already started, but she found a seat at the back, glad for the darkness.

A few minutes into the movie, a very good-looking guy and an equally glamorous woman ended up in bed together, although they'd just met.

She couldn't watch it. She walked out.

She stood in the hallway connecting the movies and tried to decide what to do. She looked at the gaudy signs for each movie, wanting desperately to be taken away from her own problems and to be transported into another world with different rules, to be someone else for even a few minutes, just to escape the reality of her own life.

She looked down the hallway to the choice of movies she had. *There's nothing here for me. Maybe I'd just better go back to my apartment.*

A few minutes later, she entered her apartment, closed the door, and began watching one of her favorite videotaped episodes of *Friends*.

Why can't my life be like that? That's all I've ever wanted— to have friends and be free to do what I wanted to do.

Friends had always worked for her before. In a way she felt like they were *her* friends. They were always there for her, no matter what.

But this time it didn't work.

She turned off the TV and all the lights in the house and sat on her couch and tried to think. She heard what sounded to be a shot or a car backfiring.

Welcome to my world, she thought.

Finally, she fell asleep.

When she woke up, it was four-thirty in the morning, and she wasn't sleepy anymore, so she splashed water on her face and brushed her teeth and went outside to take a walk.

Early on that Monday morning there was still very little traffic. The sun was like a timid actor in a grade school production, hanging in the wings until it was time to make his appearance, bringing light to the world in cautious degrees.

As she walked she thought about the little boy in the movie theater, how much happiness she had brought him in just a few minutes.

I have a baby inside me. Well, not an actual baby, but he will be a baby someday. A boy or a girl. Whatever it is, it's not his fault, and it's not her fault. How can I take away the chance to be born just because I messed up? If I do, then who will hear the laughter? Who will hear him say, "Moa?"

It's one thing to say I oppose abortion when it's just talk, when it's not a choice I'm facing. But if I'm against it in principle, then I have to be against it now, for me, or else it doesn't matter what I believe. It's not what you believe; it's what you do.

As she stopped to watch the sunrise, she knew she couldn't deny future sunrises to the baby she was carrying.

I'm not sure what I'm going to do with my baby, but one thing I am sure of, I'm not going to have it cut out.

She came to a McDonald's and ordered herself breakfast. Instead of her usual coffee and pancakes, she had eggs and orange juice.

For the baby.

79

5

Megan knew she had to tell her family she was pregnant, but she had a few days left before the rent was due, and there was still a little food in the apartment, so she hung on a little longer, hoping for some kind of miracle that would make all her problems go away.

On Monday Brianna called and invited her to Young Women Standards Night on Tuesday. "I'm going to sing. It's going to be way cool. Please come, Meggie, okay?"

"Well, I don't know."

"Please. I've worked *so* hard on my song. I want you to hear it."

What else have I got to do? she thought. *Haven't I watched enough episodes of* Friends *to last me a lifetime?*

"Okay, I'll go."

"You're awesome!"

On Tuesday night Megan sat with her mother on the second row in the Relief Society room.

How many of these have I been to? she thought. *And they're all the same. Every single one of them.*

She did like Brianna's song, though, and her sister looked so happy, Megan thought, *I'm glad I came. To show my support.*

Bishop Oldham was introduced. Big and tall, wearing a slightly rumpled suit, he looked a little out of place standing behind a table that had been covered with a lacy cloth and decorated with a vase of fresh flowers. He was obviously nervous, and just looking at him as he stood in front of them made Megan feel the same way.

"I'm sure you're all familiar with this," he said, holding up the *For the Strength of Youth* pamphlet. "How many have looked at it in the last six months? Raise your hands." He looked around. "Good. Very good. You can put your hands down now."

The bishop wiped his forehead and cleared his throat and looked down at the floor.

Oh, great, he hasn't even prepared a talk, Megan thought critically. *Way to go, Bishop.*

He looked out at each one of the girls. "How many of you have read it in the last month?"

Fewer hands went up.

"That's what I thought. Even though you think you know everything about this book, it is filled with things you need to review frequently."

Why don't you just read it to us, Bishop? That way you won't have to make it obvious to everyone that you're totally unprepared.

As if on cue, the bishop said, "Let me read some of it to you."

How much time would it have taken you to actually prepare a talk?

Bishop Oldham spent a moment silently reading, trying to find what he was looking for.

You're wasting our time, Bishop. Why don't you just admit you're not prepared and sit down?

81

He turned the page and continued to silently read. Megan looked at the Young Women president. She maintained her composure, but Megan wondered if she was getting frustrated.

He cleared his throat. "The first part is from the First Presidency. I'll read part of what they wrote."

We can read, Bishop. We don't need you to read for us.

"'You cannot do wrong and feel right. It is impossible! Years of happiness can be lost in the foolish gratification of a momentary desire for pleasure. Satan would have you believe that happiness comes only as you surrender to his enticement to self-indulgence. We need only to look at the shattered lives of those who violate God's laws to know why Satan is called the father of all lies.

"'You can avoid the burden of guilt and sin and all of the attending heartaches if you will but heed the standards provided you through the teachings of the Lord and his servants.'"

The bishop looked up from his reading. "I cannot emphasize too much the importance of living the standards talked about in this booklet. It can make all the difference in the world to you and your future happiness."

He set the booklet on the table. "Dear young sisters, these are the words of the prophets. I hope you can feel their concern. What they have done here is raise a voice of warning. I plead with you to pay attention to what they have to say. The principles they are trying to teach you are true. You may think you can ignore the warnings, that it doesn't matter how you dress and think and act, but I promise you that it isn't true. If you violate these standards, it will result in sorrow and regret."

He cleared his throat again and stared at the floor. When he began to speak again, his voice faltered. "I . . ." he pointed to the Young Women leaders, " . . . we . . . love you and hope for your happiness. We know that when any of us breaks the

82

commandments, it results in heartache, and we want to help you avoid that kind of sorrow."

He paused again and then said, "Sometimes people think they can lie to me during an interview." He pursed his lips. "Well, I guess they can. I'm not that clever to tell sometimes if someone is telling the truth or not, but I can tell you this . . ."

His voice faltered again, and he stopped talking and looked down. "Excuse me . . ." he said, fumbling for his handkerchief. After wiping his nose, he smiled and said, "You ever wonder why women cry and men blow their noses in situations like this? It must be genetics, right?"

He continued. "Nobody ever volunteers to be a bishop. It comes out of the blue, totally unexpected. I'm an engineer, for crying out loud. What do I know about counseling people with problems? Not much. But I've been blessed greatly as I've tried to learn my duties.

"When anyone hides the truth from me in an interview, it's almost as if they are lying to the Lord. Not because there's anything special about me, but because the Lord has called me to be your bishop, and he needs you to be honest. Totally honest. The thing is, unless you're truthful, there's nothing I can do to help you."

Megan felt as if the weight of a truck was on her chest, making it impossible to breathe. She wondered if anyone was noticing how flushed her face was, and, if they were, what they were thinking.

The bishop picked up the booklet and tapped it on the podium. "There can be no deviation from these principles. None whatsoever. Doesn't he say, 'I the Lord cannot look upon sin with the least degree of allowance'? Well, that's the way I have to be when you come to me. You can't say, 'Well, I'm doing just a little of this or a little of that, but it's not that serious.' You can't say that, because that's what Satan wants you to think. Besides, we don't want you worrying about the

83

consequences of misbehavior. Youth is a time to have fun and enjoy life. That's not possible if you are breaking the commandments."

Megan felt like running out of the room, but she was afraid that if she did everyone would know why, and she couldn't bear for anyone to know.

The bishop then talked briefly about the importance of dressing modestly and living the Word of Wisdom and dating good boys, preferably members of the Church. "You may think these are little things, but they often lead to much more serious transgressions."

Please, just stop, Megan thought. *I can't stand this. I don't care how bad things get, I'll never go to you. Not ever. I couldn't stand you browbeating me and making me feel like a fool for what I've done.*

The bishop said a few more things and then sat down. And then there was a song and a prayer, and it was over.

Megan had come to the meeting with her mother and Brianna, so she had to wait for them before she could go home.

"I'll be outside," Megan said to her mother.

"Don't you want some refreshments?"

"No, I just want to get back to my apartment. I've got to go to work early in the morning."

"We'll hurry."

Megan sat in the car and waited.

When am I going to let them know I'm pregnant? I only have two more days until my next month's rent is due. Maybe I should tell them tonight.

She shook her head. *No, not tonight. Not after this. Not after what the bishop said.*

She found a tissue in the glove compartment and wiped her eyes.

This might be a good time, though, because Dad is out of

town on a business trip. *So I wouldn't have to face both Mom and Dad at the same time.*

She shook her head. *I don't want to do this. I really don't want to do this. I wish I could just fall asleep and never wake up. But I can't do that. It's more than me now. It's a baby. I have to be good to my baby, no matter what.*

She tried to imagine what her mother's reaction would be. *What will I do if she tells me she knew this was going to happen? What will I do if she tells me I've disgraced the family?*

And what will Daddy say? Not much, probably. He never says much. But I know he'll be disappointed in me.

Her mother and Brianna came out to the car and got in. "Sorry we took so long," Carolyn said.

"It's okay," Megan said.

"Didn't Brianna sing well tonight?"

"I took care of it, right?" Brianna beamed.

"You did great," Megan said.

"And some people say I can't sing!"

"Who says that?"

"My choir teacher, but what does he know, right?" she joked.

"Right."

A few minutes later they pulled into the driveway of their two-story condominium.

"We can say good night here, if you need to be on your way," Carolyn said.

"Well, actually, I think I'll stay for a few minutes, if that's all right."

"Yes, of course, whatever you'd like," Carolyn said.

They ended up in the kitchen, with Carolyn loading the dishwasher, and Brianna having a piece of cake and some milk.

"Oh, we got a letter from Heather today," Carolyn said.

"How's she doing?"

"Good. They had a baptism last week."

85

"That's great."

"Here's the letter," Carolyn said.

Megan began to read.

Things are really starting to pick up here. My new companion, Sister Lofgren, and I are really working hard. We've been teaching a family of four, the Gundersons. They're really doing well. Last Sunday they even came to church. We've set their baptismal date. It's in three weeks.

I am so happy out here. I'm so grateful to the Lord to be able to tell people about the gospel.

How is everyone doing? I want to hear all your news. I brag about you all the time.

By the time Megan finished the letter, Brianna was in the living room, talking on the phone and watching TV.

Megan set the letter aside. "Mom, there's something I need to tell you," she said softly.

Her mom turned to look at her. "What is it?"

"You know I've been seeing Kurt, off and on. And, well . . ."

There was no easy way to say it. Megan took a deep breath and said, "I'm pregnant."

Carolyn stopped loading the dishwasher. She brought her hand to her mouth.

"Oh, Megan."

Megan couldn't stand seeing the pain in her mother's eyes and looked away. Neither of them said anything for a moment, then Carolyn asked, "Are you sure? Sometimes people think they're pregnant, but it's something else, like a tumor for instance. I've heard of that happening."

"I checked it with an in-home test and then went to a clinic. It's for sure."

Carolyn moved to Megan's side. "What are you going to do?"

"I don't know. Everything is still up in the air."

"Does Kurt know?"

"Yes, I told him."

"What did he say?"

"He made it sound like it was all my fault. He has no interest in getting married. Oh, he did offer to pay for an abortion, though. Well, actually, that's not true either. He offered to pay for whatever my insurance wouldn't cover."

"You're not seriously considering getting an abortion, are you?"

"No of course not. But get this, Kurt said some doctors will charge you for some other operation that your insurance will pay for. And then they just go ahead and do the abortion."

"That's not honest."

"Oh, Kurt doesn't care about that. He just wants to save a little money." She sighed. "It doesn't matter though. I'm not getting an abortion."

"So that means you're going to have the baby?"

"Yes, that's right."

"To keep?"

"Yes, of course. I could never give my baby away."

Megan's effort to hold in her emotions suddenly failed. "I'm so sorry, Mom," she whispered and buried her face in her arms on the table.

Carolyn came to her, raised her up, and wrapped her sobbing daughter in a long, tearful embrace.

Brianna came back into the kitchen. "What's wrong?" she asked.

"She needs to hear it from you," Carolyn said.

Megan cleared her throat. "I'm pregnant."

"No, you're not."

"I am."

"You sure?"

"I'm sure."

Brianna's perpetual smile collapsed, and tears sprang into her eyes. "How could that happen?"

"It just does sometimes."

Brianna put her arms around Megan and held her tight. And they cried.

"I've always looked up to you," Brianna said.

"I know. I'm sorry," Megan said. "I should have been a better example."

"I love you," Brianna said.

"I love you, too."

The phone rang.

"It's probably for you," Megan said.

"I don't care." Brianna pulled up a chair and sat next to Megan. "What are you going to do?"

"I'm not going to get an abortion. That's what Kurt wants me to do."

"No way."

"I'm serious."

"Did he tell you that?" Carolyn asked.

"He did. He makes it sound like it's all my fault."

"It's his kid, too, though, right?" Brianna asked.

"Yes, of course."

"He's trash then."

"He might change his mind," Carolyn said.

"Even if he does, it wouldn't make any difference."

"So, how did it happen?" Brianna asked.

Megan looked at her strangely, not really knowing how to answer the question.

Brianna slapped her own forehead with her open hand. "Good thing I didn't just ask my sister what made her get pregnant, right? I need to get back on my medication right away, right? What a stupid question. What I meant was . . ." She started to blush. "Was it just, like, you know, one time, where things got out of control?"

"Brianna, I'm really not sure you need to know those kind of details," Carolyn said.

"No, it's okay," Megan said. "The truth is, this has been going on since just after I met him."

"How could you go against the teachings of the Church like that?" Brianna asked.

"Brianna," Carolyn gently warned.

"What?"

"Not now."

Brianna shrugged her shoulders. "Okay. Well, answer me this then. Are you going to keep the baby when it's born?"

"I'm pretty sure that's what I'll do."

"You've got to keep it," Brianna said. "I'll help you raise it. I'm serious. I'll be the dad."

"You can't be the dad."

Brianna put her arms up and flexed her muscles. "Why not? I'd make a good dad. I can throw a ball, and I can hog the remote. Just ask Mom."

Carolyn smiled. "She's very good at hogging the remote."

"And I can spit. And I can lean under the hood of a car and hit the engine with a wrench. I'd make a great dad."

Just then Bryce came home from work at Home Depot. Seeing the three of them at the table, he stopped on his way to clean up. "What's up?"

"Megan's pregnant," Brianna said.

"Well, the hits just keep coming, don't they?" he announced, mimicking a radio announcer. "Way to go, Megan! Way to use your head. We're all real proud of you! Yes, sir! That's just great!" He started up the stairs to his room.

"Hey, come back here!" Brianna called out. "You're not at Testosterone City anymore, Bryce, so quit acting like a complete jerk."

"Don't you talk to me like that," he shot back.

"I'll talk to you any way I want to," Brianna answered. "I'm not afraid of you."

He stopped and came back down the stairs, glaring at Brianna. "What do you want from me?"

"What we don't want is attitude."

89

Bryce sat down. "All right. So you're pregnant. What are you going to do about it?"

"I'm not sure yet."

"What does Kurt want to do?"

"He wants her to have an abortion," Brianna said. "What a psychopath."

"I won't get an abortion," Megan said.

Bryce nodded his head. "All right. Next option. You could put the baby up for adoption."

"I know, but . . ."

"You're not thinking of trying to raise the baby by yourself, are you? That would be a dumb idea. You've already done one stupid thing, Megan. Don't make it two in a row." He stood up. "I've got to take a shower and clean up."

"Thank you so much for sharing your infinite wisdom with us mere mortals," Brianna shot back.

"Somebody in this family has to think rationally." He bounded up the stairs.

"There you have it, ladies and gentlemen! Mr. Sensitivity," Brianna said. "I pity the woman he marries."

"He's not so bad," Megan said. "At least with him you know where you stand."

Brianna smiled. "You could say the same thing about a charging rhino."

"Are you going to want to move back in?" Carolyn asked.

"If you'll let me."

"Of course. When do you want to move?"

"Right away," Megan said. "The rent is due tomorrow."

"Bryce and I can help you move tonight," Brianna said.

"You'd better ask Bryce about that," Carolyn suggested. "He's put in a hard day's work already."

"Yeah, right," Megan said. "Like, standing around and telling people where the hammers are is so tough."

When Bryce bounded back down the stairs on his way out for the evening, Brianna confronted him. "Megan's moving back home. We need you to help out tonight getting her moved out of her old place."

"Who made you the boss of this family?"

"C'mon, Bryce, don't be such a grumposaurus rex. We need your strong muscles and weak mind."

He fought back a smile. "Well, if you put it that way, then I'll help."

On the way across town, Megan, Bryce, and Brianna dropped by the freight door of Home Depot and gathered up some empty boxes and then headed for Megan's apartment.

All Megan had to do was throw her things in boxes while Brianna and Bryce carried them out to his pickup truck.

"What's that noise?" Brianna asked on one trip.

"That's talk radio from Mr. Podolsky next door."

"Is it always this loud?"

Megan nodded. "It's worse when he starts yelling at his radio."

"What's his problem?"

"He thinks there's a plot to destroy our way of life. He lies in wait during the day for anyone who'll listen to him. In a way, I feel sorry for him."

Brianna smiled. "I think I'll go make his day."

"What are you going to do?"

"Nothing. I'll be back in a minute."

Megan watched from the hallway as Brianna knocked on Mr. Podolsky's door.

"Excuse me, I was next door visiting my sister, and I couldn't help hearing your radio."

"You want me to turn it down?"

"No, I was wanting to know if what I heard is really true."

"Yes, and they've done it again!"

"Please tell me."

"Do you want to come in?"

"No, not really. Can't you just tell me here at the door?"

Megan went inside and continued packing, but she left the door open so she could check on Brianna.

"That is so awful!" Brianna said.

"That's just the beginning of it," Mr. Podolsky said enthusiastically.

"Oh, please tell me more. This is so interesting!"

Bryce came back for another load. "What's Brianna doing?"

"Making some guy's day." She glanced at Bryce. "You're probably thinking, 'It must run in the family.' Right?"

"I didn't say a word, did I?"

"No, you didn't."

"If you'd just talked to me." He banged the counter with his hand. "People come to me all the time. They're building this or they're fixing that. And I tell them how to do it, and they take my advice and things work out for them."

"Living a life is not exactly like remodeling a kitchen."

"I know that." He turned to face her, his hands out like he just needed the proper tool to make all their problems go away. "I could've helped if you'd asked. I know about guys. I know everything about guys."

"I know."

"You want me to pay this guy a visit and help him reorder his priorities?"

"I don't want you to beat him up."

"It's no problem, you know. I'd be happy to do it."

"He's not worth you getting in trouble."

"What do you want me to do then?" he asked.

"Just be around when I need you. And don't remind me what a fool I've been. Oh, and go easy on Brianna. This is hard for her, too."

"That's all you want from me?"

"Yes."

"I'd rather bang some heads together."

"It wouldn't do him or me or you any good."

"I just wish I could do more, that's all."

"I know." She put her arms around him and kissed him on the cheek. "You know what? You're my favorite big brother."

It was an old joke. He smiled.

She said, "If you want to help, here's another box to take out."

"That I can do." He took the box and left.

Megan could hear Brianna in the hall, trying to wrap up her conversation with Mr. Podolsky. "I'm *so* happy I got a chance to talk to you, and I just want to say, keep telling everyone about this! I'm just surprised more people don't know about it, that's all."

"Tell your friends!" Mr. Podolsky called out, his voice more excited and happy than Megan had ever heard.

"Great idea! Well, look, Mr. Podolsky, I've got to run now, but thanks for the pamphlets and for giving me the name of the radio station. Thanks again. I'll see you. I'm going now. Good-bye."

She ran inside Megan's apartment and closed the door. She had a big grin on her face. "The world as we know it is doomed. Isn't that great?"

"You're evil," Megan said with a smile.

"Well, maybe so . . . except I do feel sorry for him."

"I wonder what's keeping Bryce. It wasn't that heavy of a box." Megan looked out the window and saw Bryce standing by his pickup talking on his cell phone.

There wasn't much left to do. A few things in the bathroom, some groceries in the kitchen. The apartment was furnished, so they didn't have to move the furniture.

Bryce returned. "I've got to go back to the store. They've got a problem. It'll take about ten minutes to fix and then I'll come back."

"Okay, we'll finish up while you're gone."

"You stud, fixing the problems of the store single-handed," Brianna called out.

He knew she was teasing him but smiled anyway at the veiled compliment. "See you later."

They went in the bedroom and started to put Megan's clothes into boxes.

"So, this is where you got pregnant, right?" Brianna asked, looking at the beat-up bed frame with its lumpy, stained mattress, now visible because they'd removed the sheets.

Megan shook her head. "Let's not go there, okay?"

"You're right. Sorry." Brianna quit working. "What do I tell my friends when they come up and go, 'So your sister got herself pregnant?' What do I tell them?"

"I guess you tell them the truth."

"All my friends know I'm Mormon. What kind of great impression is this going to make with them about the Church? And what do I say to make it better? 'Yeah, she's pregnant, but it's not what she was taught all her life.' I'm sure that'll smooth things over in a big way."

"I'm sorry."

Brianna sat cross-legged on the bed with her elbows on her knees, her hands propping up her head. "And then there's the other thing."

"What other thing?"

"Bryce was active when he was little, but now he doesn't go to church anymore. You're pregnant and not married. So am I next?"

"No, you're more like Heather."

Brianna shook her head. "Nobody's like Heather. She's, like, perfect. Always has been. She sort of wills herself to not mess up. I mean it's like she's never even tempted. She just has this tremendous willpower."

"She does. She's amazing."

"But the thing is, she's never needed us. I mean the family. She always lived above whatever the family was doing."

Brianna shook her head. "I'm not like that. I like people too much. Got to be around them all the time. I'm more like you."

"You're way better than me," Megan said.

"Maybe that's just because I'm younger. Maybe I'll follow in your footsteps."

"I hope you don't."

"Me, too. At least that's the way I feel now. But who can say what's going to happen?"

"What would take you away?" Megan asked.

"That's easy. My friends. My friends mean a lot to me. The only trouble is none of them are in the Church. I don't particularly like the kids my age in the ward. They're all right, I guess, but none of them are people I like to hang with."

Megan finished packing her clothes in boxes in the bedroom. She grabbed another box to gather her belongings from the bathroom. Brianna followed.

"You had interviews with the bishop, though, right?" Brianna asked.

"I did. I lied."

Brianna shook her head. "Why?"

"I didn't want him to know."

"But if he'd known, he could have helped you. And then maybe you wouldn't have got pregnant. I always tell the bishop everything. Sometimes I wonder if he wishes I didn't talk so much, but he never says anything."

When Bryce returned, they carried the rest of her things to his pickup. Just as they were about to leave, Megan took one last chance to look out the kitchen window. "Before we go, there's something I want to tell you guys. A few weeks ago something happened. It was raining, and I was doing the dishes and I looked out and there were all these lights, like a million beacons coming from everywhere I looked. It was the most beautiful thing I'd ever seen. I don't know. It was like it was a sign from God that he loved me. It brought tears to my eyes. I prayed for the first time in I don't know how long."

"You were looking through the screen?" Bryce asked.

"Yes, why?"

"I can tell you why that happened. The screen broke the light up. It's the same thing that happens when you look at a CD. All you need is small lines, and they'll break the light up. That's not God. That's just optics."

"Okay, so there's a reason, but I can't deny the way it made me feel."

"That's just because you didn't know what was causing it. It's not a miracle."

"How can you say that?" Brianna said.

"Because I can explain it. Anything that has an explanation can't be a miracle."

"So what would be a miracle?"

Bryce shook his head. "I haven't seen any. Let's go."

◆　◆　◆

Megan moved her things into Brianna's room, the same room they'd shared before she'd moved out. Before, it had been Megan's room that Brianna was sharing. Now, it was Brianna's room that Megan was sharing.

After unpacking most of her things, Megan went downstairs to the kitchen for her favorite snack since childhood, graham crackers and milk.

Brianna was watching TV and talking on the phone. Bryce was gone to a friend's place.

Her mother joined Megan at the kitchen table. "You all moved in?"

"Yeah, pretty much."

Her mother nodded. "I think we need to call your father and see if he can come home tomorrow, so you can tell him your news."

"That's going to be hard," Megan said.

"I know, but he has to hear this from you, in person, and

it has to be done right away. If we put it off, he might hear it from someone else, and that would be very bad."

"Can you call him and see if he can come home tomorrow?"

"Yes." Her mother looked at the clock on the wall. "He should be in his motel room by now." She asked Brianna to get off the phone.

Ten minutes later Brianna came into the kitchen with the phone. "Why do you need the phone?"

"We're going to call your father."

Brianna cringed. "I'll be upstairs. If anyone beeps in, tell 'em to call back. It could be important." She ran up the stairs, then yelled down, "One point two seconds, a new world's record!" She made a hissing sound to imitate the roar of the crowd, then slammed the door to her room. And then it was quiet again.

Her mother punched in the phone number.

Walter answered it on the first ring.

A little small talk and then Carolyn said, "Something's come up . . . in the family. I was wondering if you could come home tomorrow, instead of waiting until the end of the week."

Megan could only imagine what her father was saying.

"No, nothing like that. Everyone is healthy."

A pause, followed by, "It's not something we can handle over the phone."

Megan's head was beginning to throb.

"I understand that you're two hundred miles from home, and that you have appointments set up in the morning, but you really need to come home. I'm sure you can reschedule your appointments."

Carolyn was tapping her fingernails on the kitchen table. "I can't tell you what it is over the phone. You'll have to come home for us to tell you." A long pause. "Why are you arguing with me? Why can't you just take my word that you need to be here? It won't take long. Maybe a couple of hours, and then you can go back and see your people."

97

A pause and then, "No, I can't even give you a hint. Just come home."

Megan couldn't stand it any longer. She reached over and asked for the phone.

Carolyn shrugged her shoulders and handed it to her.

"Daddy, hi, it's me, Megan. I moved back home today. . . . Why? Well, I lost my job, so I couldn't afford to stay in my apartment. . . . No, that isn't all. There is something else . . ."

"Don't tell him over the phone," her mother said. "He can come home and hear it from your own lips. This is not something that should be discussed over the phone."

Megan held her hand over the mouthpiece. "I don't want to put him out any."

Carolyn shook her head. "Don't do it. He is the father of this family. He can rearrange his schedule when there's a crisis."

"It's okay, Mom."

"It's not okay," she said with tears in her eyes as she left the room.

"Daddy, are you still there? I'm fine . . . except there is one thing . . ."

Megan dabbed at her eyes with a napkin. "You remember Kurt, don't you?"

"Is he getting baptized?" her dad asked excitedly. "Is that your big news?"

Megan covered her eyes with her hand. "No, that's not it."

"What is it then? He hasn't been in an accident, has he?"

"No, he's fine. It's something else."

"Why don't you just tell me? It doesn't look like it's something I'm going to be able to guess."

"Probably not."

Just get it over with, she thought.

"I'm pregnant, Daddy."

There was a long pause.

"I see," her father said quietly.

"I'm real sorry."

"I don't understand. We talked about chastity every month in our interview, and every month you said there was no problem. So did this just happen since our last interview?"

Tears were streaming down her face. "No, it's been going on since a little after I started seeing Kurt."

"But, how can that be?"

"I didn't tell you the truth like I should have."

"Just a minute. I need to turn the TV off."

He came back a few seconds later. "Why did you conceal the truth from me?"

"I guess I didn't want you to worry about me."

"I would have rather worried about you then than have this to deal with. Are you and Kurt going to get married?"

"No, Daddy, we're not."

"Maybe if I talked to him."

"I'd rather you didn't talk to him. It's over between us. I don't respect him anymore. I would never marry him now."

"So what are you going to do?"

"I'm not sure, except I know that I'm not going to have an abortion."

"I just don't understand why this is happening to us. They said for us to have family home evening, so we started doing that. They said for me to interview my children once a month, so I started doing that. They said for me to talk about our courtship and what it was like for your mother and me to get married in the temple, so we did that. We have family prayer. We go to church every Sunday. We pay our tithing. We go to the temple at least once a month. So what did we do wrong, that this should be happening to us?"

"It's a choice I made, Daddy."

"Sometimes . . ." Megan knew what caused him to stop in the middle of a sentence. It was something he did when his emotions got the best of him. Where her mother would just cry and let it out, her father would stop and wait for it to pass.

" . . . sometimes . . . I just don't know . . . how this could have happened to us."

There was nothing more from him for what seemed like an eternity, and then he said, "Could you put your mother on?"

Megan went upstairs to her parents' bedroom. The door was closed. Megan knocked.

"Come in."

Her mother was just sitting on the bed.

"Daddy wants to talk to you."

"I'll take it up here, if that's all right."

Megan went downstairs and hung up the phone, then went back upstairs and sat outside her parents' bedroom so she could at least hear what her mother was saying.

"No, I suppose there isn't any reason for you to come home now," she said, her voice sounding hollow.

Brianna came out of her room. "Did you tell Daddy?"

Megan nodded.

"What'd he say?"

Megan shook her head. "I don't want to talk about it now."

"Sure. I'm going to make myself a grilled cheese sandwich. You want one?"

"No."

"They're very good."

"No thanks."

Brianna clomped down the stairs.

Megan was about to leave the hallway and go to her room and finish unpacking her things when she heard her mother say, "No, Walter, I did not know you had a Scout Jamborall this weekend. But I'm quite sure that you can get some of the dads to fill in for you."

An icy silence followed.

"Yes, I understand there will be competitions for the boys, and I'm happy they've worked so hard, but I'm sure there are

100

others in the ward who are perfectly capable of being with the boys and cheering them on to victory."

The seconds passed.

Her mother said quite coldly, "I see. Yes, good-bye."

Megan waited a minute before going in to see her mother. She was sitting on the bed, her head down, her eyes closed.

"You okay, Mom?"

She looked up and smiled thinly. "Yes, of course. I'm fine." She stood up. "Do you have any laundry that needs to be done tonight?"

"No, I'm okay."

"I need to turn on the dishwasher." Carolyn started out the door, then stopped. "Your father has a Scout Jamborall this weekend, so he won't be around all that much."

"It's okay, Mom."

"Yes, of course, everything is okay," she said bitterly. "That's the way it is around here. Everything is always fine."

◆　　◆　　◆

Walter came home a little early on Friday but mainly to pack up for the Scout Jamborall. Megan was the only one home. She was in the living room watching *Wheel of Fortune.*

Her father came into the living room. "Well, I'm home."

"Did you have a good week?"

It was the question the family usually asked when he came home from a week on the road, but this time it had a warped, almost surreal quality to it.

"I mean as far as placing orders," she added.

"Pretty good week."

"Good. I'm glad."

"You doing okay?" he asked.

"I'm fine, Daddy."

Ordinarily, he would have given her a big hug, but this time he held back. "I'm glad to hear you're doing well."

"Thank you. I went to Doctor Sullivan today. He'll be the one who delivers the baby."

"I see. What did he say?"

"Everything seems normal so far."

"Good. Normal is good." He looked at his watch. "Well, I hate to run off, but I really need to get ready for the Scout Jamborall. It's the biggest they've ever had around here. I'm very hopeful that our troop will be recognized as one of the best."

"Well, good luck, Daddy. I know your Scouts will make you proud, just like they always do."

"Thanks. Scouts always do their best to do their duty."

"Yes, I know."

It was an awkward moment for both of them. Megan felt that she would never match up to her dad's Scouts.

"Well, I'd better get my gear packed."

"Can I help?"

"No, it's better if I do it. That way I know where everything is."

"Of course."

Her father went into the garage.

A few minutes later Carolyn came home from work. She went into the garage to talk to Walter.

Seated at the kitchen table, Megan could hear everything they said.

"Did you even ask anyone to take your place this weekend?" she asked.

"No, I did not."

"Your family needs you. Megan needs you."

"Why? She's already pregnant. So what would my staying home this weekend accomplish?"

"This isn't going to be easy for her. She needs us to support her."

"She lied to me, month after month. Maybe I'm old fashioned, but to me, when someone lies to you again and again and again, that shows a lack of respect. So if she doesn't

102

respect me, and if she has no interest in my opinions, and if she won't follow my counsel, then what on earth am I going to accomplish this weekend by being here instead of where I've been called to serve? At least the boys listen to what I say. That's more than I can say for anyone in this family."

"I don't want to have to carry this all by myself. Sometimes I get tired of being the one everyone else depends on. I have my limits, too."

"You'll do fine. You always have."

"I don't know how to say this any clearer, Walter. If you won't stay home for Megan, stay home for me. I need you to be here."

"Do you have any idea how much the boys have worked to prepare themselves for this weekend? If I'm not there, they'll have a tough time achieving all the goals they've set for themselves."

"I see. Well, I guess I know where I stand in your list of priorities then, don't I?"

"There will be other weekends that I'll be home. Besides, I'll be back tomorrow night."

"Yes, of course. And we'll both be tied up all day Sunday in meetings, and then you'll leave first thing on Monday. Maybe if I gave out little patches you could sew on your shirt, like they do, you'd be around more when I need you."

"What do you want me to do?"

"I've already told you what I want you to do, but you won't do it. Good-bye, Walter."

Her mother came through the side door, walked past Megan, went upstairs to her room, and closed the door.

Her father made a couple more trips inside and then backed the car out of the driveway and drove away.

The house was silent again, except for some nameless contestant on *Wheel of Fortune*, asking for the letter R.

6

Megan arranged to meet with Bishop Oldham on Saturday afternoon at one-thirty. When she arrived, his ward clerk was in the office next door working on the computer.

"Thank you for being willing to see me on such short notice," Megan said as she sat down in the bishop's office.

"No problem."

Megan closed her eyes. *I've got to start and just trust that things will go okay.*

She gave him an embarrassed smile. "I guess you're wondering why I wanted to talk to you today instead of waiting until tomorrow."

He nodded. "I'm sure you'll tell me."

She took a deep breath. "Well, yes, I will. Let me just spit it out. I'm pregnant."

He nodded. "I see."

As she talked she felt as if the room was tipping to the left and that she needed to hold on to her chair to keep from falling out. She spoke fast in a strained, high-pitched voice.

"The father's name is Kurt. He's not a member of the Church. I started sleeping with him a few months ago."

Megan cleared her throat. *At least it's out in the open now, so that's good.* "It was a dumb thing for me to do, I know, but I did it."

"Have you told your parents?"

"Yes."

"How did they react?"

"They were very disappointed."

"You understand why, don't you?"

"It goes against everything they've taught me."

The bishop nodded, then asked, "Did you start sleeping with your boyfriend before we had our last interview?"

She waited for a long time before saying, just above a whisper, "Yes."

"I see. So that means you weren't completely honest with me?"

"No. I wasn't."

He rested his elbows on the desk and covered his eyes with his hand.

"I'm real sorry," she said. "I should have told you, but I was too embarrassed."

He looked as though he had more to say but stopped and took a deep breath. "Have you thought about what you're going to do?"

"Kurt wants me to get an abortion. I thought about it, but then I decided I can't do that because it's not the baby's fault how it came to be conceived. So I'm not going to get an abortion."

"Good for you."

She was surprised he could say anything positive about this. "Thank you."

"What about you and Kurt?" he asked. "Is there any possibility you two could get married?"

She shook her head. "He's not ready to settle down. He

pretty much just wants to continue his life the way it is now. He likes the freedom to do whatever he wants. He likes to sail and backpack and be with his friends. I don't think I'd want to marry him, even if he asked me."

"Has he asked you?"

"No." She paused. "He offered to pay for the abortion, and that's the last I've heard from him." She cleared her throat. "What do I need to tell you about Kurt and me?"

"I'm not sure I understand what you're asking."

"Do I need to tell you how many times we . . . were together?"

He shook his head. "No, that's not necessary."

"Are there any details about what we did that you need me to tell you about?"

"No."

She sighed. "Good. I was worrying about that."

"Yes, of course."

The bishop didn't say anything for a few moments, then he said, "Megan, why have you come here today?"

"I needed to talk to you. You know, to confess."

"Is there something you hope to gain from that?"

"It's just something I've always heard. When you mess up, you're supposed to go talk to the bishop."

"Why?"

"I don't know. You just do."

"Megan, let me ask you something. How do you feel about what's happened to you?"

"I feel awful. I mean, I'm pregnant and I'm not married. It's embarrassing."

"Is that all it is? Embarrassing?"

"No. It's not easy. I'm going to have a baby. That really scares me."

"I'm sure it does. But I want you to think about something else. You have been taught that immorality is a major sin, haven't you?"

She panicked. "Are you going to excommunicate me?"

"Does the Church mean that much to you, that you'd care if you were excommunicated?"

She was shocked by the question. "I've always been active in the Church."

"Yes, that's true. You could often be found within the walls of this building. You were in the Church, but was the Church and its teachings in you?"

He took his scriptures from a shelf behind the desk. "Have the teachings of the Church entered your heart and mind? Or have you just gone through the motions?"

It was a painful question, one she was not willing to answer.

He continued. "Megan, I don't mean to be unkind, but what you have done is very serious. Let's read something together."

He thumbed through his scriptures, then turned the book so Megan could see it.

"This is Alma talking to his son Corianton about sexual sin. Please read verse five."

Megan read: "'Know ye not, my son, that these things are an abomination in the sight of the Lord; yea, most abominable above all sins save it be the shedding of innocent blood.'"

"What that means, Megan, is that the sin of immorality is second only to murder."

Megan didn't know what to say. She looked down at her hands.

Bishop Oldham continued, "If that was all we know, you would be in a hopeless situation, but the Lord is merciful and kind. Let's look at something else he has said."

He thumbed the pages again and pointed to a passage he had marked in red. "Read this," he said.

Megan cleared her throat and read the passage: "'Behold,

he who has repented of his sins, the same is forgiven, and I, the Lord, remember them no more.'"

"I know that is true, Megan. Because of the Atonement, the Savior is able not only to forgive but forget our sins. The question you need to ask yourself is if you're willing to make major changes in your life, so that you can be forgiven of the sin you've committed."

"Is that still a possibility?"

He nodded his head. "It's always possible."

"Are you saying that as far as God is concerned, it could be like it never happened?"

"That's exactly what I'm saying."

"I'm not sure I believe that."

"Why not?"

"It doesn't seem fair."

"In what way?"

"Well, take a girl who's always lived the way the Church teaches. Like Alexis, for example. So, basically, she's never done anything wrong. How can it be that I could be forgiven of all the things I've done wrong, and have all my sins forgiven, so that as far as God is concerned, we're both the same in his eyes?"

"I'm not saying you won't have regrets. I'm not saying you'll forget what's happened. I'm not saying there will be no natural consequences of your misdeeds, such as sexually transmitted diseases or things of that nature. There will be regrets, there will be heartache. But in time even that pain can be wiped away. The beauty of the gospel of Jesus Christ is that we can be totally forgiven of our sins, so that as far as Father in Heaven is concerned, you can start over again, clean, completely forgiven, and approved of by him and our Savior."

That was something Megan hadn't even dared hope for. She sat in stunned silence for a few moments. Then she asked, "What do I have to do?"

"It's going to take some time and some hard work on your

part. We can talk about it over the course of the next few weeks. I'll start by giving you some reading assignments. Then we'll need to get together, every week, to check on your progress."

"Do you want me to come to church?" she asked.

"Yes, of course, but there is one thing I would ask of you."

"What's that?"

"That you refrain from taking the sacrament until I give you permission."

"Why?"

"Before you partake of the sacrament again, I want you to understand its significance and what it has to do with being forgiven."

She was worried what people would think if she didn't take the sacrament, but she didn't say anything about it.

The bishop closed his scriptures and set them aside. "Megan, I'm so sorry for what's happened. I can't even imagine what you've been going through. But I want you to know that I'm here for you and that there is a way back."

She looked at him but was too emotional to respond.

"Now, what else should we talk about?" he asked.

She cleared her throat. "Well, I'm not sure if I should keep the baby or put it up for adoption."

"I'm sure that will be a difficult decision. I'd like to put you in touch with LDS Family Services. They really specialize in these kinds of issues. They won't pressure you either way, but they will help you see more clearly the consequences of the decision you make, both for you and your baby. If you want, I can call and make an appointment for you."

Megan thought about that for a moment, then said, "I'd like that. Thank you."

"Sure. Is there anything else you'd like to talk about?"

She closed her eyes. The fear she had felt in coming had been forgotten. Even though she was still pregnant and her troubles hadn't gone away, she felt calm, even a little hopeful.

She opened her eyes. Bishop Oldham was sitting patiently, looking at her, a look of kindly concern on his face. She shook her head. "No," she said. "Thank you."

◆　　◆　　◆

After Megan got home, while she and Brianna were sitting at the kitchen table, her father returned home from the Boy Scout Jamborall. Although his face had a smudge of charcoal on it and his Scout shirt looked like he'd slept in it, which he had, he was excited and talkative.

"Well, we did it! We really cleaned up! Four first place awards, the troop medallion, and a good sportsmanship award. Not bad for one troop, right?"

"I'm like 'Whoa, Nellie!' Way to go, Scout Daddy!" Brianna called out.

"Good job," Megan said, much more constrained.

"I'm very proud of the boys. They're the ones who did it."

"Yeah, but you're the one who taught 'em," Brianna said.

Carolyn came in from working in the tiny flower garden they had in their abbreviated backyard.

"If you ask me, those boys are lucky to have you," Brianna continued.

Walter and Carolyn exchanged painful and awkward glances. "I see you're home," she said with little enthusiasm.

"Daddy's troop won almost everything! Isn't that amazing?" Brianna said.

"Yes, I'm sure it is," Carolyn said in a dull monotone. "I need to finish up my work. Walter, you don't know where the pruning shears are, do you? You didn't take them with you to Scout camp, did you? I can't find them anywhere."

"I don't know where they are."

"We shouldn't have to buy pruning shears twice a year. It's a needless waste of money."

110

"Do you have some of the medals with you, Daddy?" Brianna asked.

"Yes, they're in the car. Would you like to see them?"

"I would! How about the rest of you?"

Carolyn hesitated and then said quietly, "I need to finish up outside. It looks like it might rain."

Brianna practically did cheers as Walter showed her each ribbon and award his troop had earned at the jamborall. Megan was less enthusiastic, not because she didn't value his work with the boys in the ward, but because she shared her mother's feeling of disappointment that he had not arranged for someone else to take the boys so they could face their biggest family crisis together.

Brianna left a few minutes later. Walter unpacked his own and the troop's camp equipment and stored it back in the garage.

Megan knew that her parents were going to have what could be an argument, or at least a tension-filled discussion. She didn't want to be in the house when it happened, so she decided to take a walk.

It was a hot, sunny day with few clouds, except there was still a fog bank to the west over the bay.

Because it was Saturday, people were mowing their lawns or working in their gardens. She passed a young married couple putting up a swing set for their little boy. Except for being frustrated trying to read the instructions, they looked happy. She wondered what her baby would look like at three years old, and if she'd even know. She wondered if in an adoption she would be able to even see her son or daughter.

She was just heading back when a car slowed down and stopped. Megan looked over. It was Kurt's mother. They'd met once.

She pulled over and stopped and rolled down the window on the right side of the car.

"Hello, Megan. Taking a walk?"

"Yes. It's a beautiful day."

"It is. I stopped by the house and your mother said you were out. I'm fortunate I found you. I'd like to talk to you, if that's all right."

"Okay."

"Why don't you come sit in the car?" Megan got in the car and shut the door.

Even wearing slacks and a blouse, Kurt's mother looked elegant, as usual. "You're looking good, Megan. How do you feel?"

"All right . . . so far."

"Wonderful." She cleared her throat. "This is awkward, isn't it?"

"Yeah, it is."

"Kurt told his father about you being pregnant."

"Why?"

"I'm not sure. I guess he was worried about legal and financial issues."

"That sounds like Kurt, always looking out for himself."

"I'm hoping that you and Kurt will get married."

"That would make things simpler, that's for sure."

"Of course it would. Then there would be no question about what to do."

"No, there wouldn't."

"Kurt does love you, I think."

"Does he?"

"Of course he does."

"Is that why he offered to pay for my abortion and hasn't contacted me since? Because he loves me?"

"He just panicked, that's all."

"Actually, he didn't offer to pay for the abortion. He offered to pay what the insurance wouldn't cover. And if my insurance wouldn't cover abortion, he said there were doctors he'd heard about who charge for something the insurance will cover and then will go ahead and do an abortion. So, yes, I

112

can see why you'd say he loves me. That's easy to see, now that I think about it."

"He's very concerned about you."

"Really? Is he home right now? Let's both go talk to him and have him tell us how concerned he is about me."

"Well, he's not home now. He's gone scuba diving with some friends."

She nodded her head. "I see. Well, that sounds like fun. Kurt really knows how to have a good time." Even as she said it, she began to blush, hoping Kurt's mother would not take her comment wrong. "What I meant is, he has some outdoor adventure planned nearly every weekend."

"I understood what you meant. And I quite agree."

The two women endured a painful silence.

"I'm not going to get an abortion."

"I'm happy to hear that. I'm very hopeful that his father and I can talk him into marrying you."

"How would you do that?" Megan asked.

"I would tell him he has a responsibility to do the right thing by you."

"And that would be enough, just you telling him that?"

There was a long pause. "I'm not sure."

"Well, you could always threaten to cut off his allowance."

Kurt's mother cringed. "He doesn't get an allowance."

"I'm sorry. That was a cheap shot. I shouldn't have said it. How would you get him to marry me?"

"Why do you want to know?"

Megan shrugged. "I don't know. Just curious. When a boy has everything, what do you do to get him to do what you want?"

Kurt's mother smiled. "I wish I knew the answer to that. We don't give him money. He works for what he gets."

"He doesn't seem to work very hard though."

"Well, that's because he's very good at what he does. He's always been good with computers."

"He's perfectly happy with the way his life is now. I'm sure he doesn't want a wife and a baby to get in the way of his good times."

"He's very good with children, though."

"Yes, of course, he's a real charmer," Megan said.

"How can I be of help to you?"

"I'm not sure you can."

"Please let me know."

"I will."

"What will happen to my grandchild?"

"I can't tell you that yet. Except I've decided to have the baby. After that, I'm not sure. I'll either keep the baby, or else I'll put him or her up for adoption."

"The way things are going with Kurt, I may never have a grandchild."

"That's possible. I don't see him settling down anytime soon."

"Life is too easy for him."

"It's just the way he wants it to be."

"Do you need money? I can give you whatever you want, for doctor's expenses and to pay for your stay in the hospital. Whatever you need. Just let me know."

"I will," Megan said, knowing full well that she would never ask for money.

"Would you like me to drop you off some place?"

"No, I'll just continue my walk. Thank you for coming. That means a lot to me."

"We're not enemies, you and I."

"No, not at all."

They said good-bye one more time, then Megan got out of the car and watched her drive off.

The house was quiet by the time Megan returned home. Her father was airing out the tents and his sleeping bag and cleaning up all the cooking equipment they'd used on the camp out.

114

"Where's Mom?" she asked.

"She's gone grocery shopping," her dad said quietly.

They've been arguing, she thought. *I can always tell.*

She went to her room and lay down and took a nap.

She slept through supper, not waking up until seven-thirty that night. The house was quiet, except she could hear her mother and father in the next room talking.

"I think you're being totally unreasonable," Walter said. "You want me to ask to be released from being Scoutmaster because I wasn't around here last night?"

"It's not just last night. You're always gone. I don't see why the only man in the ward who's gone all week should be taking a group of boys out camping on the weekends. You've been Scoutmaster long enough. They can get someone else."

"You know what the troop was like when I took over."

"Your number one priority should be your family, not some Scout troop. Your family needs you now."

"Needs me? What for? They don't need me. You think Bryce needs me? I don't. Megan? What can I do for her now? It seems to me like the damage has already been done. And Brianna? I can't even understand half the things she says."

"I want you to ask to be released, Walter. That's what I want. I can't face all this by myself. Do you want to talk to the bishop about having you released or do you want me to?"

"I really think you're overreacting. The Scouts don't have any more weekend activities planned for a month. I'll see if I can cut down on the days I'm out of town. I'll get an assistant Scoutmaster called who can help out. All I'm saying is give me a little time to rearrange my life. And then, if you're still not satisfied, I'll ask to be released."

After a long pause, Carolyn said, "All right, we'll give it a month."

"I will spend more time at home. You'll see. But . . ."

"What?"

"Well, because I was gone all day, tonight I need to go to

my office and get caught up on my sales reports and get ready for next week. Is that okay with you?"

"You do what you think best," she said.

That night Brianna had some friends over to watch movies, and Megan avoided them by going upstairs and reading until they left, just after midnight.

Brianna knocked quietly on the door then opened it a crack. With a Swedish accent, she said, "Room service. You want I should fluff up your pillow?"

Megan laughed. "Yes, come in."

Brianna, true to her word, fluffed up Megan's pillow. "Fluffy pillows help you sleep, yah?"

They talked for half an hour, and then Brianna got ready for bed and soon returned, talked Megan into having a prayer with her, then climbed into bed and fell asleep within a few minutes.

Megan couldn't sleep and so half an hour later she got up and went downstairs and watched an old movie on TV.

Bryce came home at two-thirty. He grabbed something to eat, then came into the living room and sat down. "You're up kind of late, aren't you?" he asked.

"I couldn't sleep."

"Got a lot on your mind?" he asked.

"Yeah."

He took a bite of the sandwich he'd made. "You want me to make you one of these?"

"No, I'm fine."

"You still thinking about keeping the baby?" he asked.

"I am."

"What would you live on?"

"I could get a job."

"You have no skills."

"I have . . . " she paused, "eight months to get some."

"What are you going to learn in that time that'll give you a

116

decent living? All I'm saying is give this kid a chance by letting a family adopt it."

"Why is everything so black-and-white to you?"

"That's just the way it is. Sometimes you got to use logic and reason. This is one of those times. Think about it."

"I will."

"Be right back." He went into the kitchen.

She was bored with the movie, so she went in to talk while he made himself another sandwich. "Are you going to keep going to church through all this?" he asked.

"Yes."

"What for? People at church won't want to have anything to do with you. So why go back? You're the exact opposite of what they want their girls to become. If they're nice to you, then it takes away from the threat they use to keep other girls in line. They can't be good to you, because if they are, the whole thing will start to unravel and fall apart."

"I'm going to try it anyway."

He shrugged his shoulders. "Suit yourself."

"I'm going to bed," she said.

"Whatever."

Megan went to bed and thought about what it was going to be like going back to church.

She sighed. *This is too hard. Everything now is so painful. Sometimes I wish I were dead.*

She opened her eyes. *I can't die though. Not now. Because of the baby.*

The next day was Sunday. Megan had told Brianna she would be going to church but felt sick when she got up, so she went back to bed.

Brianna got up, took a shower, then came back to the room they shared. "You going to church today?"

"I feel sick."

"Yeah, right. I've used that excuse, too, when I didn't want to go."

"I want to go."

"Then get up and at least try to get ready."

"I'm not making this up. I don't feel well."

"Will you ever feel good enough to go?" Brianna asked sarcastically.

"Just go away and leave me alone, okay?"

"Fine, whatever you say."

By then Megan was too mad to go to sleep. *I'll show her,* she thought, standing up, fully expecting she'd throw up. But nothing came. She walked gingerly into the bathroom and looked into the mirror. *I look awful. How can I go to church looking this way?*

And then a new thought came into her mind that brought her to tears. *It doesn't matter anymore how I look. I'm pregnant and I'm single. That makes me of no interest to anyone. Not to any guy and not to the girls my age. I am on my way to becoming invisible. So there's no reason to go to church except if I want to worship God because nobody cares what I look like anymore.*

She was about to go back to bed when another thought came to her. *Except the bishop. He'll notice if I'm not at church. And if I go, he'll come over and say hello to me. He'll be my support, even if nobody else in the ward is.*

She began to wash her face. *I'll go to church today for the bishop. In time I may have other reasons to go, but for now it will be for him.*

She still felt sick to her stomach but thought that if she had something to eat, the nausea would go away. So after getting ready, she went downstairs and had half of a banana on some cold cereal. The phone rang. Brianna answered it. It was for Walter.

"Thank you. Yes, I am proud of the boys. What they did is quite an achievement. . . . Well, I'd say Derek Adams and Jonathan would be the ones to ask to talk. . . . Well, yes, I'd be willing to say a few words, too."

118

An hour later Megan, Brianna, and their parents walked into church twenty minutes early. It wasn't until then that Megan realized that Brianna wouldn't be sitting with her because she was singing in a Young Women's choir and would be sitting on the stand. Her mother was the chorister and wouldn't join her until after the sacrament. Her father would also be sitting on the stand with his Scouts.

I'll be all alone, she thought.

Brianna went to practice with the chorus, her mother left to find some sheet music for a missionary farewell scheduled in two weeks, and her dad was busy shaking hands with some of his friends.

Megan stood alone near the door of the chapel. *How many know about me?* she thought. *Some must know. Brianna must have told some people. I never said she shouldn't. It's all going to come out anyway.*

She looked around to see if people were staring at her. They didn't seem to be, but there weren't that many people in the chapel yet. Megan felt a dull ache in her stomach. *When they find out about me, what will they say? Will they say, I'm not surprised. Will they say, I could see it coming. Will they say, Why is she even coming to church?*

Her face was flushed, and she felt sick to her stomach. *I can't go through this. I've got to get away from here. I never should have come in the first place. This is all a terrible mistake. Bryce was right. I don't belong here anymore.*

She left and walked quickly to the restroom, planning to throw water on her face and then walk home, never again to return.

She looked at herself in the mirror, something she'd been doing in that room for as long as she could remember. She had a sudden rush of memories of growing up as a member of the Church in that building. She knew every room in that building. Rooms where she'd been taught in Primary. Rooms for Sunday School and Young Women. It all came back to her.

119

All the lessons, all the treats, all the activities, all the times she'd felt the love of her teachers and leaders.

And now look at me, she thought.

Tears began to stream down her face. She couldn't stop herself.

Sister Amundson walked in. Her husband was in the stake presidency and hardly ever attended church in his own ward. She had a boy who was seven and a girl who was four. Sister Amundson had come in to assist her daughter.

Megan wiped her eyes and glanced at Sister Amundson in the reflection in the mirror. *I've got to go now.*

"Tiffany, you go ahead and go potty. I'll be right here if you need me."

Tiffany entered the stall and closed the door.

Sister Amundson touched Megan's arm lightly. "You okay?"

Megan nodded. "Yes, I'm fine."

"Are you at peace?"

It was such an odd question, one that nobody had ever asked her before. Megan glanced quickly at Sister Amundson to see if it was just a question she asked mindlessly, or if she actually meant it.

They made eye contact. The sincerity in Sister Amundson's expression was evident.

"I'm having kind of a rough time today," Megan whispered through the rush of tears.

Tiffany, in the stall, was singing a Primary song.

"What can I do to help you?"

"Nothing," Megan said barely above a whisper. "There's nothing anyone can do for me now." She covered her eyes with her hand and began sobbing.

Sister Amundson at first just put her hand on Megan's back but then drew her into a hug. "I'm pregnant," Megan blurted out.

"It's okay, Megan. We're still here for you. All of us."

"I don't think I can go to church anymore. It's too hard."

"But you're here, Megan. You've already done the hard part, just getting here."

"My mom and my dad and Brianna are all on the program today. I'm afraid I'll have to be all by myself."

"Sit with us."

"I'm afraid people are going to look down on me."

Sister Amundson smiled. "If they're going to look down on you, well then, they can just look down on me, too."

Megan bit her lip, fighting back the tears. "Are you sure?"

"Absolutely. You belong in church. No matter how bad things are, the gospel will make it better." She turned to the stall. "Tiffany, please, hurry up."

When she entered the chapel, her father came up to her. "I was looking for you."

"Sorry. You're speaking today, right? Shouldn't you sit on the stand? Sister Amundson said I could sit with her and her kids."

He thought about it for a minute. "You don't mind?"

"No, I'm okay."

"All right then. It might be better if the boys and I sit together on the stand, especially after they pass the sacrament."

"Sure, go ahead."

Megan sat near the front with Sister Amundson and her two children. "Thank you so much," Megan whispered, just as the bishop stood up to begin the meeting.

Sister Amundson squeezed Megan's hand. "You're going to be fine," she said.

Megan nodded, afraid to say anything for fear she'd lose the small amount of composure she was struggling to maintain.

When it came time for the sacrament, she tensed up, wondering if anyone would notice her not taking the bread or the water.

She was sitting on the end of the row. When the tray of

121

bread came to her, she passed it to Sister Amundson, who took it and held it while her son, Mark, took a piece and put it in his mouth. Then Sister Amundson held the tray for Tiffany to take a piece.

"Why didn't Megan take any?" Mark whispered.

"Sometimes people don't," his mother said.

"Why?"

Megan quit breathing, wondering what Sister Amundson would say.

Because they're not worthy, she thought. *Because they've messed up big-time. Because the bishop told them not to. Because they went against all they were taught. Is that what she'll say?*

"It helps them remember what the sacrament is all about, so that when they take it, it means so much more to them."

That seemed to satisfy Mark.

Megan's face was red, wondering who else had noticed she hadn't taken the sacrament. She glanced around. Everyone seemed lost in their own thoughts.

After the sacrament, Megan's mother came and sat with her in the same row with Sister Amundson and her two kids.

After the meeting was over, Bishop Oldham came down from the stand and shook her hand. "Good morning, Megan. I'm so pleased you came today." He smiled at Sister Amundson. "And that you were looked after so well."

"Thank you," Megan said.

"Could we get together after the block? Just for a few minutes."

"Yes, of course."

"It will be right after, if you could just have a seat outside my office and relax. I promise not to take too long."

Megan nodded, and the bishop moved away to catch someone else he needed to see.

Megan's mother thanked Sister Amundson, or Peggy, as she called her, for "looking after Megan."

"Oh, she was a big help to me. She kept Tiffany occupied, going through one of her books with her."

"Well, let's go to Sunday School, Megan," her mother said.

Megan was glad the Gospel Doctrine class was full of adults anxious to answer all the questions.

"How many of you did the reading for today's lesson?" Brother Halverson, the teacher, asked. Less than a fourth of the class raised their hands.

"Thanks to those of you who did. That is so helpful to a teacher to have people in the class who've read the lesson. For those of you who haven't, please read the lesson for next time. Let me ask you a question. You don't have to raise your hands, but I wonder if there is anyone here who's never read the Book of Mormon from cover to cover?"

Megan had never read it all the way through, so she was glad he didn't call for a show of hands.

"I just want to say that you will never have a sufficiently strong testimony of this work until you've read the Book of Mormon. And for those who have read it, some of you many times I'm sure, please read it again this year."

After Sunday School, Megan went with her mother to Relief Society. The lesson would have had no interest to her ordinarily, but because it was about rearing children to follow the teachings of the Church, and because she still wasn't certain what would become of the child she would have, she paid more attention.

"I need to see the bishop," Megan said to her mother after Relief Society was over and the women were filing out of the room.

"How long will you be?"

"The bishop said not very long."

"Should I take Brianna home and then come back for you?"

"I think I'll just be a few minutes."

"Okay, we'll be in the car then."

Megan sat down on a couch outside the bishop's office.

The executive secretary saw her sitting there and came over. "I don't have you scheduled to see the bishop," he said, looking down at the calendar where he kept track of the bishop's appointments.

"He said to come right after the block."

"I see. What for?"

Megan looked at the executive secretary, wondering why he would ask that.

"He didn't say," she said.

He nodded. "Sure, no problem. He should be here any minute now." He hesitated, then said, "When I asked what for, I didn't mean I needed to know. The reason I asked is because the bishop has a number of other people who have appointments, and I just need to know how long you'll be. That's all I meant."

She wasn't sure how to respond, so she just smiled and said, "Okay."

He moved on. Megan relaxed.

The bishop showed up a few minutes later, looked at those waiting for him, then said, "Megan, you're first."

She went with the bishop into his office.

He shook her hand warmly, and they sat down. "I was very pleased to see you in church today. Was it okay for you?"

"Yeah, it was. It was good."

"Maybe the Gospel Essentials class would be better for you. It's a smaller class, and the people who attend are either new converts or just starting back, like you. I go there whenever I can. Why don't you try that next week and tell me what you think."

"Okay."

"What shall we talk about today?" he asked.

"I'm not sure. I'll probably have more to talk about after I meet with LDS Family Services on Wednesday."

"Good. I'd like to know how that goes for you. If it's okay,

I'd like to see you every Sunday about this time. We won't take long. Now let me give you some more scriptures I'd like you to read before we meet next week."

A few minutes later Megan said good-bye to the bishop and went to find her mother and Brianna. She felt good, hopeful that she could change, at peace with herself, looking forward to a good week. She felt good about her decision to have the baby.

The only question now was what to do with the baby after it was born. She was hoping LDS Family Services could help her with that.

7

Megan dreaded keeping her appointment with LDS Family Services. She was scheduled to meet with a Sister Gardner. She didn't know her and wasn't sure what to expect. *I don't like having to open up details of my personal life with complete strangers, wondering what they think of me. It isn't fair for me to have to face this all by myself.*

But there was no other choice.

A few minutes later, Megan sat down across the desk from Sister Gardner. She was in her early thirties and single. Megan appreciated her friendly smile and approved of the warm and casual way she'd decorated her office with American Indian artwork.

"Did the bishop tell you why I'm here?" Megan asked.

"A little bit, but why don't you fill me in?"

She took a deep breath. "Well, I'm pregnant, and I'm not married."

"And the father?"

"He's out of the picture. He has no interest in me or the

baby. He suggested I have an abortion, but I'm not going to do that."

"Good for you."

"I want to keep my baby, but my brother thinks I should put it up for adoption. That's why I'm here."

"Well, fine, you've come to the right place. That is what we do here, explain the options that are available."

"I've been thinking that I'd really like to keep the baby."

"Of course. Many of our clients do that." She reached for a piece of paper. "Where will you be living after the child is born?"

"Well, I'll be at home right after. That's where I'm staying."

"So will you stay there after the baby is born?"

"For a while I guess, but then I'll get an apartment."

"Will you be working then or would you be a stay-at-home mom?"

"Well, I guess eventually I'll have to get a job."

"How about child care? Have you thought about that?"

"My mom can help me. She works during the day, so like if I got a night job I could have her take care of the baby while I'm at work. And my younger sister, Brianna, is willing to help, too. She likes kids and is really good with them."

"So you'll be looking for a job you can do at night."

"Yes, that's right."

"Very good. Well, we've got a worksheet here that will help you as you make your plans. What would you think about working on it at home and then bringing it back when you're done? We can look it over together as you plan for your and your baby's future. It's always better to have a plan, don't you agree?"

Sister Gardner was easier to talk to than Megan had expected, but, still, she had her doubts. "Can I ask you a question?"

"Yes, of course."

"You're supposed to try and talk me into giving my baby

127

away, aren't you? I mean, that's the purpose of the worksheet, isn't it? To get me to realize that it would be better to give my baby away."

"We prefer to call it placing the baby for adoption."

"You can call it what you will, but it's the same thing, isn't it?"

"The term *giving away a baby* implies a lack of concern for the child, but the term *placing the baby for adoption*, in my mind at least, implies a different image. But that's just because I work with this every day. The thing is, Megan, I'm happy to work with you, whatever you decide to do."

"You're sure about that?"

"I am."

"Okay. Well, I just had to ask."

"And I'm glad you did. Fill out the planning form, then we can go through it together. If you'd care to, that is."

"I guess it couldn't hurt anything."

"I don't see how."

As Megan worked on her plans over the next two days, she began to see some difficulties, which Bryce, peering over her shoulder when he came home from work the next evening, immediately seized upon.

"What are you doing?" he asked.

"Nothing. Go away."

"Don't say 'nothing.' You are doing something. Just tell me what it is."

"It's none of your business."

"Just tell me, and I'll go away."

"I'm working on plans for what I'm going to do once I have the baby."

"What's there to plan? You have the baby, you give it to the adoption agency, and you come home."

She hated his know-it-all attitude. "Gosh, Bryce, why don't I have you plan out my entire life?"

"You're not still thinking of keeping the baby, are you?"

128

"Why shouldn't I keep it? I'm going to be its mom."

"How are you going to support a kid all by yourself?"

"I'll get a job."

"And who will be taking care of your kid while you're working?"

"I'll get a night job, so Mom can take care of it while I'm working."

"Have you talked to her about it?"

"Not yet, but I will."

"Are you going to live here the rest of your life?"

"No, I'll get an apartment."

"How much do you think you're going to be making with just a high school degree?"

"Enough to get by."

"Barely enough."

"It will be enough, Bryce. Now go away and quit bothering me."

"Let me crank out some numbers for you, okay?"

She threw up her hands. "Why can't you just leave me alone?"

Bryce went into the kitchen and started rummaging through a kitchen drawer. "We used to have a calculator in here. Whatever happened to it?"

"I don't know, Bryce."

"I've got one in my car. I'll go get it."

"I don't need your help."

"No, that's just it. You do need my help. Desperately." He went outside.

A short time later he returned.

"How much was your rent in your old place?"

"I'm not moving back there."

"I know. I just need a number."

She told him what her rent had been.

"Okay, even if you get a good job and make what I make at Home Depot, by the time you pay your rent and car insurance and buy groceries there will be less than fifty dollars a month left over. You'll spend well over that on things for the baby."

"I'll go to college then, so I can get a good job."

"Good idea, Megan. And who's going to pay for college? Mom? Dad? Way to show your independence."

"I'll take classes before I go to work each day."

"Okay, well, you could do that, same as me. One class a semester. At that rate you'll be done with college by the time your child is . . ." He stopped to do some figuring. " . . . ten years old."

"It won't take that long, Bryce. I'll take summer classes."

"I put that in my estimate."

"Why are you so negative all the time?"

"Why can't you face the facts?"

"It's not for the rest of my life. I'll probably get married in a couple of years. Then things will be better."

"Who are you going to marry?"

"How should I know?"

"Hey, it should be no problem," he said sarcastically. "Every day at work guys come up to me and say, 'Where can I find a single woman with a kid, so I can get married and take on some responsibilities and debt?' And I say, 'Man, I wish I knew. I'd snap her up in a minute.'"

"I hate it when you're this way," she said.

"You mean when I'm logical? I bet you do. Sorry to burst your bubble, Megan. You can go on living in that imaginary world of yours, but don't drag some kid into it. Put the kid up for adoption. You can't feed a kid on love. You can't send him to college. You can't give him piano lessons. You can't send him to camp. You can't be there for him when he comes home from school."

She threw a couch pillow at him. "Don't tell me what I can or can't do! I'll make it just fine. You'll see!"

"What if you don't? Who's going to be the worse off? A kid

only has one chance to grow up. Why not give him the best that life has to offer?"

"Who are you to tell me how to live my life, Bryce? You're twenty-one and still living at home. And, while we're at it, why don't you show me your college degree? I must have missed it when you brought it home. And how many classes have you taken the past year? How dare you lecture me about how to live my life when you're not doing that great yourself."

He glared at her. She wasn't sure if he was going to swear at her or walk out.

When he began speaking, he spoke quietly. "Okay, maybe I could be doing better than I am right now. And maybe I have wasted my time, but the thing is, Megan, it's my life to waste. I'm not dragging anyone else down. I don't have a kid depending on me to give him or her a chance to make it."

"Some people make it in spite of their circumstances," Megan said.

"I know, some do. More power to them. Do you want to take that risk for this kid you're going to bring into the world? Because it's the one who will ultimately pay the price for your bad decisions."

In a rare display of affection, he put his hand on her shoulder. "Okay, look, maybe I have been too rough on you. And if I have, I'm sorry. All I'm saying is, why not think of what's best for the kid, okay? That's all I'm saying." And then he left.

She did think about it.

In fact, that's all she thought about.

◆　　◆　　◆

That night Thomas came over to see her. She was surprised to see him.

"Thomas?" she stammered at the door.

"Can I come in?" he asked.

"Sure, I guess so."

She wondered if he'd heard she was pregnant. And if he had, why he was coming around.

"Sit down," she said. "Can I get you something to drink?"

"No, I'm fine. I was just wondering how you're doing."

She wasn't sure how to answer, not knowing how much he'd heard about her. She sat down next to him on the couch.

"Good, and you?"

"Good, too."

"I'm glad."

There was a long awkward silence.

He's come here as a friend because he knows, she thought.

She looked down, took a deep breath, and then said softly, "I'm pregnant."

"That's what I heard, but I wasn't sure if it was true or not."

"It's true. Pretty dumb, right?"

He shrugged. "It happens. How is Kurt handling it?"

"I guess he's pretending it didn't happen. I'm not sure though. I haven't talked to him for a while."

"Is there any chance you two will get married?"

"No, no chance at all."

"How come?"

"He's not ready for that." She paused. "He did offer to pay for an abortion though. The guy is a real prince, right?"

"Are you going to take him up on the offer?"

"No."

"How come?"

"Because I think abortion is wrong."

"So what are you going to do?" he asked.

"I'm not sure. Either keep the baby and raise her myself, or . . ." She was going to say, "give her away," but she couldn't say it. It sounded so heartless. She decided to talk about it in the terms Sister Gardner had used. " . . . place her for adoption. Some couples can't have children, you know."

132

"It's not something I've ever thought about."

"Me, either. I've thought about a lot of things lately that I've never thought about before."

"You said place *her* for adoption. So, you know for sure it's a girl, then, right?"

"No. I just think of her as a girl."

"It could be a boy."

"I know."

He smiled. "So you're not going to decide on a name yet, right?"

"Right."

"Well . . ." He cleared his throat and fidgeted. "I could marry you, if that'd help you out any." He said it in the same tone of voice he'd use if he were offering to loan her his car.

His remark left her stunned. She studied his face to see if he was joking. He wasn't even smiling. *He's serious. I can't believe it.* "Thomas, why would you want to do that?" she asked softly.

"So you could keep your baby."

"You'd do that for me?"

He shrugged his shoulders. "I'm going to get married someday. So it might as well be now . . . to you."

She felt her eyes begin to sting, and she put her hand to her mouth. "I . . . I don't know what to say."

"I've got next Monday off. We could get married on Saturday and have ourselves a three-day weekend together. What do you say?"

She dabbed away the tears. "That is so . . ." She struggled for the right word. *Kind? Sweet? Thoughtful? Generous?*

"Dumb of me to even suggest?" he asked.

"No. No, it's heroic. That's what you are. That's what you've always been in my life."

"I think we could be reasonably happy, Megan."

"But we're just friends."

133

"I know, but sometimes friends get married. And if we got married, then for sure you could keep the baby."

"Would you love this baby, or would it remind you of Kurt and me?"

He paused. "I've thought about that. I love kids. I don't actually care where they come from. I mean, up to last year, I thought they came from a stork. So compared to a stork, Kurt's a big improvement."

She smiled through her tears. "You'd be the best daddy in the world, Thomas. I'm sure of that."

He stood up from the couch. "So it's decided, right? I'll take care of everything . . . the cake, the place. I can do the invitations on my computer, print 'em out and have 'em in the mail by tomorrow morning. Now if this is too fast for you, we could postpone it a week and even have a reception. If we do have a reception, what would you think about having choco-late cake with chocolate frosting? That's your favorite, right? And we'll have pizza, too. Lots of it. You know what? I bet I could get a really good deal on pizza. In fact, we could even have our reception at Leo's. Wouldn't that be great? It'll be the best wedding in history. And we'll have a drawing every fifteen minutes for a free pizza. And . . ."

She was laughing. "Stop, will you? I'm not going to marry you this weekend . . . or any weekend in the near future." As she said it, she could tell she'd hurt his feelings. And that surprised her.

He went to the window and looked out, then turned and, with a smile, said, "Of course. What was I thinking?"

"You're my best friend, though."

"You're mine, too. That will never change."

"Thanks, Thomas. For everything. I didn't think you'd want to have anything to do with me once you heard about me being pregnant."

"It'd take more than that."

She stood up, walked over to him, and put her arms

around his neck and kissed him on the cheek. "You're the best."

"Sure I am."

"Would you have really married me?"

He smiled. "I guess we'll never know, will we?"

"I guess not."

He stepped back from her. "I'd better go."

"Sure. Thanks for coming."

"Come by Leo's sometime around closing."

"Well, I'm not real comfortable being with people."

"It'll just be you and me," he said.

"How come?"

"My boss said no more parties after closing. But you can come by . . . if you want, that is."

"I'd like that. I don't get out much anymore."

"I'm working tomorrow night if you want to come by."

"I might do that."

"I'll let you make me a pizza while I clean up."

"Just like old times, right?"

"Sure, why not?" He started for the door.

"Thomas?"

"Yes."

"Thanks . . . for everything."

He nodded, then left.

The next night at nine o'clock Megan went up to her room to change. She had decided to go visit Thomas, and she wanted to wear something nice for him. Also, she wanted to decide which of her clothes she'd be able to wear for at least part of her pregnancy.

A few minutes later, she had two piles of clothes on her bed. In the larger pile were clothes she wouldn't be wearing anymore. She'd either give them to Brianna or take them to the Salvation Army.

She picked up the one tank top she owned. She remembered where and when she'd bought it, how she liked it because it showed off her body, and how nervous and excited she'd been to wear it for Kurt the first night at Leo's.

But now she viewed it much differently, almost as if it had betrayed her. She had also been wearing it the night she and Kurt had first been intimate.

She picked up the tank top and held it out to get a good look at it. *What was I thinking of? What was I trying to prove? Was I so desperate I'd do anything to get some guy's attention? Why couldn't I just follow what I'd been taught all my life? Why did I think I had a better way?*

She remembered when she was fourteen, and her mother had told her not to wear clothes she wouldn't be able to wear after she'd gone through the temple. At that time she thought the advice was stupid because she was years away from going to the temple.

She picked up each item from the pile. With each one she remembered when and where she'd bought it and some of the times she'd worn it. And she remembered the effect some of the clothes had had on Kurt.

I can't give these to Brianna. I don't want the same thing happening to her that happened to me.

I'll take them to the Salvation Army.

She was putting the clothes into a box to take to the Salvation Army when she pictured in her mind some fourteen-year-old girl buying them and wearing them and ending up abandoned and pregnant, like herself.

She carried them outside and dumped the box of clothes into the dumpster.

On her way back into the house, she thought, *I'm paying a huge price to have this baby. So why not keep my baby and do my best to give her all she needs in life? To give her away would be the easy way out. Up to now I've always taken the easy way out.*

She nodded her head and smiled. *That's it. Now I know for sure. I'm definitely going to keep my baby.*

8

Megan arrived at Leo's Pizza at eleven-fifteen. Since it was after closing, the front door was locked. She knocked for a few minutes, decided Thomas must be in the back, walked around to the back door, and knocked.

Thomas opened the door and let her in. He seemed surprised to see her. "You came?"

"Sure, why not?"

"What can I get you to drink?"

"Water would be great."

"Is that all?"

"Yeah, just water."

"You want to watch me mop the floor?" he asked.

"Really? You'd let me do that? My life would have meaning if I could do that."

He pulled a bar stool into the middle of the room for her, then got her a glass of water.

"Anything else I can do for you?"

"Dazzle me with your floor cleaning skills."

He smiled at her. "It's good to have you back."

"Thanks. It's good to be back. Thanks for . . . still being my friend."

"I will always be your friend."

"I know that now."

He began to mop. "I didn't think you'd come."

"How come?"

"I thought me asking you to marry me would freak you out."

"You did it because you wanted to make it easier for me."

"That's what friends do, isn't it?" he asked.

"Not usually. You're a special category of friend. You're the best." She paused. "Friends . . . all I ever wanted in high school was to have friends."

Thomas noticed her getting emotional. "Hey, don't get upset just because I missed a spot, okay?"

She smiled. "You're doing great." She looked around. "Remember the good times we had here with all our friends? What's happened to everybody? Where have they all gone?"

"Most of 'em went to college. Did you know that Brad Parkinson is at NYU studying film arts?"

"No, I didn't know that."

"And Mike Young is at Cal Tech, studying aerospace engineering."

"Gosh, I could see that coming back in ninth grade when we were in the same math class."

"And Andy Kukendall is back East, playing basketball at Marquette."

"He was big enough and good enough to play college ball when he was a sophomore."

"You're right." Thomas sighed. "So, you know, people move on."

She caught the melancholy in his eyes. "You're moving on, too."

He smiled faintly. "Sure I am. You don't have to move away from home to go to college."

"No."

"My sister, Elizabeth, is in her second year at Cal Poly, so she's doing good."

"That's great."

"Have you heard anything from Kurt?" Thomas asked.

"No. His mom came to see me, though."

"What'd she want?"

"She was hoping she could get Kurt and me together, and that we'd get married, so the baby would stay in the family."

"What did you tell her?"

"I told her I have no interest in marrying Kurt."

Thomas smiled. "That's fairly direct."

She shrugged her shoulders. "He has no interest in marrying me, either."

"Does that surprise you?" Thomas asked.

"In a way it does. I mean when you're in the middle of a relationship, you're sure that this is the ultimate expression of love and affection and trust. I mean, at least I felt that way . . . at first. But then you find out that for the guy you're with, it's just a game. And if it's a game, well, anyone can walk away from a game. There are always other games, and other people to play them with."

"I'm sorry things didn't work out."

"Thanks. You know what? I'm glad I came. Maybe I should help you, so you can finish up."

He shook his head. "No, while I clean up in front, make me a pizza, like old times. With a personalized message to boost my ego."

"You got it. What message do you want?"

"That we're still friends. That's the most amazing thing about all this." He said it again. "That we're still friends."

On his way to the front, as he passed her, he paused. "You want a hug?"

"I would love a hug."

He seemed a little wary. "I won't break anything, will I? I mean, you know, inside, where the baby is."

"The baby probably needs a hug, too."

When he held her in his arms, she had the feeling she'd come home, and it brought tears to her eyes.

♦   ♦   ♦

In the next two weeks, Megan met twice more with Sister Gardner at LDS Family Services. They went over Megan's plan of how she was going to manage as a single mom. Sister Gardner was a good listener and occasionally made a few suggestions or brought up things she hadn't thought about. She began to think of Sister Gardner being on her side.

Megan's waistline was beginning to grow. If she pressed her stomach, she could feel a bulge, which she learned by asking her mother was her enlarged uterus, now about the size of a grapefruit.

She and Bryce could hardly stand to be around each other anymore. Whenever they were together, he tried to talk her out of keeping the baby. Once he told her she was being selfish.

"How can you say it's selfish for me to take care of my baby?" she countered.

"Because you're only thinking about what *you* want. You're not thinking about the baby."

"Who could take care of my baby better than me?"

"Almost anyone who's married."

"You don't know what you're talking about. There are plenty of families where the parents don't get along, where the kids would be better off if they were raised by just one parent."

"I know that, but they're not likely to want to adopt a kid. And even if they did, the adoption agency would know they weren't suitable parents. Adoption is the only way to get born

140

where the parents are carefully chosen. Every other way is pure chance."

"I'll be a good mother. You'll see."

"The baby will be better off with a happily married couple than with you."

"Why should I believe anything you tell me? You sell plywood and screwdrivers, so what makes you such an authority about this?"

"Logic and reason. Something you've never been any good at."

"That is such a sexist attitude."

"Maybe so, but in this case it happens to be true."

"I don't care what you say. I'm not giving my baby away."

She continued to meet with Bishop Oldham once a week. He asked her to read the book *The Miracle of Forgiveness*. He warned her that it would be painful reading but encouraged her to read it all the way through. He was right. She didn't like having to face how far she'd strayed from the teachings of the Church. Even so, to try to do what the bishop asked, she forced herself to read a few pages each day.

With her mother at work, Brianna busy with friends, Bryce working at Home Depot, and her father gone during the week, Megan was home alone most of the time. At first it seemed strange not to be going to a job or to school. Many of her friends had summer jobs, so she had little contact with anyone. Sometimes she desperately missed Alexis, but pride prevented her from calling her at BYU or writing her a letter.

She could finish the reading assignments the bishop had given her in half an hour. The rest of her time she spent watching soaps on TV. The only reason she could think of to read more was to impress someone in the ward. But then she realized that being pregnant and single put her in the category of a person who's not going to impress very many people in the ward, no matter how diligently she reads the scriptures. Whether she read or not, she would not be asked to give a talk in sacrament meeting or to work with the Young Women in the ward.

In spite of her situation and the fact that she was beginning to show, she was becoming more comfortable attending Relief Society. She had to admit that she felt warmth and concern from many of the sisters in the ward. She did not understand why, but it was there.

Except for one woman. The bishop's wife.

♦   ♦   ♦

Diane Oldham had lived her entire life being true and faithful to the teachings of the Church. And now here she was at the top of what would be recognized as success for a woman her age in the Church—her husband serving as bishop, with them living in a new home, with money enough that they didn't have to worry, and with four beautiful children. Her oldest, twelve-year-old Rebecca, was especially talented in music and an exemplary young woman.

It was a matter of pride for Diane that she had always lived the way her leaders had taught, had kept the Word of Wisdom from her youth, had avoided watching R-rated movies, and had filled her life with activity in the Church. She was tall and had played basketball in high school, an activity that had taken up most of her time and kept her from dating much.

She had met her husband at BYU, where as freshman students they were in the same ward. When he left on his mission, she wrote to him faithfully. Then, two months before he came home, she left on a mission, and it was his turn to be supportive as a friend.

He attended her homecoming in San Mateo, driving from Provo most of Friday night to be there. They talked at her house over lunch. He had planned to leave later that day, so he would be back in Provo for his classes on Monday, but they enjoyed their time together so much that she asked him to stay another day.

That night he asked her to marry him, and she said yes.

They were married the Wednesday before Thanksgiving, just a couple of months after Diane got home from her mission. She was proud of the fact that the first time they kissed was across the altar in the temple on their wedding day.

Diane had very little sympathy for those who gave in to physical passion. It had not been a temptation for her. Looking back at her life, she was grateful she'd been chaste and, as the Mia Maid adviser in Young Women, she wished the same for all the girls under her charge.

She kept a well-organized house with everything in its place, with a beautiful flower garden, which she tended herself and took great pride in. She liked things neat and tidy and under control.

Maybe that's why the presence of Megan each week in church bothered Diane. The more apparent it became that Megan was pregnant, the more troubling it was for Diane.

All the time Megan had been growing up, she'd been the one that others looked up to for leadership. Part of it came from her appearance—her flashing, brooding, dancing eyes, and her expressive mouth, and animated laugh.

Diane had an image in her mind, that of Megan bringing her baby to church, showing it off proudly to the girls in Young Women, and all of them, the Mia Maids she taught as well as her own precious twelve-year-old Rebecca, fawning over what would no doubt be an adorable baby. *What if the girls see no bad consequences for Megan? Who will they believe? Megan, with her natural charisma? Or their leaders, older and maybe a little out of touch with the way things are now? Who will they believe?*

She worried about the way Megan was being fussed over by some women in the ward, and she resented the time Megan took up with her husband—valuable time that could

143

be better spent at home helping with the children or working around the house or in their yard and garden.

Diane knew it wasn't any of her business and that she shouldn't say anything, but she couldn't help herself.

"I worry that the girls in our ward will see how much fuss is being made over Megan and that they'll decide it's okay for them to get pregnant before they're married, too." It was a Saturday, and she and the bishop were working together in their backyard.

"How are we making a big fuss over her?" her husband asked.

"She's the center of attention. People go out of their way to make her feel welcome."

"And that's bad?"

"It could be."

"As members of the Church, isn't that what we're supposed to do?"

"How can I talk about temple marriage when my girls see this girl suffering no consequences because of her actions?"

"There are consequences."

"Is she going to keep the baby?"

"She hasn't made her mind up yet."

"If she keeps the baby, and if she brings the baby to church, then what's going to stop some girl from thinking she wants a baby, too, so people can fuss over her."

"I think the girls in our ward can see the difference between having a child out of wedlock and having one who has been born into a family that has been sealed together for time and eternity."

"Why is she still a member of the Church?"

He turned to her and shook his head. "Diane, I can't believe you'd ask me that question."

"I'm sure others are asking it to themselves. I'm the only one who has the courage to ask you."

144

"You want me to excommunicate her, so you can use her as an example in Young Women? I'm sure you don't mean it."

"She takes a lot of your time, too, doesn't she?"

"I see her once a week."

"I imagine it's the highlight of her week. I mean, you're always very optimistic and upbeat. Why does she get singled out to receive such special treatment? It's almost like she's being rewarded for bad behavior."

"This is not easy for her. She has some difficult decisions to make about whether or not she's going to keep the baby."

"Oh, she'll keep the baby. I'm sure of it."

"How can you say that?"

"So she can continue to be the center of attention in the ward."

"Diane, I don't discuss these things even with my counselors. It's not an appropriate topic."

"I will not bring it up again. I just wanted you to know how some people in the ward feel about you bending over backwards for this girl."

"You've made your point very well then," he said. "Excuse me, I need to mow the lawn."

Why can't he see my point? she thought. *Why can't he see that he's only encouraging other girls to do the same thing?*

She wondered how it would be between them now that she'd criticized him for what he was doing as the bishop. This was the first time she'd done it. In fact, it was the first time she'd found fault with any of her bishops. It was hard for her to separate their personal relationship and her role as a ward member who needed to sustain her bishop.

In other calls he's had, he's always asked me for my advice, but in this one he hasn't. I hope I haven't upset him too much. I never meant to do that. I just don't want him to make a mistake.

I'm just trying to help out, that's all.

145

After several days of watching game shows and soaps, Megan had had enough and decided to try to go an entire day with no TV.

It was a Thursday, and she had a reading assignment from the bishop. He had asked her to read fifty pages in the Book of Mormon by the time she met with him Sunday after church. He had also asked her to read two more chapters of *The Miracle of Forgiveness*. But she hadn't even begun.

I should get started. But I don't want to. I should though. What am I so afraid of?

She went into the tiny backyard of the condo and sat down at their picnic table. *This is my world now,* she thought. *An empty house, with no job. No friends except Thomas. Do people make fun of me now? Do they tell each other what a fool I was to get pregnant? And what do the people in my ward say about me? Do they wonder why I'm even bothering to go to church? Do they call me a tramp behind my back?*

Why am I so afraid of reading what the bishop asked me to read? What am I afraid of?

She was no gardener, but looking at the rosebushes she saw roses that had been beautiful days earlier but were now dying. She'd spent enough time with Mr. Podolsky in his flower garden to learn that if the bush is to produce more roses, the dead and dying blossoms need to be cut off. She went into the garage and got her mother's pruning shears and returned to the rosebush. It produced American Sweetheart roses. She sat down and began to cut away.

She became absorbed in her work, concentrating on caring for the rosebush. *If a rosebush needs to be pruned to get rid of what isn't working, why shouldn't the same be true of people, too? We get rid of what isn't working for us, and then we can go on. This rosebush is a growing thing, not doomed because of the past.*

She felt tears coming into her eyes. She hadn't expected to learn anything of value about her life by tending a rosebush. And yet she did feel comfort.

Father in Heaven, how can you still care about me when I've messed up so many times? Why do you comfort me? Why do I feel like you care about me when I've gone against everything I was taught?

She went into the condo and picked up her triple combination from the coffee table in the living room. She held it in her hands, without opening it.

What am I afraid of?

It was painful to admit, even to herself. *I'm afraid that the more I read the more awful I'll feel. Or that I'll realize that if I'd read the Book of Mormon earlier, then it would have been enough to keep me from making the mistakes I made. I'm worried that the closer I get to God, the more condemned I'll feel. And that I'll end up feeling worse than I do now.*

She closed her eyes and began to pray. *Oh, dear Heavenly Father, please don't make me suffer this alone. Please don't make my trying to get closer to you make me feel so awful that I can't stand to go on. Please don't make me bear this burden alone. It's too much for me to carry.*

If I am a damned soul as far as you are concerned, with no hope for the future, tell me now. Don't let me go on thinking I can have my sins forgiven, only to yank the hope away from me at the last minute.

Am I damned forever because of my sins? Please let me know now. Right now. Today. So at least I'll know.

She sat for a time, waiting for some impression, but nothing came. Finally, she opened her eyes, wiped her eyes and cheeks with a tissue, and set the triple combination back on the coffee table. She sat staring at it. The book had been a gift from her parents. They'd given it to her on the day she was baptized, and it had her name embossed on the leather cover.

I could at least look in the index, she thought, reaching

147

for the book. She found the word *Damnation* and scanned the entries: *Men bring damnation to their souls except they humble themselves; . . . if men have been evil, they shall reap damnation of their souls.* She continued reading the entries, stopping at: *Alma was wracked with pains of damned soul.*

That's like me, she thought. She turned to chapter 36 in Alma and began to read:

"And it came to pass that as I was thus racked with torment, while I was harrowed up by the memory of my many sins, behold, I remembered also to have heard my father prophesy unto the people concerning the coming of one Jesus Christ, a Son of God, to atone for the sins of the world.

"Now, as my mind caught hold upon this thought, I cried within my heart: O Jesus, thou Son of God, have mercy on me, who am in the gall of bitterness, and am encircled about by the everlasting chains of death.

"And now, behold, when I thought this, I could remember my pains no more; yea, I was harrowed up by the memory of my sins no more.

"And oh, what joy, and what marvelous light I did behold; yea, my soul was filled with joy as exceeding as was my pain!

"Yea, I say unto you, my son, that there could be nothing so exquisite and so bitter as were my pains. Yea, and again I say unto you, my son, that on the other hand, there can be nothing so exquisite and sweet as was my joy."

She was crying again, but these weren't tears of despair. *God still loves me,* she thought. *I am not cast off.* She fell to her knees by the couch and poured out her heart in thanksgiving for what she was feeling.

She spent the rest of the day reading everything she could find about Alma's life and about the testimony he bore throughout his life of the great gift he had been given at the worst time of his life.

Tomorrow, she thought, *I will start from the beginning and read the Book of Mormon from cover to cover.*

◆ ◆ ◆

By the time she met with the bishop on Sunday, she was in Mosiah.

"Well, you have been busy," Bishop Oldham said with a broad smile.

"It's making sense to me, too. It's so great, Bishop. I feel happier now, and I'm more positive about the future."

"Good for you. What about your reading in *The Miracle of Forgiveness?*"

"It's good, but . . . it's also kind of depressing. I mean, I can see myself and what I was so clearly now. It makes me wish I'd done better."

"You're doing well now, though. That's the important thing."

"I think so, but I'm having trouble knowing how I should feel about myself."

"How do you mean?"

"I worry about what the people in the ward think about me."

"I understand what you're saying. But that shouldn't be a concern. The bigger question is, what does the Savior think about you?"

"The Savior still loves me," she said softly.

"How do you know that?"

"I've felt it when I've been reading the Book of Mormon, and when I pray. But that doesn't keep people from talking about me."

Megan looked down at her hands and then asked, "What does your wife think about me?"

He cleared his throat. "I'm curious why you'd ask that question."

"No reason. It's just the way she looks at me."

"How does she look at you?"

149

"Like I have no business being in church. Do you know what the word *tramp* means, Bishop?"

"Yes."

"I think that's what she thinks I am." Megan sighed. "That's what I was, I guess . . . or am. Maybe once a tramp, always a tramp."

The bishop opened his Bible and thumbed the pages, looking for a passage, then he began to read:

"'And the scribes and Pharisees brought unto him a woman taken in adultery; and when they had set her in the midst, They say unto him, Master, this woman was taken in adultery, in the very act. Now Moses in the law commanded us, that such should be stoned: but what sayest thou?

"'This they said, tempting him, that they might have to accuse him. But Jesus stooped down, and with his finger wrote on the ground, as though he heard them not.

"'So when they continued asking him, he lifted up himself, and said unto them, He that is without sin among you, let him first cast a stone at her.

"'And again he stooped down, and wrote on the ground.

"'And they which heard it, being convicted by their own conscience, went out one by one, beginning at the eldest, even unto the last: and Jesus was left alone, and the woman standing in the midst.

"'When Jesus had lifted up himself, and saw none but the woman, he said unto her, Woman, where are those thine accusers? hath no man condemned thee?

"'She said, No man, Lord. And Jesus said unto her, Neither do I condemn thee: go, and sin no more.'"

Bishop Oldham set his Bible aside and looked up. "What do you learn from this?"

"The Savior didn't condemn her."

"That's right, he didn't. What counsel did he give her?"

"To go and sin no more."

"Was he sinless?"

"Yes."

"Did he understand the seriousness of adultery?"

"Of course."

"That's right. Better than anyone else. He was the one who gave the Ten Commandments to Moses. So if this woman had no reason to hope for her future, he'd be the one who would know, and, most likely, he would have told her so."

"I guess that's true. I've never thought about it like that."

"What is interesting to me," the bishop continued, "is that this woman was dragged forcefully out of her house to the Savior by a mob. And yet, after they had all left, the woman stayed there in his presence. As soon as her accusers left, she could have run away, but she stayed there. Why do you suppose she did?"

"I'm not sure."

"Well, was she terrified of him? Was she afraid he might pick up a stone and throw it at her?"

"I don't think so."

"Why do you suppose that is?"

"Because she could feel he meant her no harm."

"I think that's true."

"I don't know how to act anymore."

"How do you mean?"

"I used to be so self-confident in social settings. But now I'm not so sure of myself. Like at church. I think about answering questions in Sunday School class, but I don't because I'm afraid people would think, 'If she's so smart, and if she knows so much about the gospel, then how come she went out and got herself pregnant?'"

"How would you answer that question?"

"I'm learning things I didn't know then."

"I can see that. I encourage you to participate in Sunday School class discussions."

"I feel like I have to go through this long explanation. 'Excuse me for raising my hand. And, yes, I am pregnant. And,

no, I'm not married. And, yes, the bishop does know everything. And, no, I'm not excommunicated, even though some
of you think I should be. Now can I answer the question?'"

The bishop smiled. "I don't think you need to explain a
thing."

"Could you make an announcement, so we can get this all
out, once and for all?"

"Should I make a similar announcement for everyone in
the ward who has committed a sin recently? Would it be good
to post a list of sinners on the bulletin board? The thing is,
Megan, everyone I know is working on something. And if
they're not, they should be. This is a church where we're all
trying to do better. You're not the only one."

"But I'm starting to show that I'm pregnant."

"So?"

"Well, I mean it's pretty obvious, isn't it, what's been going
on."

"You're carrying the baby. You're thinking about the welfare of the baby. You could have had an abortion, but you
didn't. You decided to give life to your baby. In many people's
minds that makes you a little bit of a hero."

"I wish I'd lived the standards of the Church."

"I know you do."

"The thing is, now when I read the Book of Mormon, I get
so excited. It's such a wonderful book. And to think it was
there for me all along if I had just picked it up and started
reading."

"Heavenly Father sent us to earth so we could learn from
our mistakes. I'm sure that he's pleased that you're learning
from yours."

"I am. I really am. If I could just talk to the girls in Young
Women. If I could just tell them what I've learned."

The bishop cleared his throat and nodded politely.

"Can I do that, Bishop?"

He glanced away. "I'm not sure that would be for the best."

She knew what he meant. He couldn't risk her influencing the younger girls in a negative way.

"I understand."

"I hope you do."

9

A t a school dance after a football game, Brianna worked the crowd as only she could. With her out-going personality and sense of humor, she was on good terms with almost everyone in school. Every group—the preppies, the druggies, the gay-prides, the cowboys—they all loved her.

On her way to the girls restroom she passed a girl and a guy in the hall making out. They seemed nearly out of control.

It made her feel sick. *Don't go there, girl, or you'll end up like my sister.*

She thought about stopping to say something, but she didn't because she didn't know what to say. And she knew it wouldn't make any difference.

A few minutes later, in the restroom, she looked at herself in the mirror.

It's not going to happen to me.

She'd had a dream the night before that she was pregnant but couldn't remember how she'd gotten pregnant. In her dream she was trying to talk to her mother about it.

Her mother handled it well. "Well, I'm not surprised. I knew it was only a matter of time."

"How can you say that? I'm not a bit like Megan."

"You are, though. You're just like her."

No matter how hard she tried, she couldn't make her mother feel otherwise.

When she first woke up from the dream, she felt great relief that it wasn't real, but at the same time she worried that it might just be a matter of time.

The dream had ended with her saying over and over again, "I'm a good girl."

On the way back to the dance, the girl and the boy were still there.

Brianna stopped. "Not here."

The boy glanced up, looking like he was in some kind of a trance. "What?"

"Are you picking up what I'm putting down? Is the sprinkler hitting the grass? I said, not here."

"What's it to you what we do?"

"I don't care to watch what you're doing. So either quit or do it some place where people walking by can't see it."

The guy looked like he wanted to beat up Brianna, but the girl didn't want any trouble. She pulled her boyfriend by the hand. "She's right."

They were turning to leave, but Brianna locked eyes with the girl. "Be careful, okay?"

She nodded, and they left the dance.

I'm hurting, she thought. *I don't show it, but I'm hurting. Real bad.*

She hurried back to the dance where she could put on a happy face once again.

As she approached her group of friends, she called out, "Peace out, my homeys!"

155

Walter and Carolyn were seeing the bishop to renew their temple recommends. Bishop Oldham visited first with Carolyn. An interview that usually took five minutes ended up lasting half an hour.

And then it was Walter's turn.

The temple recommend interview took only a few minutes. And then Bishop Oldham leaned back in his chair and asked, "How long have you been a Scoutmaster?"

"It's been five years."

"You've done a magnificent job with the boys. How many Eagle Scouts did we have last year?"

"Seven."

"That's just amazing."

"Especially when you consider there hadn't been any for years before I took over the troop."

"You've done a great job. We'll always be grateful to you for showing us how a Scout program should be run."

"We've got some good boys coming along. The way I look at it, Bishop, it's just the beginning."

"Well, perhaps, but I think it might be time to extend a release to you and let someone else continue on."

Walter was shocked. "Did Carolyn say something to you?"

"Well, yes, she did. She thinks you need to be home more for your children. Especially now, with Megan going through her difficult time. She told me that with your traveling each week and then taking the boys camping, that you're not around much."

"I think Megan is okay now. She's back on track. And Bryce is never around anyway. And Brianna, well, she's doing okay. So I don't see how going camping one weekend a month is taking me away from my family."

"Carolyn is concerned."

"Don't release me from Scouting, Bishop. It's taken me a

156

long time to get it to where it is now. I can cut down on weekend activities for the boys for the next few months."

"Let me talk with my counselors about it, and then we'll get back to you. Believe me, trying to find a new Scoutmaster is not something I look forward to."

The next Sunday Walter was released as Scoutmaster and called to be the Gospel Doctrine Sunday School teacher.

He was devastated and resentful of Carolyn. When he accused her of engineering his release, she said, "All I did was tell the bishop our situation. I didn't ask him to release you. He made that decision himself. Don't get mad at him or me. If you believe the Lord called you to be the Scoutmaster, then you should also believe he released you. That's what happens in the Church, Walter. We serve, and then we get released. Except as parents. From that we never get released. Your family needs you now more than ever."

"They don't need me."

"They do, but you've always been gone so much that it's going to take some time before your children feel comfortable enough to come to you."

Walter spent the next Saturday cleaning out the garage, gathering all the Scout equipment in one place for his replacement, a twenty-eight-year-old novice in Scouting, to come and pick up.

This is a mistake, he thought. *This is a big mistake. The bishop should never have released me.*

It's going to be tough to watch the program I worked so hard on crumble away to nothing. And for what? So I can be home? Well I'm home today. And what good has it done? Brianna's gone all day. Megan avoids me, and Bryce is always gone. And even when he's around, he doesn't want any advice from me on how to live his life.

This is a big mistake, that's all there is to it.

After he'd been working in the garage for two hours,

Carolyn came out to see him. She brought him a glass of lemonade. "How's it going?"

"I'm almost done."

"We're going to have a lot more room around here."

"Everything I worked so hard to achieve is all going to fall apart. The new Scoutmaster doesn't know a thing about Scouting."

"He'll learn, just like you did."

"I care about the boys."

"I know you do, Walter, but someone else also cares about them, even more than you do."

"Who?"

"The Lord. Why don't you just assume that he knows what's best for you, and for your family, and for the boys in our ward? Give it up, Walter. It's not your responsibility anymore."

She turned and walked back inside.

His immediate response was to dismiss what she'd said because she'd never shared his enthusiasm for Scouting. But a short time later a new thought came into his mind.

What if she's right?

♦   ♦   ♦

On her mission in Montana, Heather read over again the letters she'd received from home in the past month. She was troubled, not by what was in the letters but because of what was missing.

The first odd letter came four weeks before. Her mother wrote: "Megan lost her job, and so she's moved back home. But she's doing really well."

Since then, in subsequent letters, there had never been any mention of Megan getting another job.

What is she doing home if she's not working? Heather

158

thought. *And why isn't she at least taking night classes? I don't understand.*

And then came the cryptic letter from her father, which read: "I've been released as Scoutmaster and called to be a Sunday School teacher."

She knew how much he loved Scouting. In many of his previous letters, he'd gone on and on talking about the progress the boys were making toward Eagle. For him to just state he had been released, with no explanation, seemed to her very strange.

Megan had written once since returning home. She wrote: "You've always been such a good example to the family. I wish we'd been closer when you were home. I could have learned a lot from you."

Something's wrong. There are no details. I still don't know what Megan is doing at home with no job and not going to college. And why would they release Daddy when he was probably the best Scoutmaster the ward's ever had?

What is going on? And why aren't they telling me?

She hated it that she'd always been put on a pedestal by the family. What it did was distance her from everyone else, so nobody brought their problems to her. Because Megan and Brianna and Bryce didn't believe she'd even understand being tempted to do something wrong, they never approached her with what they were facing. And so she had always felt isolated from everyone else in the family.

They're still doing that to me, she thought. *All I get is good news from them. Do they think I'm so fragile that I'd cave in with the truth? Well, I'm not. I've had enough bad news on my mission, faced the same problems my investigators face, helped them struggle with the repentance they need in their lives, that I can take any truth and any bad news and any disappointments my family can give me.*

If only they'd trust me. If only they'd let me in and not keep me out the way they've been doing all my life.

159

*I'll write and ask them to let me in on all the family
secrets.*

◆　　◆　　◆

Once a month, on a Sunday afternoon, Thomas's family
got together for a huge spaghetti dinner at his grandparents'
house. His three uncles and his father stayed in the living
room and argued politics or sports while the women worked
in the kitchen preparing food. The custom was that none of
the men did anything in the way of food preparation—in the
Marconi family, that was women's work.

Thomas sat with the men for fifteen minutes. They were
talking politics. Typically, the conversation was loud and
animated. He'd heard it all before.

Finally, he went into the kitchen. "Can I help?"

"You wouldn't even know what to do."

"Are you kidding? I work in a pizza place, okay? I know
my way around a kitchen."

"He wants to help? Let him help," his Aunt Beth said in a
somewhat sarcastic manner.

They let him put a glass of ice water beside every plate.

On his second trip to the dining room with a tray of
glasses, his Uncle Al called out, "You need an apron there,
missy?"

The men all laughed. Thomas smiled. *This is how we
keep everyone in their place. Men aren't supposed to help out.*

His Uncle Bill gestured. "Sit down and talk with us. The
women can see to that."

"Soon as I finish up with the water."

"Such a nice girl. She'll make someone a wonderful wife,"
Uncle Al continued.

"She'll need to do something about that figure of hers,
though."

"Someone will come along who won't mind."

160

Uncle Al burst out laughing. "That's what worries me."

I can't let them get to me, Thomas thought. He finished setting out the water glasses and returned to the kitchen. "What else can I do?" he asked.

His sister, Elizabeth, who'd heard the men teasing Thomas, came into the kitchen. She was easily the most gifted one in the family, a classical pianist, in her junior year in college, majoring in music. She had long, straight, dark brown hair and thick eyelashes and eyebrows that imbued the simplest sentence with drama and intrigue.

She put her hand on Thomas's back and said confidentially, "Don't let them get to you, Thomas, okay?"

"It's okay. They don't bother me."

They made eye contact. *She understands how oppressed I feel when I'm here.* "Can we talk?" he asked.

"I'd like that."

How come I feel that Elizabeth is a stranger, even though we grew up together? It's like we've never really talked. When we come here, it's like being in a play, and everyone acts their part. And everyone asks the same questions, like how's school going? And we obediently give the expected answers.

"Let's go in back and swing on the porch swing, like we used to when we were kids," Elizabeth said.

They walked through the kitchen and out the back door, away from the view of anyone inside the house, and sat down together in the swing.

"You okay?" she asked.

"I guess so. You know what's amazing about our family get-togethers?"

"What?"

"How many don't come. Amanda never comes. Josh, Ryan, Zach, Isaac—they all quit coming years ago. You know why they don't come anymore?"

"Why?"

"Because they don't fit in. The only ones welcome are the

161

ones who haven't stepped out of line." He turned to her. "How come we never talk about the ones we've driven away? How come it's either 'Be the same as us or stay away'? How come?"

"I don't know, Thomas."

"Me, either. I'm not what they think I am. I just play the part they've given me while I'm here. They don't know what I'm really like. And they don't even want to know."

"I feel the same way," she said.

"How about you and I agree to talk honestly about ourselves?"

She leaned her head on his shoulder. "I'd like that very much."

"Good. How are things going for you? I mean, really."

"Well, I'm very happy in my classes."

"Good."

"And I keep busy. I'm accompanying the college choir. I love doing that."

"Great."

"Although, to be perfectly honest, I'd have to say that there's something missing in my life," she said.

"What?"

In a nervous gesture, she brushed back the hair from her forehead. "Oh, gosh, this is going to seem so dumb to you."

"No, it's okay, go ahead."

"Well, the truth is, I've had such bad luck with guys."

"In what way?"

"Well, like last week, this guy in one of my classes asks me to a movie. On the way out of the theater, he suggests we sleep together. One movie and a bag of popcorn, and he's asking me that? Where did that come from? And then last month I was dating a guy. Two or three times. He treated me with respect, but then some friends of mine told me he actually prefers guys and that he was just dating me so his parents wouldn't catch on. Well, of course, I ended that. So now I'm

162

wondering where I can find just an ordinary nice guy." She smiled faintly. "Like you, for instance."

"Good luck," he said with a silly grin. "I'm one of a kind."

"Oh, man, I hope not. There's got to be more out there somewhere. But where?"

"I'll look around for you and see what I can come up with."

Aunt Beth opened the door. "Hey, you two, it's time to eat."

They returned to the house.

♦　　♦　　♦

Megan's mother, Carolyn, worked at city hall in the accounting department. Her two closest associates were both women.

Dottie had worked there the longest. Her body was starting to sag and fall apart, but her brassy, red-tinted hair stayed the same color and style. She'd long ago dropped the idea of giving her all for the job, and now the only things she looked forward to at work were coffee breaks, lunch hours, and holidays. She was the most knowledgeable one in the office, the one the bosses came to when they wanted to know something.

The other woman was Mary. Because city hall had many iron-fisted administrators, the place needed someone like Mary, who served as the heart and soul and conscience of city government. She was the one who knew when someone was having a birthday. She was the one who sent cards when someone had been sick or had problems in their family. Even so, she was undervalued by her superiors and consistently overlooked for promotions.

Although these women appeared to be very different from each other, they had one thing in common: they both had grandchildren whom they adored.

They were always showing Carolyn photographs of their

grandkids and bragging about the children's superior intelligence and wonderful accomplishments.

"Isn't she the most adorable child you've ever seen in your entire life?" Mary or Dottie would ask.

"She is. No doubt about it."

"Grandchildren are great. You've got to get yourself some."

"I will. Someday."

And now that *someday* was coming sooner than she'd ever expected. Carolyn wasn't sure, though, what Megan would decide to do—keep the baby or place it for adoption. Although Carolyn was trying to be impartial, her mind said one thing, but her heart said another. She yearned for a grandbaby. One she could fuss over and buy cute outfits for and hold in her arms and rock to sleep. She had kept the rocking chair she had used when her own children were small, and she looked forward to using it again, this time as a loving grandma.

I know I need to let Megan make this decision, she thought. *If I jump in and try to talk her into keeping the child, it might not be the best thing, either for the baby or for my relationship with Megan.*

Even so, when she went shopping alone, she often found herself diverted to the racks filled with baby clothes. She would have bought several but didn't know where she could hide them at home where nobody would find them.

With Megan pregnant, Carolyn began to fantasize about having a grandchild to love and being able to bring her own pictures to work to show off. She tried to resist the idea, but it was always there. She knew it would be emotionally difficult for her if her first grandchild were given to another couple to raise.

She did not tell Dottie or Mary that Megan was expecting a baby. She knew they would have strong opinions about what was the right thing to do, and that they would do their best to convince her they were right, and might even get her to try to talk "some sense" into Megan.

This is a decision Megan needs to make for herself. I will support her in whatever she decides to do. If I jump in too quickly, then she will feel alienated from me if she chooses to do something else.

Even though she was trying to be neutral, she did break down and buy a few things for the baby. She hid them in her bottom dresser drawer, where she hoped nobody would find them.

This is very hard for me, too, because, more than anything now in my life, I want a grandchild to call my own.

I just have to be patient, though. Be supportive and patient.

◆　　◆　　◆

Ann Marie woke up at two-thirty in the morning and couldn't get back to sleep. Weston was in the guest bedroom. Or at least that's what they called it now. It had at one time been known as the baby's room, but that had been a long time ago.

They had argued just before going to bed, and Ann Marie, in tears, had suggested he sleep somewhere else that night. And before she could call her words back, he had taken his pillow and left. She couldn't call him back because her own feelings were hurt.

He had hurt her by what he'd said, and at first she didn't think she could ever forgive him.

"All I'm saying," he had said, "is that we both need to face the fact that we're not going to have kids by ourselves. If we want to have kids, then we'll have to adopt."

"I don't want somebody else's mistake. I want a child of my own."

165

"It's not going to happen, Ann Marie. Why can't you see that? Everyone else can."

In the beginning her failure to get pregnant had been *their* problem, but their doctor had told them long ago that it was primarily Ann Marie who was responsible.

Because it was too much to bear, too oppressive a burden, she had pulled in and grown silent and moody and depressed.

And that's why she'd lashed out at Weston.

She turned on a light next to the bed and sat up. *It's strange to have his side of the bed empty. We've never slept apart since we were married. And tonight I drove him away.*

I could lose him if I'm not careful. There are so many women out there who'd do whatever it takes to make him a part of their life.

She got up and padded down the hall to the guest bedroom, opened the door, and without a word, crawled into bed next to him.

"I hope that's my wife," he said quietly.

"It is."

"Are you lost?"

"I was, but I'm not anymore."

He put his arm around her and drew her in close to him.

"You're probably sleepy, right?" she asked.

"Not really."

"Me, either. Do you want to talk?"

"Might as well," he said.

"Let's go in the kitchen and have some hot chocolate and cookies," she suggested.

"Okay."

In the kitchen she fussed with making the hot chocolate and getting out a plate for the cookies, then sat down across from him and handed him the plate of cookies—chocolate chip for her and Fig Newtons for him.

"I'm sorry for getting so emotional earlier," she said.

"I should have been more understanding," he said,

looking down at the floor, as if he were a little boy who'd been caught doing something wrong. It was a look she had grown to cherish, one of a few left over from his childhood.

He finished his Fig Newton, then reached across the table and held her hands. "There was something I should have said . . . that I didn't."

"What?"

"I will love you with all my heart whether we have kids or not. Our love isn't at risk here, no matter what happens."

She pursed her lips and nodded. "I should have said that, too." She dabbed at her eyes with a napkin. "I've always been able to solve my own problems, but I can't solve this one. That's been really hard for me to accept."

"It's been hard for me, too."

She lowered her gaze and let the tears come, tired of being strong, exhausted by having to always be in control, to always be the one that others could depend on.

He held her hands and let her cry. He'd run out of encouraging words. He, too, was on empty.

A few minutes later, she looked up and said, quite simply, "I think we should look into adopting a baby of our own."

He nodded his head and squeezed her hand.

They didn't go to sleep right away, which meant they were up way too late. They slept in the next morning, waking up too late to be on time for work. But neither of them cared.

10

Megan went back to spending time with Thomas at Leo's Pizza after closing time. She usually showed up between ten and ten-thirty at night. She'd go around to the back and knock, and he'd let her in.

Sometimes, when she was feeling good, she'd help Thomas clean up. At other times, she just sat near where he was working, and they would talk.

"You seem kind of quiet," he said one night.

"Sorry. I've been doing a lot of thinking lately."

"What about?" he asked as he wiped tables.

"My life."

"What about it?"

"I've pretty much made a mess of things, haven't I?"

"Nobody's perfect."

"I should've done better."

"Why? What makes you so special?"

"You don't even know, do you?"

"Know what?"

"Nothing."

"It must be something."

"You wouldn't understand."

"Try me."

"I'm a Mormon."

"So?"

"I shouldn't have messed up."

"What are you saying, that you're the first Mormon who messed up?"

"No."

"Then let it go. You'll drive yourself crazy trying to relive the past. It's gone. There's nothing you can do to change what happened."

"I know that, Thomas."

"Good."

"I've been reading the Book of Mormon lately. It's really helped me. I think if I'd been reading it all along, I wouldn't have made so many bad decisions."

"Books don't have the power to change people's lives."

"This one does," she said.

"That's hard to believe."

"I'll bring you a copy. You can read it and see for yourself."

He shrugged his shoulders. "Sure, whatever. I'll read it."

The next night she dropped by and gave him a copy.

A couple of days later, he called her at home. He told her he'd been reading the Book of Mormon and had some questions. She wasn't sure how to answer them, so she asked if he'd be willing to listen to the missionaries sometime at her house.

He said yes.

She got off the phone and called the ward mission leader and asked him to send her some missionaries on Sunday night. Once her mother heard about the arrangements, she called and invited the missionaries to come for supper that evening.

On Sunday there was a knock on the door at 5:30 P.M.

Megan's mother answered it and let the missionaries in, then called upstairs for Megan to come down. Brianna was at the home of one of her church friends.

"This is my daughter Megan."

The senior companion shook her hand. "I'm Elder Spaulding," he said with an easy smile. "I'm please t' meetcha." He had dark brown hair with, at least on that day, the cowlick of the century, a patch of hair sticking up from the back of his head, which he kept trying to smooth down with his hand.

He was three inches taller than his companion. Megan imagined that his height, along with his friendliness and a resonant voice, gave him an advantage over his peers. He had the easy manner of someone who had always been looked to for leadership. *I bet he was a student body president in high school. You can always tell.* Even so, she didn't resent his assumption of being in charge.

She was intrigued by his voice. It was, when he was in control, lower and more modulated than when he was excited. She wondered where he'd learned that—if it was from his mother or from a speech teacher or just because he was vain and wanted to sound like Arnold Schwarzenegger. But unlike Arnold, Elder Spaulding had a Southern accent.

"This is my companion, Elder Anderson," he said.

I'm sure Elder Anderson is perfectly capable of introducing himself, she thought.

Elder Anderson was shorter, had a round face, wore glasses, and appeared to be well on his way to going bald. He shook her hand briefly, smiled without enthusiasm, looked her in the eye for perhaps half a second and then looked down at the floor, as if greeting people was an ordeal to be endured. He glanced at the clock on the wall and then, almost as an accusation, glared at his companion.

Whoa! These two don't get along, Megan thought.

"What time is your friend coming?" Elder Anderson asked.

"Seven."

"Dinner appointments are only supposed to be an hour," he said to Elder Spaulding.

"It'll be okay, Elder. We're havin' a cottage meetin'."

"But the cottage meeting isn't until seven. We'll have half an hour unbudgeted time. We could go tracting."

"No, we'll just stay here, Elder. Relax, it's okay, all right?"

"Maybe so, but we'll be wasting half an hour," he said quietly.

"I'll take full responsibility for that half hour," Elder Spaulding said.

Elder Anderson gave up and sat down.

Megan had been worried about meeting the elders, not only because they were about the same age as she was, but also because she wasn't sure if they knew about her condition. It was one thing to tell her bishop, a man much older than she was, but it would be much more embarrassing to tell two guys her age, who had probably always been active in the Church.

"Where are you from?" she asked, trying to put them and herself at ease.

"Biloxi, Mississippi," Elder Spaulding said with a big smile. He pronounced it "Missipee." "Home of the Crawdad Festival."

"The Crawdad Festival?" she asked.

He smiled. "Yes. I can tell you've never heard of it."

"Do they crown a Miss Crawdad?" she asked.

"Yes, they do, as a matter-a-fact."

"That must be a coveted title. I mean, you know, the responsibility to represent all the crawdads in the state of Mississippi."

He broke into a big grin. "Yes, ma'am, it's not somethin' we take lightly."

"I can see that."

"I'm from Detroit, Michigan," Elder Anderson said.

171

"Home of what?" Megan asked.

"I don't know. Cars, I guess."

"No, no," Elder Spaulding teased. "Home of the driveby shootin'."

Elder Anderson's feelings were hurt. "You know what? I get that all the time, and, really, it's so unfair of people to say things like that."

"I was just jokin', Elder," Elder Spaulding said.

"Instead of just wasting our time talking, how about if we read the Book of Mormon together?" Elder Anderson suggested.

Elder Spaulding frowned.

"Mom, when will supper be ready?" Megan called out.

"Five minutes."

"Not 'nuff time to get much read," Elder Spaulding said.

Megan's dad came in, shook hands with the elders, and sat down. "Well, I understand we're having a missionary lesson here tonight."

"That's right," Elder Spaulding said enthusiastically. "We're very grateful to you and your family for takin' an interest in missionary work."

"Oh, it's not me. It's Megan. I'm very proud of her. The way I see it, some good is coming from this, after all."

Megan cringed and started to blush.

There was a long pause.

"Some good is coming from what?" Elder Anderson asked.

Walter glanced at Megan, then stammered, "Well, oh . . . I thought you both knew."

"Knew what?" Elder Anderson asked.

Megan could feel her face turning red.

"I'm sorry, Megan," her dad said. "I thought they knew."

She nodded. "It's okay. It has to come up sometime."

"Do you want me to tell them?" her dad asked.

"Yes," she said softly. "You'd better."

Her dad wiped his perspiring forehead. "I don't want you to get the wrong idea. Megan is a good girl. She always has been, but a little while ago she made a few bad decisions, and now she's having to live with that."

Megan's hand went to her face. *Don't let them see me cry,* she thought.

Her father cleared his throat. "Maybe if I'd been around more, things would be different. It's hard for me to admit that, but I've been doing a lot of thinking lately."

There was a long, uncomfortable pause. Elder Anderson was staring at Megan. Elder Spaulding was embarrassed and kept his head down. Megan was dabbing at her eyes, and her father, the man who prided himself on never showing emotion, was having trouble finishing a sentence without having to stop to gain better control of himself.

"We can't dwell on what could have been, though, can we?" Walter said. "We have to take things the way they are and try to make the best of them."

"You know what? I still don't know what you're talking about," Elder Anderson said.

"Oh, good grief," Elder Spaulding muttered. "Let it go."

"My daughter Megan is expecting a baby."

It didn't phase Elder Anderson. "So, is the father the one we're teaching tonight?"

"No."

"So how does the guy we're teaching fit into the picture?"

"He's just a friend," Megan said.

"Well, that's a relief," Elder Anderson said.

"Elder, don't talk anymore, okay?" Elder Spaulding said, shaking his head.

Megan had had it with Elder Anderson. "I'm going in the kitchen to see if I can help out."

Her mother put her to work putting salad on some plates. "How are things going in there?" her mother asked.

"It's unbelievably awkward. Elder Anderson has the social skills of a rhinoceros."

"Elder Spaulding seems nice, though, doesn't he?"

Megan shook her head. "I suppose. Except he's from the South."

"Why's that a problem?"

"When anyone talks with a Southern accent, I tend to think they're not very smart."

"I'm sure he's plenty smart."

"He comes from a town that has a crawdad festival. How smart can he be?"

"I'm sure he didn't have much choice about where he was raised."

"Maybe not, but if I came from a town with a crawdad festival, I wouldn't go around telling people about it."

Her mother smiled. "You think you might be a little unfair?"

"No, not at all."

Megan was carrying the salad plates to the dining room table when Brianna burst into the house, crying out in her cheerleader's voice, "Oh, my gosh, I've got to go to the bathroom *so* bad!" She stopped in her tracks when she saw the elders in the living room. "Good thing I didn't say that in front of the missionaries, right?" she called out, bounding up the stairs.

"That's my sister Brianna," Megan said.

"Oh, we know her," Elder Spaulding said. "They asked us t' substitute teach early morning seminary last week. Brianna answered most of the questions. She knows a lot about the gospel. We were both impressed. Weren't we, Elder?"

"Yes, we were," Elder Anderson said mechanically. "She's a lot smarter than she looks."

A short time later, Brianna came down the stairs. She had been to a planning meeting and was still wearing her Sunday clothes. "Hey, Elders, whatsup?" She high-fived both of them.

"Doin' good!" Elder Spaulding answered with a big grin. "How 'bout you?"

"Hey, today was journal writing material, you know what I'm saying?"

Elder Anderson smiled faintly.

Bryce was the next to show up. He came in through the garage into the kitchen. He'd spent his Sunday helping his boss and his wife sheetrock a family room.

"Bryce, I'm glad you're here for supper," his mother said. "How did it go?"

"Well, except for the fact that my boss is a complete idiot, it went all right. But if the man would just listen to me, we'd have been done three hours ago. But, no, he has to do it his way 'cause he's the boss."

Megan came into the kitchen.

"The elders are here," Megan said, trying to warn Bryce so he wouldn't say anything he'd regret.

Bryce swore. "What for?"

"They're going to give my friend Thomas the missionary lessons."

"Oh, great, that's all I need," he muttered. "Go ahead without me. I'll grab something after I take a shower."

Bryce walked through the living room and went upstairs without saying anything to the missionaries.

"And that was my brother, Bryce," Megan said.

"He's not active in the Church, is he?" Elder Anderson said.

"No."

"I could tell."

Elder Spaulding shook his head. "I understan' you're a cheerleader, Brianna, is that right?"

"For sure," she said. "You want to see a new cheer I just worked up?"

Before he could answer, she was standing in the living

175

room doing a cheer, which ended with her jumping into the air, kicking her legs, throwing up her hands, and shouting.

Elder Anderson lowered his gaze during Brianna's performance.

"That was amazin'!" Elder Spaulding called out excitedly when she was done.

"Well, it's better with a short dress."

Elder Anderson shook his head. "For some maybe, but not for me," he muttered.

"Is the sprinkler hitting the grass, Elder Anderson?" Brianna asked.

Elder Anderson's eyebrows raised. "What?" he asked.

"Are you picking up what I'm putting down?"

Elder Anderson turned to Megan. "I don't know what she's saying," he said privately.

"What'd you think I meant when I said it was better with a short dress?" Brianna asked.

"Well, I . . . thought . . . that . . . you meant it would . . . well . . . show more."

"How could you think that? What kind of a girl do you think I am? What I meant was I can jump higher and kick out my legs more with a short dress. That's what I meant."

"I understood that's what you meant," Elder Spaulding said.

Megan, totally embarrassed, put her hand to her forehead. *How could this possibly go any worse?*

Conversation during supper was subdued. Trying to be considerate, Elder Spaulding ate sparingly. Unfortunately, he didn't pay enough attention to Elder Anderson, who finished one pork chop, then grabbed another and started eating it.

"Isn't that pork chop supposed to be for Bryce?" Brianna asked.

"Well . . ." her mother stammered, not wishing to embarrass Elder Anderson.

Still chewing, Elder Anderson looked up to see the

disapproving eyes of everyone at the table. The pork chop was halfway eaten.

"You go ahead and finish, Elder Anderson."

"How was that pork chop, Elder?" Brianna asked, playing with Elder Anderson like a cat playing with a mouse it's caught.

"It was good," Elder Anderson said.

"Great, we'll tell Bryce that when he comes down and wants to eat. I'm sure he'll want to know what he missed."

"Sorry," Elder Anderson said. "I didn't know."

Brianna had a big grin on her face and turned to her mother. "Mom, we need to invite the missionaries over more often. I'm having a great time."

Twenty minutes later Thomas showed up. Bryce grabbed a sandwich and escaped as fast as he could because he knew that if he listened in on the discussion he'd end up arguing with the missionaries. Not that he wouldn't have enjoyed the experience, but he didn't want to hurt Megan's feelings.

The missionary discussion with Thomas went well. He agreed to read the Book of Mormon and to attend church on Sunday.

"We need to go now," Elder Anderson said, looking at his watch.

"No, stay," Megan said. "My mom baked a pie. She'll be disappointed if you guys don't have some."

"We really need to go," Elder Anderson said.

"What for?" Elder Spaulding asked. "We don't have any other appointments tonight. What kind of pie did your mom bake?" He pronounced it "pah."

"Apple. And she's got some ice cream to put on it."

"Well, bless my soul," Elder Spaulding said. "I think we'd better stay, Elder. We don't want to disappoint Megan's mom, do we?"

"All right, but then we really need to go."

They ate their pie, then visited for a while. As the elders

were leaving, Elder Spaulding sat down at the piano and began playing a hymn. They ended up singing some hymns, and before they knew it, it was nine-thirty.

"We really need to go now," Elder Anderson spoke privately to his companion.

Elder Spaulding broke into a big grin. "Oh, my gosh, you're right. Why'd you let us stay here so long, Elder? I'm surprised at you."

Elder Anderson saw little humor in the remark.

Thomas and Megan watched them go. "This was very interesting tonight," Thomas said.

"I'm glad you liked it. I'm proud of you for taking the discussions, Thomas. I'll read the Book of Mormon right along with you so we can talk about what you're reading."

"That'd be great. Well, I'd better be going." He gave her a quick hug and kissed her on the cheek and then left.

Even though there were some rough times, all in all this has been a good day, she thought. *I shouldn't be so happy, but I am.*

I wonder why?

◆ ◆ ◆

Megan had heard people talk about the missionaries bringing a special spirit into a home, and now she could see it for herself. She looked forward to each discussion. She could see the changes in Thomas, not so much in his actions but in his countenance. He smiled more, and when he prayed at the end of each discussion, it was from his heart.

Although Elder Anderson and Elder Spaulding still had their disagreements, there were times when they got along and worked effectively together.

In order to be as much help as she could to Thomas, Megan spent at least two hours a day reading the Book of Mormon. When she had a question or an insight about a particular passage, she'd write it down, then she and her mother and Brianna would talk about it during or after supper. When Walter wasn't on the road, he would join in. If Bryce was there when they started talking religion, he would usually excuse himself, although sometimes he'd stay and listen, hoping to find a weak argument he could pounce on.

Bryce got involved with the missionaries, too, but not in the way anyone could have predicted.

The elders dropped by unannounced one afternoon when Bryce wasn't working.

"Nobody's here except Megan, and she's upstairs taking a shower."

"We were just out tractin' and we're kind of thirsty. Suppose we could beg a glass of water from you?" Elder Spaulding asked.

"Yeah, sure, come on in," Bryce said.

They sat down in the living room while Bryce fixed them some ice water and a plate of cookies.

Suddenly, water began pouring through the chandelier above the kitchen table.

"Is that supposed to be happening?" Elder Anderson asked politely.

Bryce swore, ran up the stairs, and started banging on the bathroom door. "Megan, get out! Turn off the water!"

"Just ten more minutes!"

"No, now! Water's pouring through the ceiling!"

"What?"

"I said water's pouring through the ceiling! Turn off the shower and get out!"

She turned off the shower.

Bryce ran downstairs and out to the garage, bringing back a saw and a drill.

"You need any help?" Elder Spaulding asked.

"I do," Bryce answered.

179

The three of them ran upstairs. "You out of there yet, Megan?" Bryce shouted.

"I've still got shampoo in my hair!"

"We need to get in there."

"I'm hurrying as fast as I can."

"Well, it's not fast enough."

Seeing that Megan might take too long, Bryce led the elders into the adjoining master bedroom. "Okay, start pulling everything out of the closet. What we're going to do is cut a hole in the wall to see if there's a broken pipe."

The elders grabbed everything and piled it on the bed while Bryce drilled a hole big enough to get his saw started.

Hearing the saw, Megan quickly put on a robe and ran to her room.

Ten minutes later they peered into the ragged hole in the closet wall. No pipes were broken.

"Let's go downstairs and see what we can find out," Bryce said.

Downstairs, Bryce stood on the kitchen table and cut a hole in the ceiling by the chandelier to investigate further. They found no broken pipes.

"Megan, I need to talk to you! Right now!" Bryce shouted.

By this time she'd gotten dressed. She came out wearing slacks and a sweatshirt. Her hair, still not rinsed, was wrapped in a towel.

"All right, what did you do?" Bryce asked.

"Nothing. I just took a shower."

"You must have done something. What were you doing, right before I started yelling?"

"Well, I was shampooing my hair."

"And?"

"Nothing. . . . Well, I turned the nozzle up."

"You turned the nozzle up? How could you do that?"

"I always do it."

Bryce ran upstairs and into the bathroom. "That's it!"

180

He appeared at the top of the stairs. "Don't ever point the nozzle up again, you hear me?"

"What's wrong with that?"

"You want to come up here and see what's wrong with that?"

Megan shrugged. "Not particularly."

"This was all your fault!"

Megan's dark eyes flashed. "Don't you get after me, Bryce! I've been doing my shampoos the same way for years."

"Well, something happened today. The caulking around the shower has come loose, so the water got between the shower and the wall."

Megan shrugged. "Caulking is not my responsibility."

"Caulking is everybody's responsibility," Bryce answered with great solemnity.

"Don't mind him," she said. "He works at Home Depot."

Elder Spaulding nodded his head. "That, of course, explains everything."

Bryce came down the stairs. "We've got to get this cleaned up before Mom comes home. I'm going to Home Depot and get some sheetrock and popcorn spray for the ceiling."

"You need any help?" Elder Spaulding asked.

"No, it'll be quicker if I go by myself."

"We'll start cleanin' up while you're gone," Elder Spaulding said.

Half an hour later, Bryce returned. The first thing he did was cut out and replace the sheetrock in the upstairs closet wall, and then they all put Walter and Carolyn's clothes back in the closet.

Downstairs, Bryce refused help. The elders and Megan sat on the sofa and watched.

Bryce was in his glory. For him this was the perfect opportunity to show off his skills and great knowledge of home repairs. He lectured as he worked.

Finally it was time to apply the popcorn ceiling spray to

the ceiling. Bryce again stood on the table, shook the can, and sprayed. Only a few specks of the ceiling texture material actually landed on the ceiling. The rest landed on him, coating his face, clothes, arms, shoes, table, and wall.

Megan tried her best not to say anything, and perhaps she'd have succeeded if Elder Spaulding hadn't whispered to her, "Do my eyes deceive me, or is that truly the Pillsbury Dough Boy come to visit us today?"

Like a leaking balloon at first, and then, full bore, Megan broke out laughing.

"It's not funny!" Bryce shouted.

"No, of course not," Megan said, forcing her mouth to turn down. "It's not a bit funny."

Bryce slowly raised his arm to see the coating of white popcorn. "I'm going to change."

As soon as Bryce left the room, Megan and Elder Spaulding broke up, laughing in spasms, laughing so hard that tears were streaming down their cheeks. Elder Spaulding fell off the couch and grabbed his sides. For his part, Elder Anderson gave a five-second laugh and then just smiled a bit after that.

By the time Bryce returned wearing clean clothes, he had a plan. "The reason it didn't work the first time is because I held it too close to the ceiling. Now when you do that, then the air pressure bounces off the ceiling and sends the spray back down again. The first thing you should do before you try it on the ceiling is try it outside. And then you'll know better how it works."

"Good advice, Bryce," Megan said, biting her lip to keep from losing it all over again.

Because they were hoping for another disaster, they all followed Bryce outside. He tried it out, but it came out faster than he expected, so it ended up covering the tree, the fence, grass, rocks, and a flower or two.

182

Megan sank to the grass and held her sides. "That's a lot better."

Bryce, his pride hurt, headed back inside. "We'll clean that up later."

They followed him inside. "I love home repair projects," Megan said quietly, then started laughing again.

Bryce gave the second in his home repair lecture series, sprayed again, and, amazingly, had the same results as before.

Megan might have laughed but caught in Bryce's eyes his disappointment at failing once again.

"It's okay, Bryce."

He nodded and excused himself once again to get cleaned up before making another trip to Home Depot.

Ten minutes later Carolyn got out of her car after a hard day at work and started up the walk. She was puzzled by what looked like snow on part of the yard.

She entered the house. The chandelier was still on the floor, and it looked like a blizzard had attacked the kitchen.

"What on earth?"

"We can explain," Megan said.

The seconds passed. "Yes?"

"Actually, Bryce can explain it better than I can," Megan said.

"Where's Bryce?"

"Upstairs. Cleaning up."

Carolyn looked at the white-coated bowl of fruit and shook her head. "Maybe you'd better explain."

"Well, we'd better get goin," Elder Spaulding said, wanting to escape before anyone started yelling. "Nice t' visit with you and Bryce."

As the elders left, Megan heard Elder Spaulding say softly to his companion, "I've never wanted to go tractin' so much in my life."

Carolyn tried to stay mad, but as Megan explained what had happened, she ended up laughing about it, too.

Bryce left the ceiling the way it was. He had no heart to go back for round three.

◆　◆　◆

"This is so amazing!" Megan said to her family one night at supper. "I can actually understand the Book of Mormon. It makes sense to me. Sometimes I feel the Spirit so strong when I'm reading."

"I'm so happy to hear that," her mother said.

"Totally," Brianna said with a smile.

"You say you feel the Spirit?" Bryce asked. "So what good is that? What does it change? You're still pregnant. You're still planning to keep the baby."

"So?"

"So it's the wrong decision. How many times do I have to tell you that?"

"Well, I'm sorry you feel that way, but it is my life. Or are you taking that over, too, Bryce?"

"Why not give your baby to a couple who will devote their life to it? Your kid is going to spend his life being dropped off here while you go to work or to be with your friends."

"Bryce, cut her some slack," Brianna said. "She's doing the best she can right now."

"But it's all a sham. Megan, do you really think God wants you to raise this kid by yourself?"

"Yes, I do."

"With all due respect, how could you possibly know what God wants?" he said.

Brianna came right back at him. "Like you'd know anything about what God thinks, Bryce."

With that stinger, Bryce walked out.

Brianna and Carolyn looked at Megan, wondering how she'd react to what Bryce had said.

"Bryce didn't mean to hurt your feelings," Carolyn said.

184

"Of course not. That's because to him feelings don't matter."

"Don't listen to him," Brianna called out. "Keep the baby. We'll take care of it. I'll even quit school if I need to."

"Mom, what do you think I should do after the baby is born?"

The answer was a long time in coming. "Well, I think that's a decision you need to make. I'll support whatever you decide."

"I keep changing my mind from day to day, and it's driving me crazy. I've got to decide once and for all. Excuse me, I need to be by myself for a while."

Megan went to her room, closed the door, and knelt down by her bed. *I've got to decide what to do. I've got to do the right thing for my baby. Whatever that is, I've got to do the right thing.*

"Heavenly Father . . ." she began.

11

It was fast Sunday, and Megan had planned on fasting, hoping to come to a decision whether to keep her baby or to place it for adoption. But her doctor had told her it wasn't wise for a pregnant woman to go without eating, so instead of fasting she was praying to know what to do. She had thought she'd made up her mind to keep it, but Bryce's insistence that it was a bad idea kept bothering her. She didn't agree with Bryce on most things; but she respected him. He was one of the smartest people she knew. She didn't want to make a mistake on this. It was too important.

From his place on the stand, Bishop Oldham saw her enter the chapel and smiled at her. As a result of their interviews, she had come to appreciate his kindness and concern. She smiled back.

She sat on the third row of the chapel with Brianna and their father. Their mother was on the stand leading the music.

Heavenly Father, please help me to know what to do, she thought, offering a silent prayer.

She tried to pay attention to every testimony, hoping for

what could be a personal message from God to her. But there wasn't anything she could point to that would help her know what to do about her baby. By the end of the meeting, she was still undecided and discouraged and just wanted to go home.

"Will you be coming to my class?" her dad asked. "I could really use some suggestions on how I can improve."

She hated to turn him down. "All right, but please don't ask me any questions. I'm not ready for that yet."

As she sat in her dad's Sunday School class, she was impressed with all the work he'd done to prepare the lesson. It's what he did at night in motel rooms, instead of watching TV. On Saturday he had spent two hours downloading additional information from the Internet, and he gave everyone two handouts that were very informative.

Even with all his preparation, Megan noticed the members of the class seemed uninvolved in the lesson. People sat with their shoulders slumped and their heads lowered. Some were even sleeping.

Because there was so much material to cover, it was almost like a lecture. Walter asked very few questions, and most of the questions could only be answered by gospel scholars. Even so, several people stopped after class and thanked him for the excellent lesson.

"Good job," she said enthusiastically, moving up to the front.

"Really?"

"Sure, there was so much new information. You really worked hard on that lesson, didn't you?"

"I did. I learned a lot."

"I'm sure everyone else did, too."

Women were starting to come in for Relief Society. Megan wanted to get out of the room before anyone could ask her to stay to the meeting. Keeping her head down to avoid the gaze of the sisters, she said good-bye to her dad and slipped out the door.

Three hundred miles away, Ann Marie Slater stood at the pulpit to bear her testimony. "I would like to bear my testimony that I know that God lives and that Jesus is the Christ and that we have a living prophet on the earth today." She paused, pulled a tissue from the box next to the pulpit, and held it in her hand.

"I'm here today to also ask your forgiveness."

She dabbed at her cheek with the tissue.

"I've been having a hard time lately. I've felt angry at God and had uncharitable feelings toward members of this ward. I know that's not right, but that's the way I've felt. I'm trying to work on that. I know I'm the one at fault. Please, if I've seemed unfriendly, I'm sorry."

She closed her testimony and sat down.

After sacrament meeting Colleen Butler, the Young Women president, cornered Ann Marie. "Let's go talk, okay?"

"I'd like that."

They ended up sitting in Colleen's car in the parking lot.

"Have I offended you?" Colleen asked.

"No, not at all."

"You want to talk about it?"

Ann Marie nodded but hesitated. "This is so embarrassing." She took a deep breath and then said, "It's about me not being able to get pregnant. We've tried so hard, and nothing has worked. It's always been frustrating, but we've recently been told there's not much chance we'll ever be able to have a baby. Then when someone like Melissa Partridge gets pregnant, without even trying . . . it seems so unfair!"

She put her hand over her eyes but was unable to control the flood of tears. Colleen fished a tissue out of her bag and handed it to her.

Ann Marie pinched her nose with the tissue and wiped at the tears on her cheeks. "When I was growing up, all I ever wanted to be was a wife and mother. But sometimes we don't get what we want, do we? No matter how hard we pray about it."

"I'm sorry I haven't been more of a support to you."

"What's hard is what this has been doing to Weston and me." She shook her head. "We both want the same thing, but sometimes it's like we're competing or something."

She went on. "Things have always come easy to me, but I've had to face the fact that I can't do everything, that some things aren't just a matter of trying hard, or having a good attitude, or never giving up. I can't do the one thing that most women take for granted will happen to them. I've had to concede that it's not going to happen to me." She took a deep breath. "That's been hard for me to accept."

She wiped her eyes. "Do you have another tissue?"

She took it and wiped her nose. "I'm so grateful to Weston for being so patient with me. We've decided to look into adopting a baby. Of course, we have no idea how long that will take."

She sighed and shook her head. "What I said in church must have seemed strange to people, but I felt like I needed to apologize to the ward."

She smiled through her tears and looked at Colleen. "I'm sorry to unload on you, but just talking has helped. I'll be all right."

Ann Marie took a deep breath and pulled down the visor to look at herself in the mirror. "I'm a mess."

Colleen reached across the seat and put her hand on Ann Marie's. "Any time you need to talk, just give me a call."

"Thanks. I will." Ann Marie looked at her watch. "Well, let's go get ready for Young Women."

◆   ◆   ◆

Megan was on her way out of the Relief Society room when Kristin saw her. She was two years older than Megan,

189

but they'd been friends in high school. Kristin had fallen in love and gotten married her first year at BYU—had married a returned missionary and was now pregnant with her first baby. She and her husband, Justin, were temporarily living in an apartment in Kristin's parents' basement.

"You want to sit with me in Relief Society?" Kristin asked.

"Well, I don't know . . . I wasn't going to stay."

"C'mon. If the lesson gets boring, we can compare notes about our pregnancies."

Megan hesitated, then nodded her head and followed Kristin to Relief Society.

During the opening song, Megan's mind wandered.

What am I doing here? Kristin and I have a few things in common, but not the most important things. She's married and I'm not. When she found out she was pregnant, she was happy. She has a husband who will support her when she's down. I don't have anyone. Her family is proud of her. Mine is ashamed of me.

The teacher began the lesson. "I have a copy of the 'Proclamation to the World' that I'll pass out to everyone. I thought I'd just have everyone take a turn reading one sentence and then we'll talk about it afterwards."

As one of the women in the ward read the part that said that the powers of procreation are only to be used by a husband and wife, Megan wondered if other women were curious what she thought about that. *What do they think, that I'm going to argue against that? I should get up and leave. The only trouble is that if I leave, I'll have to crawl over Kristin to get to the aisle.*

What am I doing here? Why do I come here each week? Why don't I just quit and give up and stay home?

I'll wait until the next person starts to read, and then I'll go.

Another woman began to read: "'The family is ordained of God. Marriage between man and woman is essential to His eternal plan. Children are entitled to birth within the bonds of matrimony, and to be reared by a father and a mother who honor marital vows with complete fidelity.'"

Megan, her mouth wide open in astonishment, reached for Kristin's copy of "The Family: A Proclamation to the World" and quickly found the paragraph that had just been read.

She read it again. *Children are entitled to birth within the bonds of matrimony, and to be reared by a father and a mother who honor marital vows with complete fidelity.*

Tears began to well up in her eyes. *That's it. That's my answer. I have to do what's best for my baby. I will place my baby for adoption.*

In tears of relief, she leaned over and gave Kristin a big hug. "Thank you for getting me to Relief Society," she whispered.

♦   ♦   ♦

On nights when a missionary discussion was scheduled, Megan's mother invited the missionaries and Thomas to have supper with the family. Sometimes Thomas wasn't able to come for supper because he was either working or in class, but the missionaries were usually able to make it.

Having the elders to supper gave Megan and her family a chance to get to know the missionaries better. In time they learned that Elder Spaulding had a girl waiting for him. She was someone he'd met his first year at BYU.

"Do you have a picture of her?" Megan's mother asked.

"Well, yes, I do, as a matter-a-fact," Elder Spaulding said with a big grin. "I carry it in my wallet, next to my heart." He smiled. "Of course, I also carry a picture of the car I left behind, too." He pulled out his wallet and passed the picture of a pretty blonde. "Ain't she a beauty?"

Elder Anderson fidgeted.

"What's her name?"

"Melissa."

"How did you meet her?" Megan asked.

"Craziest thing. We met in a Laundromat. She stole my detergent. I set it down one minute, and then the next thing I know, she's carryin' it out of the place. I'm not talkin' a small box here. I'm talkin' a 'conomy-sized box, enough for like an entire semester. Well, I couldn't let her get away with that, so I went after her. I caught up with her jus' before she was goin' into her dorm. I called after her, so she stopped.

"So she looks at me and says, 'Yes?' So I go, 'You have my Cheer.' And she's all, 'What is up with this guy anyway?' I point to the box and say, 'That's mine.' And she goes, 'No, it isn't. I bought this yesterday.' So I go, 'You may have bought a box of Cheer yesterday, but it wasn't that box. Maybe you left your box in your apartment.' And she goes, 'Well, I can check, but I'm sure I didn't.' So she goes inside and comes back about a minute later with a second box of Cheer, and she's all, 'I'm so sorry.' And I'm all, 'Hey, don't worry about it.' So she invites me for supper the next day, and I meet her roommates and everythin', and she and I get along really good after that. So I started hangin' around and lovin' every minute I could spend with her." He chuckled. "I tell people, I've had Cheer ever since the day I met her."

"Elder," Elder Anderson warned.

"I'm almos' done. Anyway, the point is, 'fore long we were talkin' about gettin' married after my mission. So that's where it stands now. She bakes me cookies about once a month."

"Well, that must be a treat," Megan's mother said.

"Not really. To tell you the truth, they're pretty awful. Seems she's on a molasses kick. Claims it will keep me from gettin' sick. So she makes all her cookies with molasses instead of sugar. Each one weighs about ten pounds. Elder Anderson likes 'em though, don't you, Elder?"

Elder Anderson nodded.

"Course you'd expect that. He likes anythin' that's hard."

Elder Anderson was about to speak, but Elder Spaulding cut him off. "Not me, though. I like things easy. 'Easy does it.' That's my motto. Do the easy things first, and then maybe you'll never have to do the hard things. You know what I mean? Like what we're doin' here tonight. Teachin' Thomas, that's easy. Goin' tractin' in a rainstorm? That's hard . . ." With a sideways glance at his companion, he continued, " . . . hard and not all that productive."

Elder Anderson protested. "We had an hour left. I wasn't ready to just close up shop."

Elder Spaulding suddenly looked over at Megan, Brianna, Bryce, and their mother. "I'm sorry. We shouldn't be havin' this discussion in front of you, should we? We'll talk about this later, Elder."

Elder Anderson nodded his head. "You're right. I'm sorry for bringing it up here."

"Remind me never to serve a mission," Bryce said.

"It's the greatest two years of a person's life," Elder Spaulding said enthusiastically.

Bryce laughed. "Right," he said sarcastically. "I can see that, hearing you two argue."

"I love my companion," Elder Spaulding said. "He knows that, don't you, Elder?"

Elder Anderson gave the expected answer. "I suppose."

"This is good preparation for marriage," Elder Spaulding said.

"How's that?" Bryce asked.

"It teaches you how to work out problems with someone who doesn't think 'xactly like you do. Elder Anderson an' me, well, we're not the same. We both look at things differently. But I respect him. I'm learnin' to work with him, and he's learnin' to work with me, so that's good."

"You want to know who you two remind me of?" Megan asked.

193

"I'm not sure we do," Elder Spaulding said with a smile.

"Tigger and Eeyore. Elder Spaulding, you're Tigger. You're bouncing all over the place all the time. Elder Anderson, you're more mellow and thoughtful, and you always try very hard to live the mission rules. So that's good, too. I think you make a good team."

Elder Spaulding locked his arm around Elder Anderson's shoulder and pulled him into a momentary hug. "We *are* a good team," Elder Spaulding pronounced. Elder Anderson just looked uncomfortable.

After that it was hard for Megan not to want to call Elder Spaulding Tigger, which he constantly lived up to, as, for example, after supper, when he jumped up and started clearing off the plates. "What can I do? You want me to stack the plates in the kitchen? I can do that. Whatever you want. You cooked this wonderful meal for us. The least we can do is help clean up."

"Brianna can take care of that."

"No need. No need at all. Let me do it. Brianna, you've had a hard day."

"Okay, thanks."

"You should help him," her mother said.

"Why? He's doing okay by himself."

"It's your job."

"I know, but he wants to do it."

They heard a loud crash in the kitchen.

"Don't worry! It's not a plate or anythin'!" Elder Spaulding called out.

"What is it?"

"Jus' the fish bowl. But don't you worry none. I got all but one of the little buggers. He's under the 'frigerator, but I'm movin' the 'frigerator, and I'll have him in water 'fore you know it."

Elder Anderson shook his head.

"I got it!" Elder Spaulding called out. "They're okay."

194

He came out of the kitchen, carrying a Tupperware bowl with the fish in it. His pant legs were wet from the fish bowl breaking on the floor.

Brianna ran to him. "I love my goldfish! To me, they're part of the family," she said, choking with emotion.

Megan looked on in amazement because she knew Brianna hated the goldfish.

"Which one went behind the fridge? Tina or Buffy?" Brianna asked, peering into the plastic container.

"I don't know."

"Buffy has a little red mark on her side. I got her from my best friend just before she moved away. It was her last gift to me. She said, 'When you look at this goldfish, you'll remember the good times we had together.' I don't know what I'd do if anything happened to Buffy."

"I don't think she got hurt none when she hit the floor 'cause she jus' kept wrigglin', like she wasn't even stunned."

Brianna faked heartache. "First the fall and then not being able to breathe. She must have been *so* scared. And then being behind the refrigerator, wondering if anyone would even know she was back there. Poor Buffy." Brianna covered her eyes and pretended to cry.

"I feel real bad."

"And then there's Tina. She's had a hard life. One time the cat knocked her bowl off the counter and had her cornered. She even took a swat at her. I came home just in time. She didn't eat for days after that. That's when I first started calling her Tina. Before that she was a two-pound trout. And now look at her."

Elder Spaulding, his gaze on the floor to indicate his great sorrow, looked up to see Brianna's cheesy smile. "You've been funnin' me all this time?" he asked.

Brianna laughed. "Yeah, pretty much."

"I'll get you for this. I was feelin' worse and worse, the more you talked."

"I got you, didn't I?"

"I'll get you back."

"I don't think so. You're a missionary. You have to be good."

"No, I *will* get you. You just wait and see. Sometime when you're least expectin' it."

"But if you do that, then I'll have to get you back, so there'll be no end to it."

"And that'll be my fault?"

"Yes, you should just accept the fact that you can't win."

Megan watched with amusement the feuding between Elder Spaulding and Brianna. It was like a brother and a sister at each other, like the way Megan and Bryce had been when they were growing up.

A few minutes later, Thomas showed up for his weekly lesson.

After the opening prayer, Elder Spaulding asked, "Were you able to get any readin' done since the last time?"

"Well, I read some. Not everything, though."

"What did you read?"

"I read the pamphlet you gave me, and I read a few pages in the Book of Mormon."

"That's real good," Elder Spaulding said.

"Really good," Elder Anderson agreed.

"What did you think of what you read?" Elder Spaulding asked.

"It was okay. It kind of made sense. It's all new of course."

"Be sure and write down any questions you might have as you're reading, and then we can talk about them," Elder Anderson said.

As the discussion proceeded, Megan was surprised what an effective teacher Elder Anderson was. She'd always thought of him as the weaker of the two missionaries, the one who'd rather be doing something else than what they were doing.

He's not a bad guy, she thought. *He just wants to make the best use of his time. There's nothing wrong with that.*

At the end of the discussion, Elder Anderson asked if Thomas had any questions.

"Just one. These lessons, they're about me joining your church, aren't they? I mean, it's not just me learning more about it. It's about me becoming a Mormon, isn't it?"

"If you knew it was true, wouldn't you want to be a part of it?" Elder Spaulding asked.

"I'm not sure I could live up to all that's expected of a member of your church."

"You could do it, Thomas," Megan said.

"You didn't though, did you?"

Megan felt devastated. "That's true. I didn't, but I'm trying to change. People can change, Thomas. Even you and even me."

"Why do I have to change? I'm already living the way Mormons are supposed to live."

Megan felt once again the sting of regret that she hadn't been a better example to Thomas.

"Isn't knowing the truth important to you?" Elder Anderson asked.

"All churches think they have the truth."

"That's right. They do. But there is a way to find out if what we're tellin' you is the truth," Elder Spaulding said.

"How's that?"

"By continuin' to learn what we believe and then prayin' to ask God if it's true."

"And you think he'll answer me?"

"We know he will."

"What if he doesn't?"

"Then you're off the hook."

Thomas nodded. "Sounds fair."

Megan, for the first time in her life, ached to talk about her growing testimony—about the truths she had discovered

197

in reading the Book of Mormon. But she kept silent because she didn't feel that what she would say would have much impact with Thomas because he'd seen her at her worst. And so she sat there quietly, silently praying that Thomas would someday feel the way she did now about the Church.

Thomas agreed to continue with the discussions, and he even set a date for baptism, although he kept saying that he hadn't made up his mind about it yet.

After the discussion the elders stayed and had dessert and sang a few songs, with Elder Spaulding again at the piano.

After the elders left, as Megan helped clean up in the kitchen, her mother asked, "What do you think of Elder Spaulding?"

"He's okay, I guess."

"I agree. You and he seem to get along well together."

"Mom, he's a missionary, and I'm not married and pregnant. It's not exactly the best timing for either one of us. Someday he'll go back home and marry Melissa, the Cheer girl."

"You don't know that for sure."

"I don't want to talk about this anymore, ever, okay?"

"Of course, whatever you say."

They didn't talk about it anymore. But that is not to say that Megan didn't think about it. She did almost every day. And felt guilty doing it.

It's because I have nothing else to think about, she thought, lying in her bed that night. *My life is so isolated now. I stay in the house by myself alone all day, and I don't go out much because I'm beginning to show and it's too awkward to have friends from high school come up and start asking questions, and so I stay in the house, and the only guys I see all week are Thomas and the missionaries. Elder Spaulding is a good missionary, but he's nice, too, and easy to talk with and has a good sense of humor.*

I guess it's possible I might be falling for Elder Spaulding, but that's because he's such a good example of a worthy priesthood holder. And because he's on a mission and dedicating his life to God. I'm not sure I'd like him that much if he wasn't on a mission.

Maybe it's not that I'm falling in love with him. Maybe it's just because he's nice to me and doesn't seem to be judging me harshly because of my past. Maybe that's it. Or maybe it's because he acts like he's got all the time in the world for us when he's here.

I'm sure that's it. It's not that I'm falling for him. It's that I respect Elder Spaulding for putting people first. That's what it is.

I wonder what his Melissa is like? I hope she's wonderful. I hope she waits for him his whole mission. I hope they get married a few weeks after he gets home from his mission.

I hope I come to my senses soon.

I can't let Elder Spaulding suspect anything because that would ruin everything. I have to keep telling myself that I'm not thinking clearly now and that I have to be strong and not cave in to some silly fantasy that would ruin everything for Thomas and his chances to become a member. I have to keep my feelings to myself.

There, that's taken care of. I've got things under control.

I wonder if I could get a picture of Elder Spaulding. That would be great.

She smiled and closed her eyes and soon fell asleep.

12

Megan had gained seven pounds. It was obvious to her family that she was expecting, but her mother said she didn't think most people would notice.

On the day the elders were to give Thomas his last discussion before his baptism, they showed up before anyone else except Megan was home.

She seemed surprised to see them but let them in and then excused herself and went upstairs to change clothes.

"We shouldn't be here with just Megan," Elder Anderson said as they sat down in the living room.

"Brianna will be showing up soon."

"We'll be here until ten again, won't we?" Elder Anderson asked.

"Probably."

"The president said—" Elder Anderson began.

"I know what the president said, okay? You don't have to remind me every five minutes."

"You don't even care what the rules are, do you?"

Elder Spaulding, red-faced, barely under control, turned

to confront his companion, "And that's all you do care about, isn't it? You didn't come out here to baptize, did you? You came out here to harass your companions. Well, Elder, if that's your goal, let me congratulate you because you're a big success."

The elders quit arguing when Brianna showed up.

An hour and a half later, Brianna, Bryce, Megan, and Carolyn sat down with the elders to supper.

Elder Anderson didn't say much at all, but Elder Spaulding tried to make up for it by being even more talkative and charming than usual. Even Bryce was enjoying himself.

After finishing supper they waited another half an hour, but Thomas didn't show up. After forty-five minutes, Megan telephoned his house. Thomas answered. It was a short conversation.

Megan hung up. She turned to the others, feeling as though she'd been kicked in the stomach. "Thomas says he's decided to quit taking the discussions."

"Why?"

"He says his entire family has always been Catholic. It's been good enough for them, so it's good enough for him."

"We need to talk to him," Elder Spaulding said.

"He said he doesn't want to talk to you guys anymore. He just wants to go back to the way things used to be."

They sat in silence for a few moments.

"I can't believe it," Megan said. "Why would he quit taking the lessons when he was so close to being baptized?"

"Maybe if he'd had a better example," Elder Anderson said softly.

Megan, painfully, took a deep breath. "You mean if I hadn't been sleeping around before he started taking the discussions?"

"No, no," Elder Anderson stammered. "You don't understand. I didn't mean it like that. I was talking about Elder

Spaulding and me, if we were getting along better. That's what I meant."

Tears burning her eyes, Megan got up to leave.

"Please, don't go," Elder Anderson pleaded. "I was talking about Elder Spaulding and me. Not about you. I would never say that about you."

"Don't worry about it. But it is true. I should have been a better example. Thomas is the best friend I've ever had, and if he doesn't join the Church because of me, well, I don't know what I'll do."

Megan went to her room. A few minutes later she heard the elders leave and watched through the window as they drove away.

She stayed in her room the rest of the night, listening to music and agonizing over Thomas's decision. Brianna came in and tried to cheer her up, even inviting her to go to a movie with her.

"Thanks, but I think I'll just stay here. I don't want to go where any of my old friends will see me."

"How about I put a pillow under my sweatshirt? Then people won't notice you so much."

Megan couldn't help but smile. "Sure, that would solve all our problems."

"For sure. Come be with me and my friends then. They won't care."

"No, I'll just stay here. I'm fine, really."

Brianna bent down and wrapped her arms around Megan. "I love you."

"I love you, too. I'm fine here, really."

"Well, then, I'll be going."

A while later Carolyn opened the door a crack. "You okay?"

"Yeah, I'm okay."

"Can I get you anything?"

"No, but thanks anyway."

Megan was sitting up in her bed with a comforter wrapped around her. Carolyn came and sat on the bed and reached for her daughter's hand. "Sometimes people decide not to join the Church—not because of something a member said or did, but just because it's such a big step in a person's life. Sometimes people aren't ready to take that step." She sighed. "So I don't think you should blame yourself because Thomas decided to stay with his own church."

She nodded. "I know. It's just such a big disappointment, that's all."

"Of course it is."

"It's everything coming at me all at once. Like, I worry so much about what's going to happen. When you were pregnant the first time, were you ever afraid of what could happen in the delivery room?"

"Yes, of course, it's only natural to worry about that."

"Like, what if the baby is born deformed or stillborn or dies right after it's born? And I'm not sure I can take all the physical pain that goes with having a baby. I mean, there's all these things. And if I was married, I'd have a husband who could be with me and support me and help me get through whatever happened, but I don't have anybody."

"You have a family who will be there for you."

"Mom, why doesn't Kurt ever call me? Why doesn't he care about this life that he's helped to create? How can he just walk away like it never happened? Did I mean so little to him that he won't even call and ask how I'm doing? Why was I so stupid to think he cared about me? And how can he go on like everything's the same? Well, for me nothing's the same. And it never will be."

"I can't answer any of those questions. He's the only one who can."

Megan shook her head. "It's not that I want to see him or have him in my life. I don't. I just can't understand someone who would walk away from this and pretend it never happened. I was so wrong about him."

They talked for another hour, sometimes as mother and daughter, but sometimes, when talking about having a baby, they talked as friends, two women, who shared a common bond.

Carolyn excused herself at nine-fifteen. She usually talked to Walter every night at that time. At nine-twenty the phone rang.

Five minutes later Carolyn returned.

"Your father is coming back tonight."

"What for?"

"I told him about our talk. He was wondering if you might like a priesthood blessing—tonight or tomorrow."

"But . . . he never comes back before Friday."

"I know, but he is this week. It'll take him about three hours to get here. You think you'll still be up?"

"I'll be up for him if he's coming all that way just for me."

"Good. He'll be pleased."

She wanted to prepare herself as much as she could for the priesthood blessing from her father. And so she took a bath, put on Sunday clothes, and sat down and read in her Book of Mormon.

Brianna came home just after ten o'clock. She noticed Megan's Sunday clothes.

"Whatsup?" she asked.

"Dad's going to give me a priesthood blessing."

"Is he home?"

"Not yet. But he's coming."

Brianna thought about that for a minute. "That is so cool," she said. "Can I listen?"

"Sure. But it'll be a while. He's driving back."

Her dad arrived at twelve-thirty, found Megan sitting in the living room, and asked if she would like a father's blessing. Then he changed into his Sunday clothes.

To keep Bryce from barging in when he came home, they put a note on the front door telling him what they were doing and asking him to be quiet until the blessing was completed.

They gathered in the living room, with Brianna and Carolyn sitting on the couch and Megan seated on a dining room chair her father had brought into the room. He asked Carolyn to say a prayer, and when she was finished, he placed his hands lightly on Megan's head. He closed his eyes and, calling her by name, began. " . . . by the authority of the Melchizedek Priesthood, I lay my hands on your head . . . "

By the time he finished, they were all in tears.

But this time they were happy tears.

◆   ◆   ◆

A few days later, Megan showed up at Leo's Pizza after hours. Thomas seemed surprised to see her.

"Can I come in?" she asked.

"Please do."

Thomas was mopping the floor in the dining area.

"What can I do to help out?" she asked.

"Actually, I've pretty much got things under control," he said.

"Sure."

He worked for several minutes without either one of them saying a word.

"We're both kind of quiet tonight, aren't we?" she finally said.

"Yeah, we are."

Another unbearable silence followed.

"Would you rather I just go home and let you get your work done?"

"No, don't go," he said quickly.

She gave a sigh of relief. "Good. I don't want to go home."

"What *do* you want?"

205

"I want it to be like it used to be between us."

He nodded his head. "Me, too."

"It's okay if you don't join the Church, Thomas. I can understand that."

He shook his head. "It just got to be too much, that's all. My family especially."

"Sure, I understand."

He quit working and stared at her for the longest time.

"What?" she asked.

"Can a guy ask a girl for a hug?" he asked.

"Oh, yeah! I'd love that."

He draped his long arms around her but didn't hold her tight like he used to. She knew it was because he was afraid he'd hurt the baby inside her.

"This feels so good, Thomas."

"I know. It really does."

"Do I feel different now?"

"A little."

"I've missed not having you come around," she said.

"I've missed it, too." He pulled away enough to make eye contact. "But it's for the best, as far as my family goes."

"Okay."

"Besides, all churches do good."

"That's true. They do."

He caught the look in her eye. "But what?"

"Just give me five minutes, and then I'll never bring it up again."

"Okay."

"Let's sit down for this, okay?" she asked.

She sat down across from him, and she held his hand in hers, not out of any kind of romantic feelings, but more because she wanted him to somehow sense how strong her testimony was.

"You know me better than anyone else in the whole world. I've told you things I've never told my parents or Brianna or anybody. You know the worst about me. But, Thomas, I also want you to know the best about me, too. I have to tell you how much I've changed in the past few months. I know for myself that the Book of Mormon is true and that Jesus Christ is my Savior and that he loves me. And I know that Joseph Smith was a prophet of God. I know it by the influence of the Holy Ghost. Can't you feel something while I'm talking to you?"

He didn't say anything for a moment, then said, "I do feel something."

"What do you feel?"

He smiled. "That you're squeezing my hand really hard."

She blushed and pulled away. "Well, that's it then, isn't it? I gave it my best shot."

"You did."

She grabbed a napkin and wiped her eyes. "Sorry to get so emotional."

"It's okay."

She stayed a few more minutes and then left.

◆　◆　◆

On Sunday Thomas went to mass with his Grandmother Marconi. She was by far the strongest in her faith of anyone else in the family. His parents never went to church. His three uncles also never attended, though they were the first to defend it.

It had been his Uncle Al who had talked him into not meeting anymore with the Mormons. "Our family already has a church. It would break your grandmother's heart if you threw away all you've been taught your whole life. We're a family, and we got to stick together. If you put as much time and study into your own religion as you have the Mormons, you'll see it's just as good and, I'm sure, a whole lot better."

It was an argument that was hard to refute. Family had

always been a big thing, and Thomas knew his grandmother would never understand his willingness to give up their traditional religion. To keep peace he agreed to stop meeting with the missionaries. Everyone in the family was relieved. He got phone calls of support from his extended family all that week.

And so when Sunday came around, he envisioned the entire family at church with him—his mom and dad, his uncles and aunts, and all his cousins. He started phoning Saturday morning, inviting members of his extended family to go to church. But everyone was busy, what with work and needing time to rest up from a hard week, and doing some shopping.

And so he went to church with his grandmother. The sermon that day was entitled, "New Wine in Old Bottles."

At first Thomas didn't pay much attention to the sermon. But then a question rang out from the pulpit: "What did our Lord mean when he said that we cannot put new wine in old bottles? Did our Lord form a task force suggesting small changes that might be made? No, he had to start over with completely new ideas. We must also take stock of ourselves and throw out those things in our patterns of thinking which are not in keeping with God's will for us." The sermon went on to other themes, but Thomas felt like the message he'd heard was a message from God.

As he and his grandmother left the church, Thomas shook the priest's hand. "Your sermon today was inspired."

The priest smiled. "Thank you very much. We hope to see more of you from now on. Your uncle told me you've recently made a wise decision. I'm very pleased."

Thomas smiled, but only halfheartedly. "I find myself changing in ways I never dreamed. It's almost like God is leading me in a certain direction."

"I'm sure he is," the priest said with a broad smile.

That afternoon the family got together for their traditional Sunday spaghetti dinner.

As Thomas entered the living room, Uncle Al grinned and asked, "So tell us about the Mormons. How many wives did they promise you if you'd join up with 'em?"

"None."

"No wives? Right now that sounds good to me! I've got one I'd like to get rid of! So how do I join?" Uncle Al laughed until it brought up phlegm, and he started coughing out of control.

"Seriously, what could they possibly say to you that would cause you to even think about leaving the church our family has been in for hundreds of years?"

"They say that just like in Bible times, God called a modern-day prophet named Joseph Smith."

"Yeah, right, like God couldn't come up with a better name for a prophet than Joe Smith."

"I knew a Joe Smith once . . . ran a pawn shop in Cleveland."

Thomas let the comments continue, deciding that nobody wanted a serious discussion. He glanced at Elizabeth. Her head was down, as if she were in a storm trying to stay upright while facing a stiff wind.

"I have a question for you all to consider," Thomas said. "What's worse, to give allegiance to a church you don't attend and beliefs you don't try to live, or to try to find a set of beliefs that has the power to make you a better person?"

Everyone stared at him, stunned. Family members didn't ask questions like that at occasions like this.

"Well, you can look all you want but not where you been looking," Uncle Bill said. "The way I heard it, the gal who got you studying with the Mormons got herself pregnant with some guy she met at a bar. She don't exactly sound like Mother Teresa there, right? I'm not sure she's the one you should go to for spiritual guidance."

Elizabeth came to him, put her arm around him, and

asked, "Thomas, while we're here, could you look at my car? I can't get the oil light to go out."

Still in a combative mood, Thomas nodded his head and followed Elizabeth out to her car in the driveway.

They sat in her car. "What about your oil light?"

She shrugged. "Looks like you fixed it. Thanks."

"No problem."

"Don't let them get to you," she said.

"I won't."

"You think you might become a Mormon?"

He shrugged his shoulders. "I'm not sure. But I do think I'll go back and meet with the missionaries again. Megan talked to me the other night and told me how much the teachings of her church mean to her. She asked me if I felt anything."

"I don't understand. What did she think you'd feel?"

"She thought God would let me know that what she was telling me is true."

"Did that happen?"

Thomas sighed, "Yeah, I think so, but I didn't admit it."

"How come?"

"Afraid of change I guess." He sighed. "But now that I've had a chance to think about it, I've decided to give it another try."

"Let me know how it goes."

"I will."

Elizabeth pursed her lips. It was something she'd been doing all her life when she couldn't decide whether or not to say what was on her mind.

"Go ahead and say it," Thomas said.

Instead of looking directly at him, she stared at the steering wheel of her car. "This is embarrassing to talk about, but, the fact is, I feel lonely so much of the time. Not so much in the daytime, you know, with classes and accompanying the choir, getting ready for concerts. Mainly at night, when it's late

210

and there's nobody to talk to. I can't find anyone for me. Well, I could, I guess, but not what I'm looking for."

"What do you want me to do about that?"

"That's such a guy response." She smiled and shook her head. "I don't need you to *do* anything, except maybe to listen to me whine."

He started chuckling. "New whine in old bottles."

She looked at him with a puzzled expression.

"It's a play on words. It's funnier on paper. You know, w-h-i-n-e, as opposed to w-i-n-e."

"Give it up, okay? Tell me something. What are Mormon guys like?"

"Well, you'd probably like Elder Spaulding, except you can't like him."

"I can't like him? Why's that?"

"Not for two years. Well, less now. What I'm trying to say is he's a missionary. They don't date for two years."

"Two years, huh?"

"That's right."

She nodded her head. "I guess I'm a missionary, too, then. It's been about that long for me."

"But they have other guys who aren't on missions."

"How could I check out the ones who aren't on missions?"

"You could come to my next discussion with the missionaries and then go to church with me."

She broke into a wide grin.

◆　　◆　　◆

On Thursday Elizabeth went to Thomas's next discussion and met Elder Spaulding and Elder Anderson, who were delighted to have Thomas back and to have him bring his sister along.

On Sunday Elizabeth and Thomas entered the chapel and

sat down. Because they weren't members, they'd made the mistake of coming early.

Elder Spaulding and Elder Anderson, on their way to correlate with the ward mission leader, stepped into the chapel and welcomed Thomas and Elizabeth to church and then left for their meeting.

"Elder Spaulding seems like a nice guy," she said.

"He is. Very nice."

"Did I ever tell you that for the past little while I've been trying to decide if I should switch?" she asked.

"Switch to what?"

"That I might give up on men and turn my attention to women."

He raised an eyebrow. "No, you didn't mention that."

"Well, I was thinking about it. I've had such rotten experiences with guys. After a while, you start to wonder." She paused. "Do you want to know why I was thinking about it?"

He cleared his throat. "You know what? I'm not sure I do."

"It was because I started to think all guys were scum."

"I'm a guy."

"Not you, of course. Just everyone else. It's not that I had any great attraction for those of my own gender. It's sort of like if you're answering a multiple-choice question and there's only two choices and you're pretty sure the answer isn't A. So then you start to think that maybe B is the right answer. So, I was thinking B because A had worked out so badly for me." She smiled. "But now I'm thinking A might not be that bad of a choice."

"What happened to change your mind?"

"Meeting Elder Spaulding."

Thomas cocked his eye at her.

She said, "I suppose there are others just as nice as him. But I guess it's kind of like the first time you see a PT Cruiser. You always remember the first one you see. And then, before

212

you know it, you see them all over the place. It's very encouraging."

"I suppose."

"Thomas, I've got a confession to make."

He faked a scowl. "You know what? I wish we'd come late
like everyone else."

"My confession is that I checked out the website for BYU.
They have a men's chorus . . . full of really decent looking
guys."

"That's sort of what you'd expect for a men's chorus."

"But these look like nice guys." She smiled. "I have a
whole new mission in life."

"What?"

"To go to BYU and accompany the men's chorus."

"I wish you and the men's chorus every happiness."

"See that young couple with the baby?" she asked.

Thomas turned to look at them. "What about them?"

"They seem nice, don't they? Happy in a domestic kind of
way. I guess what I'm trying to say is I want to be like these
people. I want to marry a member of the BYU Men's Chorus
and have children and come to church with four diaper bags.
What do you want?"

He sighed. "I'm thinking about getting baptized."

She nodded her head. "Me, too."

"You have to actually know something about the Church
first."

"Okay then, after that, I'll get baptized."

"Why?"

"I think the BYU Men's Chorus would expect that of me."

"We'll have to tell the family then."

"We will someday," Elizabeth said.

"I mean, before we're baptized."

"That seems like a bad idea. Why don't we just, every
Sunday, say we're going to Wal-Mart. Who would know the
difference?"

"No, we have to tell them."

She shook her head. "Here comes World War Three."

♦   ♦   ♦

When the ward mission leader learned that Elizabeth wanted to learn about the Church and that she had a crush on Elder Spaulding, he made arrangements for the sister missionaries to teach her at his home.

Elizabeth received two lessons a week, which helped her catch up with Thomas.

Three weeks later they were both ready to be baptized.

Thomas and Elizabeth agreed to tell their family about their decision to get baptized. They were prepared to do so at the next Sunday family dinner.

"When do we tell them?" she asked.

"After dessert."

"Why after dessert?"

He flashed her a grin. "It's pecan pie. I want to get some before they throw us out."

"Is that what you think will happen?" she asked.

"I'm not sure what will happen."

They waited until they had finished their dessert and then Thomas stood up.

"Elizabeth and I have an announcement to make. We're going to become Mormons."

The announcement had the effect of freezing everyone in time.

"So what's the punch line?" their uncle asked.

"It's not a joke. We're going to become Mormons. We're getting baptized next Saturday. You're all invited."

"What's he talking about?" Grandmother Marconi asked.

"They're changing churches."

"We're Catholic," she said. "We've always been Catholic. We will always be Catholic."

"That's good . . . for you . . . but not so good for us," Elizabeth said.

"Mormons? Who are they?"

"They're the ones with the choir," Elizabeth answered.

"We have choirs."

"They're in Salt Lake City . . . in Utah."

"You're moving to Utah?"

"Well, maybe," Elizabeth said. "You see, BYU has a men's . . ."

"Not now," Thomas said to her privately. "One family crisis at a time, that's my motto."

"Our family has been Catholic for hundreds of years."

"True, but we think we'll like this better," Elizabeth said.

"You can't go around changing religions like you do a shirt. You have to have a reason."

"We have a reason."

"What's your reason?"

"They have a prophet."

"You're joining their church because they make a profit? We make a profit, too."

"Not that kind of profit. A prophet like Moses."

"What about Moses?"

"Is Moses a Mormon?"

"No, he's dead. They have a prophet just like Moses."

"Can he walk across the Red Sea on dry ground?"

"I don't know. It hasn't come up yet. Besides, he lives in Utah."

"Then he's not just like Moses. Can he send a plague of frogs?"

"No."

"If you ask me, you're not getting your money's worth."

Their grandfather stood up. "You're not joining the Mormon Church, so just forget about it."

The conversation quickly changed to sports for the men and to children for the women.

215

Thomas and Elizabeth walked outside.

"They don't believe we'll do it."

"But we will, won't we?" she asked.

"Yes, I think we'd better."

"It's going to change a lot of things," she said.

"I know."

"I want to become better friends with Megan."

◆   ◆   ◆

On Monday, during the day, Elizabeth dropped by the house to visit with Megan.

They sat in the living room. At first it was a little awkward.

"How are you doing?" Elizabeth asked.

"Okay, so far."

"Good. Expecting a baby is a big deal, isn't it?"

"It is. It's the hardest thing I've ever done."

"Have you been sick a lot?" Elizabeth asked.

"Not too much. It's other things."

"Sure. Thomas and I are getting baptized."

"You are? When?"

"Next Saturday. Can you come to it?"

"Of course!"

Elizabeth paused. "I wanted to thank you for getting Thomas interested in the Church."

"I wasn't the best example. He's been great, though. He's helped me get through this."

Elizabeth smiled. "He's like that, all right." She cleared her throat. "What can you tell me about Elder Spaulding?"

"Elder Spaulding? Well, he's from Biloxi, Mississippi. Home of the Crawdad Festival."

"The Crawdad Festival?"

"That's what I said. Anyway, he's got just a few months left of his mission. Oh, there's a girl waiting for him. Of course,

216

it's been two years since they've seen each other, so who knows how that will go."

"And you, what about you? Are you hoping this girl doesn't wait?"

"Well, I've fantasized about it from time to time. But there's no reason to expect we'll ever be more than just friends after he goes home."

"I'm not sure how this works with missionaries."

"Basically, it's best to back off until they go home."

"And then?"

"He'll go back to his friends and family and then pretty much forget all about us, except maybe he'll tell about teaching Thomas when he gives his homecoming talk in church." Megan nodded her head. "Basically, that's how it works."

"Okay. I had to ask. I didn't know."

"Sure, I understand."

"Do you love him?" Elizabeth asked.

She hated it that she was blushing. "I respect him. I guess you could say we're friends. But that's all."

Elizabeth pulled a video out of her backpack. "Well, if he's not in the picture, I have here a video of the BYU Men's Chorus that I think you might be interested in. I don't have all their names yet, but I'm working on it. It's one of the wonders of the Internet. BYU has a stalker-net that has been very helpful."

They watched the video, laughing hilariously as they singled out the ones they liked. "Oh, baby, sing that Bach!" Elizabeth cried out.

Megan soon caught the spirit of it. "Oh, yeah, Mr. Bass Man! I'm yours, baby, yes, sir!"

Brianna came home in time to join in the silly frenzy. "Uuuuh, baby, I'm your biggest fan! Sing the tenor like a man!" she shouted.

The three of them ended up on the floor in pain because they were laughing so hard.

"So, when are you going to go to BYU with me?" Elizabeth asked Megan. "We'll room together."

"That would be great." She patted her tummy. "I've got a few things I need to take care of first."

"Okay, you take care of business, girl, and then we're out of here. Just the two of us."

"That sounds so fun."

Elizabeth stood up, extended her arms, and, mimicking Buzz Lightyear from the movie *Toy Story,* called out, "To the BYU Men's Chorus . . . and beyond!"

◆　　◆　　◆

The day before Thomas and Elizabeth were scheduled to be baptized, Elder Spaulding and Elder Anderson dropped by to see Megan.

"I just wanted to make sure you'd be at the baptism Saturday," Elder Spaulding said.

"I'll be there."

"Good. I'll be leavin' right after the baptism. I'm being transferred."

She was stunned. "Transferred? Where?"

"The president said he needs me in the mission home. One of the elders in the office got sick and had to be sent home. So I'll work there until I go home."

She felt awful. "Oh, I see. I know you can't write to me on your mission, but I hope you will after you get home."

"You know I will."

"No, I don't know that, but I hope you will."

"Well, anyway, thanks for sharin' the gospel with Thomas."

"I enjoyed having him taught here. You did a good job."

"It wasn't me."

"No, of course not, but you know what I mean." She wanted to say something but wasn't sure what to say. *Some*

218

days just knowing I was going to see you kept me going. A dozen other thoughts ran through her mind. But, in the end, she said nothing.

"I'll always remember you," Elder Spaulding said, extending his hand.

Elder Anderson quickly interjected, "Elder, we need to go. We have an appointment in ten minutes."

Elder Spaulding nodded. "Well, I'll see you at the baptism, and then we can say good-bye."

"I'll be staying," Elder Anderson said.

She didn't care if Elder Anderson stayed or left, but she didn't want to hurt his feelings. "Okay, good."

Elder Anderson cleared his throat. "I've said some things I regret. I hope you won't hold it against me. I'm trying to do better. I wanted you to know that now I can see some good things about Elder Spaulding, and I'm going to try to be a little bit more like him."

She was surprised to hear that from Elder Anderson. For just an instant, she saw him in a new light. *He's like me in some ways. Trying to change, trying to be better. I'll try not to be so judgmental about him from now on.*

She walked them to the door and said good-bye.

◆   ◆   ◆

On Saturday she got up early so she could do her hair in time for the baptism. It had been scheduled in the morning to allow Elder Spaulding to catch his Greyhound bus to the mission office.

She was up early enough to get in Bryce's way as he got ready for work. "What are you doing up so early?" he asked.

"Thomas and his sister, Elizabeth, are getting baptized. I wanted to look nice for that. Also, Elder Spaulding is being transferred today."

"You fixing up for Elder Spaulding?"

219

"No."

"I bet you are, aren't you?"

She hated it that he knew her so well.

"Can I give you a little advice? I think washing your hair is not going to make that much of a difference to Elder Spaulding. Why should he pay any attention to you after his mission when he'll have his pick at any of the Church schools?"

"You're such a total jerk sometimes, Bryce."

"Maybe so, but I'm right, and you know it."

She breezed past him and went to her room and closed the door and crawled back in bed. She cried herself to sleep.

She would not have gone to the baptism at all were it not for Brianna, who got up an hour later and got ready to go, coming into their room every few minutes to tell Megan to get up and get dressed.

"You got to get up now, or you'll miss the baptism."

"I'm not going," Megan muttered.

Brianna grabbed the covers and ripped them off the bed. "You gotta go! I don't care how tired you are! You got to do this for Thomas and his sister!"

"Leave me alone."

"What is your *problem?*"

"Elder Spaulding is being transferred today."

"Do you want me to get a tissue so we can cry about it? So what? Elders get transferred all the time. That's not the point. The point is Thomas and Elizabeth need you to be there for their baptism."

"Don't you understand?"

"Understand what?"

"I'm in love with Elder Spaulding."

Brianna scowled. "Oh, good grief. That's not supposed to happen."

"I know that. I couldn't help it."

"So because you love him, you're going to miss your last

chance to see him before he leaves town? Sure, that makes perfect sense."

"Just leave me alone."

"It's not going to happen. You're going to the baptism, one way or another. I'd suggest you put on some church clothes, but, hey, I'll take you in a blanket if I have to."

Brianna prodded and poked and finally got Megan to a standing position.

"Look at me, I look pregnant."

"That's not exactly news to anyone. Put on something and let's go. You can do your hair on the way."

"Don't boss me around!"

"I will boss you around until you get your senses back."

Megan stood in front of her closet and picked out a loose skirt and an overblouse.

"Yes! We're on the move now! You da mama!"

Megan turned around and scowled at her.

"It was a compliment, okay?"

Ten minutes later they left the house for the baptism.

◆　　◆　　◆

It was like most baptismal services, with all the right people in attendance: the bishop, the ward mission leader, the man and his son who would be Thomas and Elizabeth's home teachers, Walter and Carolyn, and all of the missionaries in the district.

Megan and Brianna sat in the back.

"Isn't this great?" Brianna whispered.

Megan nodded. Even though she couldn't stand the thought of Elder Spaulding leaving, she was thrilled that her best friend and his sister were getting baptized.

"You made it happen," Brianna whispered.

"I wasn't a good example for him."

"Maybe not at first, but now you are."

221

After the opening song and prayer, Brianna gave a talk about the importance of being baptized. In her talk she almost entirely avoided jargon. For her it was like speaking a foreign language. Sometimes she would stop, as if she were searching for the way to say things in plain English.

And then it was time for the baptisms. They gathered by the font as Elder Spaulding and Thomas entered the water together.

And then Elder Spaulding baptized Thomas. After Thomas surfaced he threw his arms around Elder Spaulding, and they hugged each other.

And then as Thomas went up one set of stairs, Elder Spaulding turned to escort Elizabeth into the font. Dressed in white, with her long, dark brown hair hanging down to her waist, she looked like an angel.

Elder Spaulding took her hand and began, "Elizabeth Marconi, having been commissioned of Jesus Christ . . ."

And then he baptized her.

She came out of the water with the biggest smile anyone had ever seen from her, but she did not hug Elder Spaulding. She had learned the rules.

◆　◆　◆

Thomas and Elizabeth were confirmed a week later in sacrament meeting. Elder Spaulding had been transferred, and as the holdover from the original companionship, Elder Anderson confirmed both Thomas and Elizabeth. Megan cried tears of joy as she listened to the blessings they were given.

After the closing hymn and prayer, Elizabeth and Thomas stood up and put their arms around each other.

"I feel so good now," Elizabeth said. "How about you?"

"Me, too."

"It's true, isn't it?"

"It is."

"Isn't that nice that it's true?"

"It is. It's very nice."

They embraced again, brother and sister in a family, and brother and sister in the gospel.

Brianna leaned over and whispered in Megan's ear. "You made this happen."

"No, not me."

"Who then?"

She pointed at her stomach. "This baby made it happen."

Brianna put her face down close to Megan's stomach and called out softly, "Way to go, baby."

13

When Weston came home from work, Ann Marie ran to meet him. She excitedly threw her arms around him. "Come see what I've done today!"

Ann Marie had informed her boss she could only work part-time until their baby came and that then she'd be quitting for good. She'd spent the extra time working on the baby's room. She and Weston now stood in the doorway, arms draped around each other, and looked in at what would be the nursery for their baby.

In one week's time, she'd painted the room a color that the paint store called "Georgia Peach," made some cute animal cracker curtains for the window, had new carpet installed, and purchased a crib and a changing table, blankets, a month's supply of diapers, and one of the new glider-type rocking chairs so she could rock her baby to sleep.

Weston shook his head in wonder. "This looks great!"

"It's been so much fun!" She kissed Weston on the cheek. "I'm so excited. It's going to happen, isn't it?"

"Sure it is." Weston paused. "Sooner or later."

"I've got an idea. Let's have family home evening in here tonight."

"We never have family home evening."

"I know, but we need to start, don't you think, so it's a part of our life when the baby comes."

Weston nodded. "Whatever you say." They headed into the kitchen. "What's for supper?" he asked.

She made a guilty face. "I have no idea. I was working so hard on the baby's room."

"But we will eat, right? I mean, I think we should. It'll set a good example for the baby if the parents eat."

Ann Marie laughed. "I'm hearing a desperate man here, aren't I? Okay, okay, I get your point. I've been having way too much fun lately, haven't I?"

"It's fun for me, too. Do you want to call out for pizza?"

"That'd be great. I'll go downstairs and get some ginger ale." She started down the stairs but stopped and said, "I've got an idea! Let's have a picnic in the baby's room."

"You sure you want to do that? I mean, what about the new carpet?"

"It's okay if we spill. I need practice cleaning up the carpet for when the baby comes."

Ann Marie put out a red and white checkered tablecloth on the floor of the nursery. They were careful and didn't spill anything. Ann Marie was almost a little disappointed because she'd bought an arsenal of cleaning products in preparation for the baby.

"Let's have the lesson right here on the floor, okay?" she said.

"I don't know how it is for you, but sitting on the floor isn't as easy as it used to be," Weston said, getting to his feet.

He helped Ann Marie up, too. "You're right, but we'll get used to it. Let's take a break. We'll meet back here in ten minutes."

"Why do we need a break?"

"Well, we've got to have refreshments. And you need to work on a story."

"What story?"

Ann Marie started singing the Primary song, "When the family gets together." She added, "See, Daddy tells a story, Mother leads us in a song."

He scowled. "Oh, good grief, we're not really going to sing, are we?"

"We have to."

"I'll go warn the neighbors."

She burst out laughing. "It's not going to be that bad."

"Look, you're talking to a guy who once received a call from the bishop not to be in the youth choir."

"That doesn't matter. You'll get better."

"We're actually going to sing every Monday night?"

"We are. Every Monday night. No exceptions. Okay, you work on your story, and I'll get the refreshments. Do you need to go potty before we start?"

Weston laughed and shook his head. "Potty? You've gone too far this time."

"Sorry, I'm just practicing."

Ten minutes later they were sitting again on the floor in the baby's room.

Weston asked Ann Marie to say the prayer. And then, using a newly purchased copy of the *Children's Songbook,* they sang "Families Can Be Together Forever." By the time they finished, they were fighting back the tears.

And then it was time for a story. Weston read from a book of children's stories Ann Marie had purchased during the week.

" . . . I think I can . . . I think I can . . ."

Ann Marie loved the story. "Tell me another one."

Weston smiled. "You think our child will ever say that?"

"I'm sure of it. You're really very good. Lots of good vocal inflection."

He modestly shrugged. "Well, it's better that way." He put his arm around Ann Marie. "I love you, Annie."

Nobody called her Annie, except Weston, and only when they were alone.

"I love you, too."

"We're not setting ourselves up for heartache, are we?" he asked.

"How do you mean?"

"There are so many couples like us, and so few babies. There is no guarantee in this that we'll get a child."

She pursed her lips. "I know."

"I worry about you, that's all." Positioning himself behind her, he wrapped his arms around her waist and kissed her on the back of her neck.

They gazed up at the crib.

"What are you thinking?" she asked after a minute or two.

"How bad my hips are hurting right now."

She leaned back and they fell over. They ended up on their backs laughing.

"You think I should wallpaper the ceiling? I saw a cute pattern at the paint store. Little farm animals."

"Do we really want our kid thinking animals crawl on the ceiling? I don't think so." He stood up, offered his hand, and then pulled Ann Marie up. "Are we done yet?"

"No, we've got to have a lesson."

"Can we do it at the kitchen table? If I spend any more time on the floor, I'll need hip replacement surgery."

"Okay, we'll adjourn to the kitchen."

Before they began the lesson, she set a plate of chocolate chip cookies on the table.

"You made cookies?"

"Yeah."

"How come?"

"That's what moms do."

"Not anymore. Now they buy them."

"My mother made cookies for us. Sometimes she'd have them ready for us when we came home from school."

"Are you going to actually let me have one of these, or are you saving them for when our child is in first grade?"

"You can have as many as you want."

"Thanks." He reached for one.

She put her hand on his. "After the lesson."

A grin spread across his face. "You want me to do the lesson? I've got one that'll take about thirty seconds . . . and then we can get to the cookies."

"No, I'm going to do it."

"How long will it take?" Weston asked.

"Why are you asking?"

"The cookies look very inviting."

"Am I going to have to put these away, so you'll be able to concentrate on the lesson?"

"You're absolutely right. Here, I'll put them in the pantry."

He kept his back turned to her as he opened the pantry door.

"Weston?"

"What?"

"What are you doing?"

"Nuffing."

"Did you have a cookie?"

"Um-uhm," he said.

"How many cookies did you have?"

Without turning around, he held up one finger.

"There's more than one in there."

He held up two fingers.

"You're setting such a bad example."

He looked around.

"For who?" he mumbled, continuing to chew.

"The baby."

"Why don't we wait until the baby shows up?"

"It's just a matter of time," Ann Marie said.

228

"I hope so."

"Somewhere out there is a girl who is determined to do the best for her baby. She's been to LDS Family Services, and she's thought about her particular situation. Maybe marriage to the biological father isn't the best option for her. So she's wondering what to do. It's not an easy choice. And everybody has an opinion on the subject. But someday she'll learn about us and will sense how much we want a baby in our home, and maybe Heavenly Father will help her decide to trust her baby to us."

"I just don't want you to get hurt by getting your hopes up too high."

She nodded. "I'm going to be all right. Which brings us to our lesson."

She opened her Book of Mormon to Ether, chapter 12, and handed it to Weston. "Will you please read verses 23 through 25?"

Weston began to read:

"'And I said unto him: Lord, the Gentiles will mock at these things, because of our weakness in writing; for Lord thou hast made us mighty in word by faith, but thou hast not made us mighty in writing; for thou hast made all this people that they could speak much, because of the Holy Ghost which thou hast given them;

"'And thou hast made us that we could write but little, because of the awkwardness of our hands. Behold, thou hast not made us mighty in writing like unto the brother of Jared, for thou madest him that the things which he wrote were mighty even as thou art, unto the overpowering of man to read them.

"'Thou hast also made our words powerful and great, even that we cannot write them; wherefore, when we write we behold our weakness, and stumble because of the placing of our words; and I fear lest the Gentiles shall mock at our words."

"Thank you," she said. "That's all for now. Something struck me about this. Moroni was doing what I do sometimes."

"What do you mean?"

"Think about it. There's a thousand years of history contained in what his father had abridged. A thousand years of written documents. And yet Moroni picks out the best writing from that thousand years to compare what he and his father were able to contribute. I do that, too. In fact, I think I've been doing that most of my life."

"Making comparisons?"

She nodded. "I remember in high school wishing I could be as beautiful as Shauna Mortensen, or as gifted a violin player as Judith Carter, or as good at basketball as Jill Dunn. And these were the very best in our school. Well, that's what Moroni is doing here, isn't it? He wishes he could write like the brother of Jared, the best writer over a thousand-year period."

"I see what you mean. I do that, too."

"What's interesting to me is what advice the Savior doesn't give Moroni."

"I can tell you've thought about this a lot."

"It's what you can do when you're not working full-time, and you have time to think. Okay, here are some things the Lord could have told Moroni. He could have said, 'Maybe if you wrote it out on paper first, got your rough draft, then worked it over, made the corrections you need to make, then I think things will work out a little better for you.' That's the 'Just buy a self-help book and work a little on it every day' approach. But that's not what the Savior said."

"You're not saying it's bad to try to learn new skills and get better at something, are you?" he asked.

"No, not at all. But it's not the approach the Savior used with Moroni. Okay, another thing the Savior could have said to Moroni. He could have said, 'It's not that bad, actually. And,

230

in fact, you'd be surprised if you knew how many millions of people are going to have a life-changing experience as they read the Book of Mormon.' But he didn't say that. What did he say? Would you read verses 26 and 27?"

Weston began reading:

"'And when I had said this, the Lord spake unto me, saying: Fools mock, but they shall mourn; and my grace is sufficient for the meek, that they shall take no advantage of your weakness;

"'And if men come unto me I will show unto them their weakness. I give unto men weakness that they may be humble; and my grace is sufficient for all men that humble themselves before me; for if they humble themselves before me, and have faith in me, then will I make weak things become strong unto them.'"

"Thank you," Ann Marie said. "That's what the Lord said. His grace is sufficient for all those who have faith in him. I love that. It brings me such comfort."

"We all need that, don't we?"

"I know I do. There's one more lesson I've picked up. It's found in verse 36, when Moroni prays that the Gentiles will have grace, that they might have charity. Once again, the Lord brings him up short. Will you read verse 37?"

"'And it came to pass that the Lord said unto me: If they have not charity it mattereth not unto thee, thou hast been faithful; wherefore, thy garments shall be made clean. And because thou hast seen thy weakness thou shalt be made strong, even unto the sitting down in the place which I have prepared in the mansions of my Father.'"

"Here's how this applies to me," Ann Marie said. "I've tortured myself, wishing I could be like the women in the ward with a large family. I've gone with the self-help approach. I know as much about how babies are made as any woman I know. I've also tortured myself wondering if the reason why I haven't been able to have children is because of something

231

I did when I was growing up. I've agonized over every action, every harsh word, every sin I've ever committed, looking for the one sin so serious that in his wrath God would punish me by making me unable to have children."

She used a napkin to dab at her eyes. "But, in the end, I am left with what the Lord said to Moroni. I've been faithful, I've seen my weaknesses, and that's all that counts. My disappointment that my life hasn't turned out exactly the way I envisioned is lifted from me when I realize that all the Lord requires from me is to be faithful. Nothing else matters. Just being faithful."

She reached for Weston's hand. "Whatever happens, it's going to be all right. The Savior has promised us that, and I believe him with all my heart. So don't worry about me, okay?"

Weston leaned across the table and kissed her on the forehead. "Do you have any idea how much I adore you?"

"Actually, I think I do." She got up and went to the pantry. "Who wants cookies?" she asked.

"I do!" Weston said.

"I do!" Weston said, imitating a teenage boy.

"I do!" Weston said, imitating a teenage girl.

"I do!" Weston said, imitating a five-year-old boy.

"I do!" Weston said, imitating a three-year-old girl.

Ann Marie made a worried face. "You know what? I'm not sure I made enough for everyone."

"You didn't," Weston said with a big grin.

And, sure enough, he was right.

14

At four months Megan's doctor did an ultrasound test. She was blown away by the images on the screen as he moved the sensor around on her abdomen, pointing out the baby's head, legs, and even the heartbeat. He froze the frame at one point and said, "Well, he's going to be a little man." That reality would ripple through the lives of many people.

♦   ♦   ♦

Megan's regular clothes were now too snug. She went shopping with her mother for loose fitting and casual outfits to wear around the house and a couple of nice maternity dresses for church.

In previous visits with Sister Gardner of LDS Family Services, Megan had outlined the qualities she wanted in the couple who would be adopting her baby.

In her next visit, Sister Gardner gave her letters from three couples who, in general, met Megan's requirements. Glancing at the way the letters began, Megan saw that the people did not know her name. She assumed it was to protect her privacy. They signed their first names but not their last name. Also, Megan had no idea where they lived. She could understand that was to protect their privacy.

"Can I take these home?" she asked.

"Yes, of course. Take your time. There's no hurry. Take all the time you need."

"Are all these couples active in the Church?"

"Yes."

"What about being sealed? Will they be able to have my baby sealed to them in the temple?"

Sister Gardner nodded. "Yes, that's right. After the adoption is final."

"Can I meet with them first and then decide?"

Sister Gardner paused. "Well, if possible, we'd like you to come to a decision without us bringing them in."

"I'm not sure I can make a decision like this without meeting them."

"I understand. Do your best, and please make this a matter of prayer. Heavenly Father knows which couple would be best for your baby."

"What about later? After my baby goes home with the couple I choose, will I find out how he's doing?"

"Yes. You'll receive a letter each month, along with pictures. They'll send the letters to us, and then we'll forward them to you. The same is true of the letters you send to them."

"How long will that last?"

"For at least six months. After that, when the adoption is final, then the amount of correspondence you have is whatever you and the adoptive parents feel comfortable with."

Megan ran her hand over the folder. "It's a big decision."

"That's right. Maybe the biggest you'll ever make. Be sure to pray about it."

"I will, for sure."

At home, after reading the letters, she offered a prayer, asking for help in making the decision.

After the prayer, she still didn't know.

◆　　◆　　◆

Diane Oldham was primed for war when her husband walked in the door on Sunday afternoon, a full three hours after the block of meetings ended. She was waiting for him at the door.

"I need to talk to you, Bishop," she said with anger in her voice.

"When?"

"Now. Right now."

"Can't I eat first?"

"How many people did you talk to after meetings today?"

"I don't know. Five or six, I guess."

"You didn't eat before you talked to them, did you?"

"No."

"Well, then, I deserve as much. I am a member of your ward, aren't I?"

"Okay, let's talk."

"Not here in front of the children. Let's go some place. We can talk in the car."

He couldn't help but let out a troubled sigh. He had been looking forward to coming home and relaxing.

He put his tie back on. "Yes, of course."

"You don't need to put your tie back on."

"It's no problem."

She felt a tinge of conscience for being one more burden he had to carry, but there was no one else she could go to except her bishop.

They drove to a neighborhood school and parked.

"Today in Relief Society I got a new visiting teaching route. Megan's name is on it. You did this, didn't you?"

235

"I had nothing to do with it."

"I don't believe that for an instant. You must have said something to someone in the Relief Society presidency."

"I didn't say a word."

"Then how do you explain me being assigned to her?"

"I have no explanation."

"I'm not assigned to her mother, just Megan. It makes no sense. You must have said something."

"I didn't."

"I will not visit teach her."

"Then you should talk to someone in Relief Society, not me."

"Can't you take care of it?"

"No, I'm sorry. I can't. The assignment didn't come from me. You'll have to explain your reasons to Marilyn Mortenson."

"I will. Don't think I won't. I'm not going to back down."

They drove home. As soon as the car stopped, she got out. "We've already eaten, so if you want something, get it out of the fridge. You can warm it up in the microwave just as well as I can."

"Yes, of course."

She turned to confront him. "Don't you be nice to me. I know you're behind this, one way or another."

He got out of the car. She came around to the driver's side, got in, and drove off.

A minute later she was met at the door of the Relief Society president's house by a three-year-old boy. "Is your mother here?"

He nodded and walked away.

She thought he was going to get his mother, but minutes passed. She stepped inside and waited.

And waited.

"Hello?" she said quietly.

No one answered, but she could hear voices. She walked toward the sound of the voices.

"Hello?" she called out again.

The source of the voices was a TV in the living room. The boy who'd let her in was sitting in front of the set, watching a video about Daniel in the lions' den.

"Hello?" she called out.

"Is someone here?" It was Marilyn Mortenson's voice. Diane took a few more timid steps into the hallway, came to a room, and looked in. There on a large couch with blankets draped over them were Marilyn, two of her kids, and her husband. Everyone else was asleep, but Marilyn and Diane made eye contact.

"I'm sorry," Diane said. "Your boy let me in. I didn't mean to just barge in. I'll go now."

"No, that's fine. We were just taking a nap, that's all. Sunday is such a busy day for us that by this time of the afternoon, we're completely wiped out."

Marilyn managed to untangle herself from the arms, legs, and knees of her children and husband. She was wearing a baggy sweatshirt and some yellow sweatpants.

Diane envied the scene that she'd barged in on. *We never do that on Sundays. It looks so good. I wish we spent more time like that.*

"I am sorry," Diane said.

"It's no problem, really. Let's go in the living room."

The living room had newspapers scattered all over the floor. There was also a box of Cheerios turned on its side, with its little round O's scattered everywhere.

"Looks like Adam has been having a good time while we were napping, doesn't it?" she said, getting down to clean up.

"You don't have to clean up for me."

"All right, I won't," she said, getting up again. "If you can overlook our Sunday mess."

"I can."

237

"Fine. Please sit down. Can I get you something? A glass of water? Some lemonade?" She smiled. "Cheerios?"

"No, I'm fine. I won't take much of your time. I just needed to ask you a question about my visiting teaching. I just wanted to know why I was assigned to Megan Cannon."

"We thought it would be better to have someone who can pour some time into Megan."

"Why did you choose me?"

"Well, I'm not sure, except to say we talked about it at a presidency meeting."

"My husband claims he didn't put you up to it."

"Of course not." She paused. "Is there a problem?"

Diane closed her eyes. *Yes, there's a problem. The whole ward is coddling Megan, turning her into some kind of a celebrity. If we paid as much attention to the girls who don't step out of line, then there would be less of this going on.*

That's what she wanted to say to this woman, still warm from the combined heat from her husband and her children, who had been caught in the act of napping on a Sunday afternoon after church while their little boy, totally unsupervised, made a mess of the house.

She's no better than me, and yet she's the Relief Society president.

"I'm just curious why you've assigned me to be her visiting teacher?" Diane said.

"I'm not sure what you want me to say. Do you want me to say we fasted and prayed about who should visit teach Megan? Well, I'm sorry. We didn't, but I did feel good about our decision. For one thing, you don't work. And your children are all in school. We were hoping you and Sister Baker could visit her during the day when she's all alone."

You can't even keep your house under control. Why should I believe God would guide your decisions?

Adam wandered into the room with a half-gallon of ice cream and a large spoon.

"Adam, you're having a real good time, aren't you?" Marilyn asked with an amused smile.

He smiled back.

"You know the rules, Adam. Let me have the ice cream."

He handed over the ice cream. She took it into the kitchen, returned it to the freezer, and came back into the living room.

"You need to clean up the mess you made, Adam."

"It's too hard for me," he whined.

"You start and I'll help."

Adam sat down on the living room floor and picked up a few Cheerios and put them in the box.

Transfixed, Diane watched the scene playing out in front of her. For every Cheerio Adam placed in the box, his mother did a handful.

"He's not much help at this age, is he?" Diane said.

"He's doing as much as he can. When he does as much as he can, then I step in."

Diane watched this for a few minutes and then the thought gradually came. Diane repeated the words: "He's doing as much as he can, and then you step in." Diane pictured Megan on her hands and knees, picking up the consequences of her mistakes. Who would step in and help her?

"Is there a problem with the assignment?" Marilyn asked.

The image in her mind had disarmed Diane. "No, I just wanted to check with you, that's all."

"I see."

"I'd better be going now."

Have I been wrong all this time? Diane thought.

As she drove home, she felt the gentle tugging of conscience she associated with the influence of the Holy Ghost. *I have been wrong, but there's still time to change.*

When she arrived at home, she found her husband in the kitchen with a full plate of food but not eating because he was on the phone.

She took his fork and took a small taste of the food. It was room temperature. She put it in the microwave to reheat it, then wrote him a note: "Who is it?"

Still listening, he wrote back: "Brother Snyder."

Brother Snyder was a member of the stake high council. She gently removed the phone from her husband's ear. "Hello, Brother Snyder? How are you? Can I ask you a question? Have you had your dinner?"

"Yes, of course," he said over the phone.

"Well, my husband hasn't. Can you call back in a couple of hours? Yes, thank you. Bye."

The microwave dinged. She removed the food and put it in front of him.

"Eat," she said gently.

"How did your meeting go?"

"Good."

"Who's going to visit teach Megan?"

"Sister Baker and I."

"Really?"

"Yes."

"How come?"

"That's who Father in Heaven wants."

She found a box of Cheerios in the cupboard. "After you finish eating, can we take a nap together?"

"We don't take naps." He seemed confused. "Do we?"

"I think we should start."

He yawned. "I guess I could stand a nap."

She put the box of Cheerios on the kitchen table.

"What's that for?"

"In case anyone gets hungry."

"I'm not sure I understand what's going on."

"I know."

"But I like it."

They had a wonderful Sunday afternoon nap together, joined later by their dog, Blue.

Two days later Diane and Sister Baker visited Megan. Barbara Baker, a woman in her mid-sixties, gave the visiting teaching message for the month, then asked Megan, "How are you doing?"

"Good. I mean, considering my . . . situation. I'm doing all right."

"How do you spend your time? You're not working are you?"

"No. I'm mostly just here at home. With everyone else gone during the day, I have a lot of time by myself. I've had a chance to read quite a bit. I'm on my second time reading the Book of Mormon."

"That's wonderful."

"Yes, it's been very helpful."

"Do you ever get discouraged?" Diane asked.

"Honestly? Yes, I do. When I think about how I've messed up and how complicated my life has become, it's hard. I hate that I've hurt people. Not just my mom, but Brianna and Bryce, and my dad. I'm afraid a lot of the time, too, especially when I think about actually having this baby. And when I think about my baby and how he deserved to be born to a mother who'd lived a better life . . ." She sighed. "When I think about those things, then I get very discouraged."

"It must be hard."

"Also, I know I've disappointed a lot of people in the ward. I'm sure they feel bad for my mom, who did everything she could to teach me how to live my life."

"We have such high hopes for our youth," Diane said.

"Can I be perfectly honest? Sister Oldham, I know you've never said anything to me, but I've gotten the feeling that I've been a great disappointment to you."

"Megan, I will be honest with you, too. I've really struggled with my feelings about your situation."

"I can understand that. I went outside the bounds of morality when I truly knew better."

"No, it's not so much that. We all make mistakes. But I've been worried that if we made it too easy on you, or if we made too much of a fuss over you, other girls would think that what had happened to you was no big deal. Or maybe even follow your example—so they could get the same kind of attention."

Megan nodded her head. "I can understand why you'd think that."

"It wasn't anything against you personally."

"Okay. Also, I suppose you were probably aware of how much of your husband's time I was taking."

"Yes. He works very hard at his calling. Sometimes he gives so much there's not much left for him to give our family."

"I'm not meeting with him that often anymore."

"He never tells me who he's meeting with or why."

"That's probably good, that you don't know."

"Yes. I'd rather not know."

"I'm usually okay during the week. As long as I have my morning prayers and read the scriptures, but when I leave the house, then things happen that make me feel bad."

"What kind of things?"

"Like when I meet one of my friends from high school and they ask me what I'm going to do, and I tell them I'm going to place my baby for adoption. And they say, 'I could never do that,' like I'm cold and heartless to even be thinking of letting my baby be adopted."

"Just the opposite is true, though."

"I know. It's because I love him so much that I want him to have more than I can give him. I can't give him a father who will love him. I can't give him a situation where his mother can stay home and be with him all the time. I can't give him any of that."

"I think it's commendable that you're thinking of his welfare more than your own," Sister Baker said.

"That's the way I see it, but my friends from high school don't see it that way." She paused. "And then there are the people who think I'm a fool for not having had an abortion. To them, seeing me getting bigger, knowing I've given up all my social life, to them I'm a fool. That's hard to take, too."

"I'm sure it is," Diane said.

"Sometimes it's hard to go to church, too."

"Is it?"

"Yes. I'm still not allowed to partake of the sacrament. That was one of the things the bishop asked of me while I go through the process of repentance. At first it didn't mean that much to me, except that I was embarrassed to have the deacons wonder about me. But now, after studying the gospel so much, I can see the value of the sacrament, and I want to take it, but I can't."

Sister Baker smiled. "I raised four deacons. Believe me, they don't think about things like that. Heavenly Father was wise to appoint twelve-year-old boys to pass the sacrament."

"That's good to know." Megan focused her gaze on the floor. "Also, at church, I can tell by the way people look at me how they feel about me."

Diane wiped her eyes. "I'm sorry I've been one of those."

"Thanks for admitting that." Megan cleared her throat. "To tell you the truth, when you called and said you'd been asked to be my visiting teacher, I didn't know what to expect. I wondered if you were going to come and tell me what a sinner I've been. The thing is, I know that. I'm not sure you could say anything that I haven't said to myself."

"I've had a change of heart."

Megan smiled. A thin, little smile.

Diane had only intended to pat Megan's arm, but it turned into a hug that left them in tears.

"God sent you both to me, didn't he?" Megan asked.

"Yes, I believe he did."

243

15

Megan was talking to her mother about how they were going to decorate for Christmas when suddenly she stopped talking. With a look of astonishment on her face, she put her hand on her stomach. "Oh, my gosh! I can feel the baby moving. Here. Put your hand here."

Carolyn gently placed her hand on Megan's tummy and felt a tiny movement. "Well, hello, little one. We're glad you've come to say hello."

"This is so amazing!" Megan cried out. "I'm really going to have a baby, aren't I?"

"Looks that way."

"My little baby."

"Yes, what a thrill it is to hold your baby in your arms and count all its fingers and toes. Every birth is such a miracle."

Tears of joy began to run down Megan's cheeks.

Over the next few days, she made sure each member of the family had a chance to feel the fluttering motions of her baby. Brianna put her mouth close to Megan's tummy and sang to it. Bryce was too self-conscious and pulled away after about two seconds. Her father smiled broadly as he felt the motion.

"Too bad we can't tell Heather about this," Megan said.

They still had not told Heather about her pregnancy, using the excuse that they didn't want her to worry or be diverted in any way from missionary work.

Megan tried to get Thomas to feel the motion, but he was too embarrassed to even try. "We're best friends, but I'm not sure you want me doing that."

"C'mon, I'm wearing this heavy sweater. It'll just feel like there's a mouse inside my stomach, that's all."

He felt uneasy. "How about if I just take your word for it?"

Elizabeth wasn't at all bashful. "Wow, there is something in there after all, isn't there?"

"I think so," Megan said happily.

"Have you decided who you want to adopt your baby?" Elizabeth asked.

"Not yet. I'm still working on it."

As Megan read and reread the three letters Sister Gardner had given her, one couple kept coming to the top, the couple whose first names were Weston and Ann Marie. When her mother read over the letters, she also rated them very highly.

And so Megan prayed.

And prayed.

And prayed.

After a week she'd come to a decision. It would be Weston and Ann Marie.

"I'll let them know," Sister Gardner said. "You can be sure, they'll be thrilled."

Arrangements were made to meet the couple in Sister Gardner's office.

Megan wanted this first meeting to be special. She decided to buy a baby outfit and present it to them as a token of what she would be giving to them in a few months.

She went shopping by herself for a baby outfit that her son could be blessed in by his father.

It was the Christmas season and even on a Wednesday morning Wal-Mart was packed with people. Megan went to the racks with baby clothes and slowly looked at each one, excited to be doing something for her baby.

And then it struck her. *This is the only time in my life I'll buy clothes for this baby. I won't ever buy him socks and I won't ever buy him shoes and I won't ever buy him a white shirt for church. This baby, who is stretching and rolling around inside of me, will never call me Mommy. He won't nurse from me or be changed by me or be cuddled at night when he's crying. I'll never read to him. I won't be the one to teach him to ride a bicycle. He'll never come to me in tears with a scratched knee.*

This is it. All I will ever give to my baby is this one little outfit.

It was too hard. On the verge of crying, she had to leave the store.

She hurried to her car and drove to a park and sat in her car and mourned the loss that was to come. *How can I do this? How can I give up my child?*

She drove to Home Depot and went to the information desk and asked them to page her brother.

A few minutes later, Bryce showed up.

"What's wrong?"

"I need to talk to you."

"You look terrible."

"Where can we go to talk?"

"Lumber."

They ended up in a cavernous room, stacked to the ceiling with forests' worth of lumber.

"So, what's wrong?"

She told him about shopping for an outfit for her baby.

246

"It's not the only thing you're ever going to give your baby," he said.

"What else am I going to give him?"

"A mom and a dad who've been waiting for years for him to show up. That's better than any set of clothes you could ever buy."

"This is so hard, Bryce."

His first reaction was to discount what she was saying because it involved the emotions, but then, in a rare display of concern, he said tenderly, "I know it is. It's probably the hardest thing you'll ever do. I wish I could make it easier." He bit his lip. "I do that here, you know, for people with projects. But for this project I'm pretty much at a loss to know what to do to make your pain all go away."

"Could you give me a hug?" she asked tentatively.

"On company time?"

"Yes."

He smiled faintly. "Usually they frown on us hugging the customers."

"I'm not a customer."

"Then I guess it'll be all right."

He held her in his arms and then kissed her on the cheek.

"Sometimes it's almost like you're . . . well, a real human being," she said.

He chuckled. "We'd better not let that get around, okay?"

"Okay."

"Can I interest you in a load of plywood while you're here?"

"You know, I just bought some the other day."

"Well, come back when you want some more. I'll give you a good deal."

He walked her to her car and hugged her again before she got in.

He even watched her drive off.

Megan returned to the store and bought an outfit her son could wear when he was blessed in church.

♦   ♦   ♦

Sister Gardner asked Megan to take a seat in a small conference room while waiting for Weston and Ann Marie to arrive. Her heart pounding and feeling more anxious than she ever remembered being, Megan sat alone with her thoughts. *How can I be sure this is right? What if these people are weird? I mean, they're strangers, and here I am thinking of giving them my baby. Just giving him to them?*

The clock on the wall had a minute hand that jumped ahead every sixty seconds. It was now ten minutes after the scheduled meeting time.

I wonder what they think of me? I don't know what Sister Gardner has told them. They probably think I'm some little tramp, who goes around sleeping with guys and getting pregnant. I'm not though. That's not the way it was.

In the silence of the room, the minute hand jumped to fifteen minutes after the hour.

"We're so sorry we're late," she heard a woman's voice say. "We got lost."

"It's no problem. We're just glad you arrived. Please come with me, and I'll make the introductions."

Megan stood up as Ann Marie burst into the room, full of apologies.

"We took a wrong turn," Weston added.

The man reminded Megan of someone who could have played the sheriff in a western movie. He was tall, lean, and big-boned, with broad shoulders. He was wearing slacks and a white shirt and tie for the occasion, like he might wear to church, but the cowboy boots gave him away.

His pretty wife was also tall, wore a dress, and had her

blonde hair pulled up, seemingly more to get it out of the way than to show it off.

Sister Gardner introduced them by their first names and then gestured for them all to be seated at the conference table.

"Megan has prepared a list of questions. Megan?"

Ann Marie was smiling but looked nervous. Weston was unable to keep his big hands still on the tabletop.

Megan pulled out a paper and unfolded it in front of her.

She looked at Weston. "You'll be the daddy for my baby. Can I ask you a question? What was your dad like when you were growing up?"

Weston cleared his throat. He smiled as he said, "I grew up on a farm, so my dad always had work for us to do. But he didn't just tell us what to do. He worked alongside my brothers and me."

"Was he good to you?"

"He was. He wasn't the kind to take vacations, but every so often my dad would just take the day off with us, and we'd go fishing or even just float down the river in inner tubes."

Megan looked at her notes. "Were you afraid of him?"

Weston chuckled. "Well, we never talked back to him, but that was because we respected him. But, no. We weren't afraid of him."

"Did you love him?"

"Our family wasn't one to *talk* about love. But I loved him, and I knew he loved me. Because of how much time he spent with me and all the things he tried to teach me—not just about farming, but about other things, like always telling the truth and being honest and working hard . . . things like that."

"Was he religious?"

Weston smiled. "I never think of him like that, but I guess he was. He served as a bishop for six years, so that probably counts as being religious. He didn't preach much, though, if that's what you mean. Right now he and my mom are temple ordinance workers, so they've turned out okay, I guess." He smiled as he said it.

Megan turned to Ann Marie. "How long have you been trying to have a baby?"

"It's going on nine years," she said.

For a moment Megan saw in Ann Marie's expression the pain and anguish that had played out over that time, but then Ann Marie covered it up with a weak smile.

Then she said, "Having a baby has been the most important thing in our lives. But when you're doing everything they say, and nothing happens . . . month after month . . ." She hesitated. "I'm sorry. I'm sure you don't want to know any of that, do you? I'll just say that, eventually, when we couldn't go on the way we'd been going, we talked it over and finally decided to try to adopt." She cleared her throat. "We've been waiting for such a long time. I promise you, we'll give him all the love he deserves."

Weston put his arm around Ann Marie's shoulder. "You'll never find a better mother than this gal."

Megan looked into their hopeful faces. It was a strange situation. Even though she was so much younger than they, she could feel them wanting her to like them, hoping she would be impressed enough to grant them their desire.

Her heart went out to them. They were obviously good people. Sister Gardner had recommended them, and they wanted this so much. It felt right. Her own heart pounding, she folded up her notes and reached down and picked up a gift-wrapped box she had set on the floor next to her chair.

She slid the box across the table to Ann Marie and said, "May I be the first to congratulate you both."

Ann Marie brought her hands to her mouth, then turned to look at her husband, tears springing into her eyes. He put his arms around her and held her without speaking.

They opened their gift to find a baby outfit. Ann Marie

250

took it out of the box and held it, just looking at it, tears rolling down her cheeks.

After a time Ann Marie said, "Five years ago we bought a tiny pair of cowboy boots in hopes that someday we'd have a little boy to fill them. They've been on our mantle ever since, and now, finally, we're going to have a boy who can wear them."

"Thank you for this . . . outfit," Weston said, fighting to keep from bawling.

"We have a gift for you, too," Ann Marie said. She stepped into the next room and brought back a beautifully wrapped present. Megan opened it. It was a photo album. "This is for you to keep the pictures we'll be sending you of your baby."

Megan felt a rush of emotion, as did Ann Marie, and they met in a big hug.

The thought ran through Megan's mind as she was being held by Ann Marie, *I'm giving my boy far more than I could ever give him by myself. I'm doing the right thing for him. And that's what counts.*

◆　　◆　　◆

Two Sundays before Christmas, Megan attended her dad's Gospel Doctrine class.

It was another masterpiece. Her dad used excerpts from Handel's *Messiah* along with video clips of the General Authorities bearing their testimonies of the Savior's mission.

It was a wonderful presentation and brought many compliments after class.

But like all of his lessons, there was no class participation.

Megan wished there had been time for class members to talk about their testimonies of the Savior, because if there had, she would have told what he now meant to her.

That night her father came to her. "How did you think the lesson went today?"

251

"It was a wonderful lesson."

"Yes, I've had many compliments. Several people want copies."

"Every week you just get better and better," she said.

"Something's missing though."

"What more could you have done?"

He put his hand on her shoulder. "You know what this reminds me of?"

"What?"

"Our father-daughter interviews when we used to hide the truth from each other. When I pretended that I wanted to know details about your life, and you pretended to tell me the truth. I mean, we have gotten beyond that, haven't we?"

"We should have by now," she said with a sigh. "After all we've gone through."

"So tell me what you really think about my lessons."

"I'm not a teacher. I wouldn't know what to tell you."

"Tell me how you feel."

She let out a deep sigh. "You talk about the Savior each week, and I sit there almost overcome with my gratitude to him for providing me a way to be forgiven of my sins, and I want to bear my testimony, but you don't ask anyone to do that. Sometimes I feel like your lessons are designed to get people to compliment you for being such a great teacher."

She grimaced. It was a harsh thing to say, and she was fearful he would take offense. He didn't seem to, though.

"What should I do differently?"

"I think members of the class need opportunities to bear their testimonies about what the Savior has meant in their lives."

"How can I do that?"

She shrugged her shoulders. "I don't know. I'm not the teacher."

"Let me think about it, and I'll get back to you."

"Sounds good."

He was about to leave when she said, "Dad?"

"Yes?"

"If we're being honest with each other, then why don't we tell Heather I'm expecting a baby?"

"We haven't wanted to distract her from her mission."

"If I were her, I'd be insulted not to be told the truth."

"Let's go talk to your mother about this."

Five minutes later they agreed to tell Heather.

Megan told her on the phone on Christmas Day when Heather called to wish them a merry Christmas.

"I knew something wasn't right," she said. "I'm glad you told me."

"We don't have family secrets anymore," Megan said. "So don't you keep anything from us either, okay?"

"It's a deal," she said.

◆　　◆　　◆

Elizabeth was dead set on going to BYU winter semester. She had a high enough GPA, and her audition tape featuring her on the piano was enthusiastically received by the music department. She phoned often enough that she finally gained provisional acceptance, with the understanding that she'd only take evening classes during her first semester.

After she was accepted, Elizabeth worked on talking Thomas into going with her. Since he was working and only taking one class a semester, she argued he could do the same thing in Provo, where he could enroll at UVSC while waiting to get into BYU.

She eventually wore him down, and he agreed to her plan. Out of respect for their family, they attended one last Sunday family supper. It was the first one they'd attended since joining the Church.

"Where you two been?" Uncle Al asked. "Your grandmother asks about you all the time. You're breaking her heart by never coming around anymore."

"It's good to see you again, too," Elizabeth said.

"So, you got that Mormon thing out of your system yet? I knew it was just a matter of time before you gave up on it."

"Not really. We're moving to Utah."

"No, you're not. You wouldn't be that heartless—to abandon your family."

"You know what, Uncle Al? We'll miss you telling us how to live our lives," Thomas said with a good-natured grin.

"I hope you know you're going to break your grand-mother's heart."

"Sometimes I think you say that just so you can control us," Elizabeth said. "We'll talk to Gramma. I think she'll be glad for us. We're going to get a college education."

"You think there's no colleges out here? Is that what you think?"

Elizabeth smiled politely. "Nice to see you again."

On January 3 they left for Utah. All the way there Elizabeth insisted they listen to a CD of the BYU Men's Chorus.

16

egan's baby was growing. Now, when she felt him
moving, she could sometimes distinguish between
a tiny arm or leg and a head or buttocks. The baby's
heartbeat was strong enough to be heard with a stethoscope.

In January life seemed to slow down to a crawl for Megan.
No more missionary discussions. No going to Leo's Pizza to
talk to Thomas. No friends she'd known in high school to
visit with. They'd written her off, either because she was going
to have the baby or else because she was going to place it for
adoption.

Her due date was May 10. At times it seemed that date
would never come. And at other times, she wished it wouldn't;
she knew there would be a great sense of loss in giving up her
baby, who, by now, seemed to have a personality, communi-
cating to her with his kicking and tapping on the walls of the
place that was his home until he would be born.

She spent her days at home, mostly alone. Brianna worked
after school, and so she was gone a great deal of the time.
Bryce continued to work full-time at Home Depot.

And, of course, her father was always gone, leaving each Monday, returning every Friday, on the road all the time. It was a pattern she'd grown up with.

But near the end of the month, he announced to his family that he'd told his boss he was tired of being gone all the time. The company found him a place in the home office. It paid less but at least he'd be home every night.

On his first day at his new job, he came home happier than Megan had ever seen him. To celebrate they all went out to supper.

Also, in January Elder Spaulding went home from his mission. Megan didn't get to see him off. It would have meant a long drive to the airport. And, besides, she hadn't been asked.

Ann Marie and Weston wrote several letters to Sister Gardner, and she passed them on to Megan. They were excited and making preparations. They sent photographs of the baby's room.

She still met occasionally with Bishop Oldham, but they were running out of issues that needed to be resolved. She had faithfully gone through the process of repentance he had outlined. She'd read the Book of Mormon twice since she started meeting with him. She had also finished reading *The Miracle of Forgiveness,* and they had discussed each chapter in detail.

"Is there anything else we need to do?" he asked after one of their visits.

She thought for a minute. "There is one thing, Bishop. I feel like I've made a lot of progress, but when will I know I have been forgiven?"

He leaned forward across his desk. "I can't give you a time. That is something that only you and the Lord will know. The only thing I can tell you is that if you keep going on the road you're on, the time will come when you will know in your heart that you are forgiven."

He leaned back in his chair and studied her face. "I think it's time for you to begin partaking of the sacrament again."

She closed her eyes and tried to keep from crying. "I would like that very much."

"Do you understand why I asked you not to partake of the sacrament?"

"So that I would appreciate its significance?"

"That's right. The sacrament is a sacred ordinance. If we partake of it, knowing that we are unrepentant, it no longer becomes a blessing to us. I wanted you to be ready."

She grabbed a tissue and wiped her face. "Thank you very much."

"There's something else about the sacrament. Let's look at the prayers."

Bishop Oldham flipped through the pages of the Doctrine and Covenants until he found what he was looking for. He had Megan read the two prayers.

Then he asked, "When we partake of the bread and water, who do we remember?"

"Jesus Christ."

"That's right. And what do we say we are willing to do?"

Megan looked at the prayers again. "Take his name upon us."

"And?"

"Always remember him and keep his commandments."

"You made that same promise when you were what?"

She looked at him without understanding.

"When you were eight years old . . ."

"Baptized?"

"Exactly. So, when you partake of the sacrament, you are really renewing your baptismal covenant. Does that make sense?"

"I never thought of it in that way."

"Now consider this. When you were baptized, it was for what?"

257

"The remission of my sins."

"Megan, think about that. When you partake of the sacrament worthily, after having truly repented, you can be as clean and acceptable to the Lord as you were when you were baptized. Can you think of anything more wonderful?

"As you take the bread and water, think about what he did for you. Remember the price he paid in Gethsemane and on the cross. If it weren't for the Atonement, none of us would have any hope. But because he has already paid for our sins, he can forgive them. Listen to the words of the sacramental prayers and be grateful for his love and mercy. That's what I want you to do."

"I will. I promise I will."

"Then I'm not sure we need to continue meeting on a regular basis. If you have problems, please let me know, and we can talk, but, otherwise, I think we're done here."

"I'll try not to have to come back."

He smiled. "I'll miss talking to you."

"Maybe out in the hall," she suggested.

"Let's do that."

He stood up and shook her hand and walked her to the door.

"Thank you for all you've done for me," she said.

"If you've been comforted, that's come from the Savior. He's the one you should thank."

"You know what I mean."

"Yes, of course."

She wanted to give him a hug but didn't.

The next Sunday she partook of the sacrament. It was an amazing experience to her.

It was a holy day.

April, Ninth Month

For Megan life revolved around her family and the baby she carried.

When she lay in bed at night, she could sometimes see her whole tummy change shape as the baby moved. It was getting harder to move around. Her stomach seemed to be in the way whatever she did, and because she was retaining water and her ankles were swollen, walking became a challenge. Her lower back also sometimes ached.

As general conference approached, Megan began to look forward to watching it. It was the first time in her life she'd ever felt that way—not just because the talks and music promised to be good but because she had heard that if members of the Church will approach the experience prayerfully, and listen carefully, they will receive promptings that will help them answer some of their questions and worries.

It was with that hope that she faithfully listened to each session of conference.

What she wanted to be assured was not so much if God could forgive her for what she'd done, but to know if he would hold it against her in some way, if she would forever be on his list of those who had messed up and had to set their lives back on course.

She wanted some assurance that she could still have all the blessings promised to members of the Church.

And, to her amazement, that was the topic of Elder Richard G. Scott's conference address. She felt as though he were speaking directly to her when he said:

"If you have repented from serious transgression and mistakenly believe that you will always be a second-class citizen in the kingdom of God, learn that is not true. The Savior said:

"'Behold, he who has repented of his sins, the same is forgiven, and I, the Lord, remember them no more.

"'By this ye may know if a man repenteth of his sins—behold, he will confess them and forsake them. . . . ' (D&C 58:42-43).'

"To you who have sincerely repented yet continue to feel the burden of guilt, realize that to continue to suffer for sins when there has been proper repentance and forgiveness of the Lord is prompted by the master of deceit. Lucifer will encourage you to continue to relive the details of past mistakes, knowing that such thoughts can hamper your progress. . . .

"When memory of past mistakes encroaches upon your mind, turn your thoughts to the Redeemer and to the miracle of forgiveness with the renewal that comes through Him. Your depression and suffering will be replaced by peace, joy, and gratitude for His love.

"How difficult it must be for Jesus Christ, our Savior and Redeemer, to see so many needlessly suffer, because His gift of repentance is ignored. It must pain Him deeply to see the pointless agony both in this life and beyond the veil that accompany the unrepentant sinner after all He did so that we need not suffer."

It was the answer she'd been looking for.

◆　　◆　　◆

MAY 29, PAST DUE

A little after two in the afternoon, Megan's labor pains began. At first she thought it was just false labor, but when the pains became worse, she became concerned.

Since The Home Depot was only five minutes away, compared to where her father and mother worked, Bryce had been designated the one for her to call when she needed to go to the hospital.

260

As she reached for the phone, Bryce was at that moment talking to the most amazing young woman he'd ever met—a brunette with short hair that bounced when she turned her head, high cheekbones that made him wonder if she was part American Indian, and blue eyes that reminded him of a deep lake. She said she was planning to add a garage to a house she'd just bought, but, unlike so many young women who wandered the aisles of Home Depot, trolling for guys, she didn't seem to need help. That bothered Bryce. Women customers always needed him. But this one didn't seem to.

"I could give you some tips about this if you'd like," he said.

She looked up from the list of supplies she needed.

"No, I'm okay."

"A lot of people forget to cut the top plate so it breaks at the center of a stud."

"I know that, but thanks anyway."

"You sure?"

"Positive. I've been helping my dad build houses since I was twelve."

"Then why did you come here?" he blurted out.

"For supplies."

He felt himself blushing. "Oh, sure."

She went back to studying her list of materials. He just stood there and stared at her.

She looked up. "Don't you have some other customers who actually need help?"

"Look, if you want, I could come out on my day off and help you."

"Why would you want to do that?"

"I'd like to get to know you."

"Is that why you work here, to meet women?"

"I've never done this before."

"Yeah, right," she scoffed.

261

"Forget about me. Let's talk about your project. Are you telling me you couldn't use a hand?"

"Are you any good?"

"Better than you."

"Now I know you're lying."

"Try me out and see."

"Well—"

"Give me at least a try. If I don't work out, then you can just tell me to get lost."

"Well, okay."

"I'll need to know your name and address and phone number."

She said, "My name is Jordan Taylor" and had just written her phone number on a scrap of paper when one of Bryce's coworkers hurried over to him. "Bryce, your wife called. She's in labor. She needs you to give her a ride to the hospital."

Jordan threw up her hands. "You're getting my address while your wife is about to have a baby?"

"No! You don't understand! I'm not married."

She glared at him. "You are *so* pathetic."

"No, it's not like that. She's my sister. We live just a few blocks from here. That's why she called me. To take her to the hospital."

"Just give it a rest, okay?"

"I've got to go now, but I'll call you." He stuffed the paper with her number on it into his pocket and turned and ran for the door.

Five minutes later Bryce burst into the house. "I'm here! Let's go!"

Megan was sitting on the couch in the living room, her arms wrapped around her sides as she rocked back and forth, writhing with pain.

"Just give me a minute, okay?"

"Sure. Do you need me to get you anything upstairs?"

"No, I've got it all here in this bag."

"I'll take it out to the car."

She nodded.

"He carried her suitcase out to the car and then hurried back.

She stood up. "I think I can move now."

He held his arm out for her to hold as they slowly made their way to the car.

He opened the car door for her and helped her in, then raced around to the other side of the car, jumped in, and backed down the driveway.

"How much of a hurry are you in?"

Her eyes were closed. "Just drive the way you usually do. That'll be fast enough."

A few minutes later, when a stoplight changed to green, Bryce gunned it, pushing Megan's head against the headrest. She grimaced with pain.

"Go easy, okay?"

"Oh, sure, sorry."

The admittance process went smoothly, and ten minutes later Megan was lying in a bed in the Women's Center, in the room where she would give birth and also be staying. She paid no attention, but unlike a normal hospital room, it was nicely furnished, with subdued lighting and a bed that had a brass rail headboard.

While the nurse was settling Megan in, Bryce called his parents and told them to come right away.

Then, just when she was so close to delivery, things slowed down dramatically.

"You want to go back to work?" she asked.

"No, I'll stay here with you."

She smiled. "Thanks."

It was quiet, except for the occasional sound of a woman in the next room, who was in the last stage of delivery and cried out in pain whenever she had a contraction.

"She sounds like she's having a rough time," Megan said.

"Sounds like it."

"I suppose I'll be just like her before very long."

"I suppose." Bryce paused. "I met this incredible girl today. She's going to build a garage."

"What made her incredible?"

"She didn't need my help. She said she's been building things with her dad since she was twelve."

"What is she like?"

"Well, she knew not to buy the top grade two-by-fours. That's where a lot of people go wrong. You don't need that for a garage."

"I meant what did she look like?"

"She looked real good."

Megan smiled. "You're going to make me pry this out of you, aren't you?"

"I could hardly keep my eyes off her."

"Describe her to me."

"She looks like a girl who'd sell backpacks on the Home Shopping Network."

"So, you like her then, right?"

"Yeah, pretty much." He sighed. "She has kind of a bad impression of me, though. When one of the guys came to tell me you'd called, he said that my wife was having her baby. Naturally that put a damper on our relationship. I tried to explain, but I'm not sure she believed me. I have her number here if you want to call her."

She gave him a wry smile. "Maybe later. I'm kind of busy here now."

Carolyn was the first to arrive. Her face was full of concern. "Megan, how are you doing?"

"The pains slowed down for a while, but they're starting to come back."

"Your father should be here any minute."

"Good. What about Brianna?"

"She's working. I haven't tried to get hold of her."

"I think you should."

"She might not be able to get off work."

"Maybe not, but she should be told." Megan paused. "Remember, no secrets, no holding back."

"I'll call her work and see if I can talk to her."

Carolyn left the room, and Bryce came to stand at the side of Megan's bed. She didn't have much energy to carry on a conversation, so he just stood there, keeping her company. Whenever she felt a labor pain, she would take hold of his hand and squeeze.

"Megan, you know what? I'm sorry I chased you through the house with the vacuum cleaner when you were little."

"I can't remember that."

"You were about four years old. You were screaming. I think you really thought I'd vacuum you up."

"Why would I think that?"

"Well, maybe because that's what I said I was going to do."

She smiled weakly. "That would explain why I have an irrational fear of vacuum cleaners."

"There's more," he said.

"Not now, Bryce. Just hold my hand."

A labor pain came. She squeezed.

"That's quite a grip. You been working out?"

"Would you go tell Mom to phone Sister Gardner and tell her I'm in labor? Then she can call Weston and Ann Marie."

Megan, now alone, waited for the next contraction. It was all she could really think about—how bad would it be and how many more of them were yet to come.

After a few minutes, her mother came in to be with her. "I phoned Sister Gardner. She said she'd call the adoptive parents."

"Mom, I'm really scared."

265

"Of course you are. It is a scary experience, especially the first time."

"Was it for you?"

"It was. Very much. But I got through it, just like you will."

Her dad came in the room.

"Daddy, can I have a priesthood blessing?"

"Yes, of course."

"Ask Bryce to assist you."

"Bryce? He'll never do it."

"Maybe not, but ask him anyway."

Her dad left to go ask Bryce.

Bryce returned. "I can't do that."

"I wish you could."

"I know. Me, too."

"You're one of the most honest guys I've ever known, Bryce. If I can change, anyone can. Even you."

He nodded his head but didn't commit to anything.

Walter returned and, with Carolyn and Bryce in the room, he laid his hands on her head, took a deep breath, and in a quiet voice blessed her that she would get through the birth process safely and have a healthy baby.

Megan kept her eyes closed after the blessing as the tears ran down her face. Carolyn was crying, too.

◆　　◆　　◆

The night dragged on.

Ann Marie and Weston arrived at the hospital a little after three in the morning. Ann Marie knocked on the half-open door and then stepped into the room. She took Megan's hand. "I'm sorry you're in so much pain. I wish I could take some of it."

"I know."

They talked about details for a few minutes, and then Ann Marie left to allow a family member to be with her.

The doctor, an older man who was substituting for Doctor Sullivan, broke her water about three-thirty in the morning. The contractions that followed were intense, about two minutes apart, and lasted about a minute each.

The nurse instructed Megan not to move during contractions, but the next one was so painful she thrashed around a bit until it was over.

"How am I supposed to hold still?" she complained. "It hurts!"

As the pain momentarily subsided, she closed her eyes and said a silent prayer. She asked Father in Heaven to help her get through the ordeal and to bless the baby.

Right after that she was given an epidural, which took away much of the pain.

Later, during hard labor, Megan began shaking uncontrollably due to a reaction to the epidural. Nothing could stop it.

"Would you like another blessing?" her dad asked.

"Yes, please."

As he put his hands on her head and gave her a blessing, the shaking subsided. Her dad promised her she would have control over her body and that her baby would come quickly.

She was in tears when he finished his blessing. "Thank you."

The doctor examined her and said she had some more pushing to do.

She didn't think she could stand any more of this. Even though there were people in the room—the doctor, a nurse, her mother—she closed her eyes and spoke softly, "Father in Heaven, if I ever needed you, I need you now. When it comes time to push, I need you to push this baby out for me."

"What's she doing?" the doctor asked Megan's mother.

"Praying."

The doctor rolled his eyes but made no comment.

Megan opened her eyes.

He explained the process of pushing and had her do three, small, practice pushes just to make sure she understood. And then he turned to the nurse. "I'm going to grab a cup of coffee. Call me when you need me."

The next contraction was beginning.

"Okay, Heavenly Father, I need you to take this baby out," she said softly.

She pushed.

"What's she doing?" the doctor asked.

"Having a baby?" her mother asked.

Megan pushed, and the baby's head came out.

"Good grief!" the doctor said, rushing to get his gloves on. "I can't believe it!"

Megan heard the sound of a baby crying. "Thank you, Father in Heaven."

"My sentiments exactly," the doctor said.

◆　　◆　　◆

After the baby had been bathed and wrapped in a receiving blanket, the nurse laid him in her arms. "Will you be nursing the baby?" she asked.

"No."

The nurse returned with a bottle.

It was, at once, the happiest and saddest day she'd ever known. As tears streamed down her face, she looked at and touched and spoke to her baby. He was the greatest miracle she had ever experienced. She loved him more than she had ever loved anyone before in her life.

17

It began with an offhanded comment by one of the nurses. "I know I should admire you for giving up your baby to a married couple, but it's not something I could ever do. I love my children too much to do that."

The remark devastated Megan so much she began to have doubts if she was doing the right thing.

When they take him away, I will lose everything, she thought.

Her mom and dad showed up a while later. They had gone home for a few hours of sleep and were just coming back.

"Can we see the baby?" her dad asked.

A few minutes later, Walter picked up his grandson for the first time.

"Oh, he's a fine one, that's for sure. Look how strong he is. Look how he's holding onto my finger."

"He is so adorable," her mother said.

"I wonder if we could get a picture of me holding the baby," her father said.

"I brought my camera," Megan said. "It's in my bag over there."

"I can take the picture," Carolyn said.

"No, you both have to be in it. Let's see if we can get a nurse to do it."

A minute later the picture was taken of Walter and Carolyn proudly showing off the baby. And then they took several pictures of Megan with him.

Then it was her mother's turn to dote on the baby. As Megan watched her mother hold her baby boy and coo, Megan realized she had been the recipient of the love her mother was now showering on this child.

"To tell the truth," Megan said, "I've been thinking about keeping him."

"Really?" her mother said.

"Things were so clear to me before he was born. Now, with him here, it's harder to think clearly. And then this nurse said she loved her kids too much to ever be able to give them away."

"It's because you love him so much that you're doing this. You're thinking of his welfare above your own interests," her mother said.

Sister Gardner of LDS Family Services dropped by an hour later and asked Megan how she was doing.

"I'm having a tough time with this," Megan said. "I'm having second thoughts."

Sister Gardner nodded. "I can understand that."

With tears in her eyes, Megan asked, "Why did I ever agree to give up my baby?"

"Because you based your decision on what would be best for the child."

Megan broke down and sobbed.

Sister Gardner sat by her side and held her hand.

"I love my baby," she sobbed.

"Of course you do, Megan."

There was nothing that could be said. No magic words to make it all better.

"I want to talk to Bryce. Where is he?"

"I'll go ask your mom to get him."

Forty-five minutes later, Bryce showed up. "You wanted to see me?"

"I want you to hold my baby."

"Sure, no problem."

A few minutes later Bryce was holding her baby.

"Isn't he the most wonderful baby in the world?" Megan asked.

"He is, no doubt about it. I think he looks a lot like me when I was a baby."

Megan smiled through her tears. "That's why he's wonderful?"

"Yeah, pretty much," he said with his mischievous grin.

"While you're holding him, you tell me that I should go ahead and give him away."

She'd never seen Bryce emotional. He fought it, but she could tell because he brushed a hand underneath his right eye. "It's best for the kid, Megan. That's what I've always said. It's the truth, and you know it."

She nodded, then asked him to leave, so she could be alone with her baby boy.

After he left, she began to sob. But this time it was not out of desperation or being torn by indecision. She could not doubt the validity of her former decision.

She was going to place her baby. And it cut her to the very core of her existence.

◆　◆　◆

A day later, an hour after Megan had been released from the hospital, she placed her baby in Ann Marie's arms. Ann

271

Marie leaned forward and kissed Megan on the cheek. "Thank you for giving us such a wonderful baby."

Ann Marie smiled through her tears as Weston stepped forward to give Megan a hug. "I promise you, I'll be a good daddy."

"I know you will," she said, barely able to speak.

Ann Marie and Weston turned and left with their new baby.

That night, at two-fifteen in the morning, Megan got out of bed and went downstairs. Her mother must have heard her because she came down to check on her.

Megan was on the patio in the backyard, looking up at the stars.

"He'll see the same stars I will."

"That's true." Her mother put her arm around her. "He'll be all right."

"I know he will. My question is, will I?"

"You did the right thing."

"I did the right thing for him."

"Yes. That's what mothers do."

"My little angel has gone away."

Her mother brought her into her arms just like she'd done when Megan was little. "Oh, Megan, I know it's hard. I wish I could make it easier."

"The baby was the one who got me back on the right track," Megan said.

"Yes, I guess, in a way, that's true."

"And now he's gone. I feel so empty, like there's nothing left, that all the good in me left with him."

"That's not true."

"How do you know that? I'm not sure who I am anymore."

◆　　◆　　◆

A Week Later

Megan had slept until ten in the morning. She got something to eat but delayed getting into the shower, waiting for the mail to come. She had already received some pictures of Joshua from Ann Marie and Weston and was hoping there would be some more that day.

She heard the sound of mail being shoved through their slot next to the front door and went to see what had come. There was nothing from Ann Marie and Weston, but there was a letter from Elder Spaulding.

She tore the letter open and sat down on the couch. There was a letter and a wedding announcement, with a photograph of him and Melissa, the girl who had waited for him. As Megan began to read his letter, she could just hear his Southern accent.

> Dear Megan,
>
> Well, as you can see, I have big news! I wanted you to be one of the first to know. Even though it'd been two years, the moment I saw Melissa when I got off the plane, standing there holding a silly balloon in her teeth with a rose in her hair, I just started laughing. She said she didn't want me to feel any pressure from her, so she decided to make it funny. Well, we started laughing, and we haven't stopped yet.
>
> In many ways she reminds me of you. I think she even looks a little like you. She's been busy while I've been gone. She'll graduate from college this spring, so she'll be able to work some while I'm going to school.
>
> We're getting married right after she graduates.

273

I know that's not very far away, but, the truth is, we can't wait to be married. It's the right time (after my mission), the right place (the temple), and we're totally in love. We both hope you'll be able to come to our reception.

I sure enjoyed knowing you and appreciated being able to teach the gospel in your home. Those were great times.

Well, I got to run. Melissa and I send our love.

Your favorite elder, James Spaulding.

◆　　◆　　◆

So, that's it then. No surprise there. I must have been delusional to think that anything would ever come from my friendship with Elder Spaulding.

Still, though, he did help me get through a tough time in my life, and for that I'll always be grateful.

It's just that I feel like I'm on empty. No hopes. No plans. Nothing to look forward to, except a letter and some pictures once in a while.

She got up to make herself a cup of peppermint tea. As she was filling the cup with water, she suddenly started to sob. She set the cup on the counter and surrendered to the grief.

When she had finally cried herself out, she took a shower and got dressed and went out to look for a job.

18

LIFE GOES ON

Megan reserved every Saturday night to help her dad with his Sunday School lesson. After reading everything they could about effective teaching, they had agreed that effective teaching involved asking questions that would encourage participation from everyone in the class and, at the same time, bring the influence of the Holy Ghost.

"That's what I need," her father said, "not more research, but good questions."

They began to learn from the scriptures how the Savior used questions in his teaching.

This was their project, and Megan loved it because it gave her time to spend with her father, and, she hoped, to help him.

And, on one Sunday, she herself was blessed by what they'd learned.

"In the last year, how has your testimony of the Savior's atonement increased?" Walter asked in the middle of his lesson.

At first there was no response.

Megan and her dad had talked about what he would do if there was no response.

"Just wait," she had said. "People need time to respond to the prompting of the Holy Ghost."

And so, on that Sunday, her father waited.

Ten seconds went by.

And then thirty.

And then Megan raised her hand.

"Megan?" he said with a smile.

"In the past year, I have learned that Jesus Christ is my Savior, and that he loves me, and that he has forgiven me. He knows me by name, and he thinks about me, and that, more than anything, he wants me to have joy in this life and in the eternities to come. That's how my testimony of the Savior has grown in the past year."

"Thank you, Megan," her dad said.

Five other hands went up.

By the time the class was over, there was not a dry eye in the room.

After the class no one approached Walter to tell him how impressed they were by all his preparation. They were too overcome by the Spirit to do that.

Megan was the only one to come up to him.

They embraced and hugged each other.

"I'm so proud of you," her father said, his voice choked with emotion.

"I'm so proud of you, too, Daddy."

♦   ♦   ♦

Megan got a job working as a reservation clerk at a motel. It was the perfect job for her because she got to meet new people every day. She enjoyed making them smile and helping them have a pleasant stay.

Sister Gardner passed along pictures and letters from Ann

Marie and Weston. They wrote every week. Little Joshua was healthy and growing fast. Megan cherished every picture and every detail about him.

♦　♦　♦

"That was definitely a smile," Weston said, looking down at Joshua in his mother's arms.

"I don't think so. It's too early for him to be smiling."

"He's very advanced for his age."

Ann Marie shook her head. "It's gas, Weston."

"Okay, there may be a little gas here, but that doesn't account for his smile. He's smiling because he made gas. He thinks it's very funny."

"Oh, right."

"Look, I don't expect you to understand this. It's pretty much a guy thing."

She burst out laughing. "You are pathetic."

"There it is again. Are you saying that's not a smile?"

"Go away."

"No. I'd rather be here with him."

"Me, too."

"You know what? I'm thinking of canceling cable. Nothing can compete with watching your son smile back at you."

She kissed him on the cheek. "I'm so happy."

"I know. Me, too."

"I think a lot about Megan. How much love she showed to this child. I'm very grateful to her, and I always will be. She gave us the gift that nobody else in the world could give us."

"Let's take some more pictures of Joshua and send them to her."

"We just did two days ago."

"But now we have news."

"What's our news?"

"He's smiling now."

Joshua made a tiny sound.

"Wait a minute," Weston said. "Was that a *Ma?* I think it was. Let me go get my camera."

Ann Marie started laughing as Weston went to get the camera. She gazed down at her baby. "Your daddy is so funny! Yes, he is! He is. He's so funny. You're going to have such a fun time with him. Just you wait and see."

◆　　◆　　◆

One night after her parents had gone to bed, Megan fell asleep on the sofa reading her scriptures. She was awakened by a strange, chattering noise. She looked over at the door and, much to her delight, saw a mother raccoon demonstrating to her three babies how to go through the cat flap, find the kitchen, pull out the bag of cat crunchies and have a good meal.

Megan had to work hard to stifle a giggle as she saw the raccoon babies march in through the flap and then back out, over and over.

She heard a car door slam and Brianna say good-bye to her friends.

The raccoon family made a quick exit through the cat flap.

Brianna opened the door and turned on the light. Megan sat up.

"Brianna?"

"That's me."

"You'll never believe what just happened."

Brianna looked at the mess on the kitchen floor. "Hmmm. You've been nibbling cat candy again, haven't you?"

"No, they were raccoons. A mother and her three babies. They came in through the cat flap."

"No way!"

"I was asleep on the couch when they came. It was so funny! I wish you'd been here to see it."

"Maybe they'll come back. I want to see this."

They turned off all the lights, scrunched down on the sofa, and threw a blanket over themselves.

"It's okay, everyone's asleep," Brianna called out quietly to the raccoons.

Megan poked her in the ribs. "You've got to be quiet."

"Right."

Ten seconds passed. "You ever going to date?"

Megan laughed. "That's not being quiet."

"Just answer my question."

"Yes, I am, when I'm ready."

"I know a guy. His brother just got back from a mission."

"I'm not ready for that."

"Do you miss Elder Spaulding?"

"Not that much, actually. What I liked most about him is that he honored his priesthood." She paused. "You know what? More than anything I miss Thomas."

"Call him then."

"No, he's in Provo, surrounded by thousands of coeds."

"So what? Call him anyway."

"What for? We're just friends."

"But he's the best friend you've ever had. That's got to count for something."

"I'll call him sometime."

"Let's call now." Brianna grabbed the phone and called information.

"Provo, Utah . . . Thomas Marconi . . . Thank you. I just want to say I think you people are doing a great job. I know it's not easy pretending to be a computer twenty-four/seven." She hung up. "Now, that wasn't so hard, was it?"

"Don't call him."

"Why not?"

"It's too late."

"We're up, aren't we?"

279

Brianna started to punch in the numbers. Megan grabbed for the phone. They started wrestling on the couch and giggling.

Brianna broke free and stood up, shielding the phone. "Resistance is futile."

"Give me the phone."

"Don't get loud and vibrant on me," Brianna said.

"Don't call him."

"I'm calling him." Brianna punched in the first two numbers. Megan lunged at her.

They ended up on the floor, laughing as they wrestled for control of the phone.

And then Bryce walked in, stood at the edge of the living room, and watched.

"What is going on here?" he asked in his sternest voice.

Brianna tried her best to be the well-meaning and sincere victim. "I need to make a phone call, and Megan won't let me."

"That is such a lie. She wants to phone Thomas."

"It's a free country. I can phone anyone I want."

"Give me the phone," Bryce said in his best commanding voice.

"Do what he says," Megan said.

Brianna handed over the phone.

"Frankly, I'm surprised at the two of you," he said.

Brianna mimicked him. "Frankly, I'm surprised at the two of you."

"I will keep the phone in my room for the night," he said.

As he walked off, Brianna whispered in Megan's ear, "Let's get him."

They tackled him on the stairs. "Oh, now, you two be careful! Don't get me riled."

Brianna ran into the garage and came back with two plumber's helpers. "I'm going to suck the brains out of you with this, Bryce."

"Where do you get this stuff?"

"That's what you did to me when I was about five years

old," Brianna complained. "You chased me around the room with these."

"She's right. You were such a pest, Bryce," Megan added.

He laid the phone on the stairs. "You know what? I give up. I'm too tired for this. I'm going to bed now. I'll leave the phone here. I just hope you two will show a little maturity and good sense." As he turned to go up the stairs, Megan and Brianna grabbed for the phone.

They tried, but neither one of them could wrest it away from the other.

"Truce?" Megan asked.

"Truce."

They returned to the couch to wait for the raccoons to make another appearance—and fell asleep that way, loosely entangled with each other on the couch.

◆　　◆　　◆

If they had called that night, they would not have reached Thomas. He had a date with a girl in his ward.

Thomas and Elizabeth worked at a pizza place near campus. Thomas was the manager. And so, when the date was over, Thomas dropped by to talk with Elizabeth and help her clean up.

"How'd it go?" she asked.

He grabbed a mop and a bucket. "It was okay, I guess."

"Just okay?"

"We didn't talk much."

"Whose fault is that?"

"I tried. I asked her a lot of questions. She answered them with either a yes or a no. Do you have any idea how many questions you can run through in an hour that way? I actually know how old she was when she got her smallpox vaccine."

"I'm running out of girls in my ward I can line you up with."

"I know."

"Why don't you just say it, Thomas?"

"Say what?"

"You miss Megan."

Thomas started mopping. "Megan is just a friend."

"I know that, but as far as I can tell, she's the only friend you've ever had who's a girl. Maybe that's worth pursuing."

He shrugged his shoulders but didn't tell her not to try to get them together.

The next day Megan received an unexpected phone call from Thomas.

"Guess what? I've just been named the manager of a pizza place in Provo. It's brand-new, and you should see the kitchen! It's state-of-the-art! The decor is terrific, and the owners insist that the waiters know how to sing in Italian. There's even an artificial waterfall in the middle of the dining room. Oh, and we have great bread sticks that we bring right away when someone shows up to order. It's such a great place, but it's missing one thing."

"What?"

"You. Come and work here with me. You could room with Elizabeth, if you want. They just had a girl move out. It'd be perfect. Whuduya say? It'd be like us at Leo's, except maybe ten times better."

She tried to think of a reason why she couldn't leave town but couldn't come up with any.

"Are you sure you want me?"

"Are you kidding? Of course I want you. It'd be just like old times."

"When would you need me?" she asked.

"Right away. This weekend, if possible. That's when we're the busiest."

"I can't just pack up and move to Utah."

"Why not?"

"Because—"

"Because why?"

"I'm thinking, I'm thinking, okay, don't rush me."

"Look, this is just a business proposition. I mean, I wouldn't want you thinking it was anything but that. Good business . . . and because of our being such good friends. That's all it is."

She could hear Elizabeth in the background. "You're making such a mess out of this, Thomas. Give me the phone."

"I'm not making a mess out of this."

"I said give me the phone."

"Well, all right, but I wasn't making a mess out of it."

Elizabeth came on the line. "Megan, hi, this is Elizabeth. How are you doing?"

"Real good."

"How's your baby?"

"Real good. I get pictures at least once a week. He's growing so fast."

"I can't wait to see those pictures. Look, Thomas and I both really want you to come out here. Thomas is a complete grump without you around to brighten his day."

Megan could hear Thomas grumbling in the background, "That is *so* not true."

"It is true, Thomas, and you know it. Now go away so Megan and I can talk in private."

"Where do you want me to go?"

"Outside or in the hall, I don't care. Just get out of here."

Megan smiled at hearing the two of them carry on.

A few seconds later, Elizabeth resumed their conversation. "Megan, I know Thomas wants you to believe this is just business, but, between you and me, it's way more than that. If you care anything about him, even if just as a friend, please come out here and spend some time with him. And then if nothing comes of it, well, then fine. At least you'll have had some good laughs—and also some excellent pizza."

Megan tried to think of what she should do.

283

"I need a little time to think about this," she said.

"Of course, take all the time you need," Elizabeth said.

Just do it, Megan thought.

No, I can't just pick up and move.

Why not? Thomas will be there, and Elizabeth. It'll be great.

If I do it, Thomas might think there's more to it than just friendship.

It's because of you being best friends that he asked you. It's not the worst thing in the world, to be Thomas's friend.

No, it's not. It's the best thing in the world.

Then just do it.

She could hear Thomas in the background. "Can I come in now?"

"No, I'll tell you when you can come in," Elizabeth said.

"Why are you taking so long?"

"We're talking."

"You're not talking to her. You're talking to me."

"And that's because you're still here. I want you out of here. Go sit in the car."

"I don't see why I have to sit in the car when I'm the one who called Megan."

Megan began to laugh. She decided to end their good-natured bickering.

"Elizabeth, I'm going to do it. I'll be there in two or three days."

"She's going to do it!"

"Let me talk to her!"

Thomas was the next to speak. "You're coming?"

"I'm coming."

"I can't believe it! That is so great! Give me your email address, and I'll send you directions on how to get here."

A few minutes later, she hung up the phone.

She felt very happy and very excited about her future.

And, also, a little hungry for a really good pizza.

LDS Family Services

LDS Family Services is a private, nonprofit corporation that has been established by The Church of Jesus Christ of Latter-day Saints to provide licensed, child placement services and to help Church members and others resolve social or emotional problems. The agency also provides help to LDS Native Americans, refugees, and other members of minority cultures. All services provided are consistent with gospel principles.

Birth Parent Services

Helps birth parents apply gospel principles to their decisions about the child.

LDS Family Services assists individuals involved in a pregnancy out of wedlock or an unplanned pregnancy. Available help includes counseling, foster care, education and medical assistance, adoptive placement of the child, if desired, and understanding from caring professionals and volunteers. Birth parents are encouraged to use gospel principles to make decisions in the best interests of all concerned. These services are offered confidentially, and referrals are accepted from any source, without concern for clients' religious affiliation.

Adoption

Assures temple sealing of adoptive children to worthy families.

LDS Family Services provides licensed adoption services to Latter-day Saint families. The agency may also help families identify other resources that can help with adoption. The goal of LDS Family Services is to ensure a successful adoption, including the temple sealing of the child to the adoptive parents.